LOCKE BROTHERS SERIES

VICTORIA ASHLEY
JENIKA SNOW

LOCKE BROTHERS SERIES

THE LOCKE BROTHERS

Whispers of the Locke Brothers fill the town, facts and reality twisted to fit what these motherfuckers believe they know about us. That we're sadistic bastards, incapable of any real emotions or fear. Maybe they're not wrong about that...

Aston Locke – Damaged
Sterling Locke – Savage
Ace Locke – Twisted

We taught ourselves how to love in the best way we know how. When it comes to giving our heart away, we do it with everything in us. We may be dangerous sons of bitches, but we love hard as shit...

Meet the Locke Brothers today to see what makes them so Damaged, Savage and Twisted.

DAMAGED LOCKE

LOCKE BROTHERS, 1

Cover model: Brook Dede

Photographer: Wander Aguiar

Cover Designer: Dana Leah, Designs by Dana

Proofer: Lea Schafer

Aston Locke

Whispers of the Locke brothers fill the town, facts and reality twisted to fit what these motherfuckers believe they know about us.

That we're sadistic bastards, incapable of any real emotions or fear.

Maybe they're not wrong about that.

That is, until I set my sights on Kadence King, getting just as drawn to her as I am the darkness. It's the first time I've felt anything in a long time.

But would she really be scared knowing the depth, the lengths I go with my brothers to make any fucker who crosses us pay?

I need a woman who can accept me for who I am.

For what I am.

I'm hoping like hell it's her, because I want nothing more than to claim her as mine...

Kadence King

I know Aston's dangerous, know people fear him. But I want him. I'm drawn to him, just as he's drawn to the darkness.

I should be afraid of him, should turn the other way, but I can't. I've gone mad and let him in my room, in my life, allowing him to consume me.

He possesses me, dominates me. Aston Locke shows me what it means to want to be claimed by him and only him.

And when he tells me I'M HIS, I have no doubt that's the truth.

Because in the end it's what I want too.

No matter how dangerous he is...

WARNING: Damaged Locke is a short co-written, kind of twisted love story from NYT Bestselling Author Victoria Ashley and USA Today Bestselling Author Jenika Snow. If you like it hot and a little rough... this is the book for you. 18+

1

Aston

I close my eyes and lean my head back as I take a long drag off my cigarette, letting the harsh smoke fill my lungs and calm my nerves.

Standing here in the blackness of the night, preparing for what the fuck my brothers and I do, never gets easier for me.

Although, I've convinced myself we do this shit for all the right reasons, some might believe we're the spawns of the fucking devil.

A blond-haired, blue-eyed evil son of a bitch to be feared.

That's what everyone sees when they look at me.

I can't say I've done much to prove them otherwise.

Whispers of the Locke brothers fill the town, facts and reality *twisted* to fit what these motherfuckers believe they know about us.

That we're sadistic bastards, incapable of any real emotions or fear.

Maybe they're not wrong about that.

My eyes open at the sound of Sterling and Ace grabbing their shit out the back of the Expedition before closing the door.

A light on across the street has my attention pulled in the wrong direction until I feel Sterling hit my arm, dragging my attention back.

"Here." He slams my sawed-off shotgun into my chest with force. "Stop holding your dick over here and take this shit."

Grinning, I yank it from his hands.

"Who wants to do the honors tonight?" Ace asks while swinging his expensive-ass titanium hammer around with pride. "Maybe Aston can just blow the damn thing down."

"I've got it, motherfuckers." Reaching into his pocket, Sterling slips on his brass knuckles and stalks up to the door, checking to see if it's locked.

It must be, because two seconds later, he's kicking the door open and walking inside as if he owns the place.

Ace flashes me a crooked smile as he pushes away from

the black SUV and walks past me, running his hand over his hammer. "Put a pep in your step, baby brother. The place is wide fucking open. I call dibs on the biggest one."

Lifting a brow, I calmly make my way up the steps with my shotgun over my shoulder as Ace disappears into the house, most likely searching for some big motherfucker to take down.

And so it begins.

The dark, twisted ways of the fucking Locke brothers.

Stepping into the dirty house, I look around to see four guys inside. Four perverted, sick motherfuckers that deserve to lose their dicks and their lives for the shit they pulled last week.

These mind-fucked tweakers can't be any older than nineteen to twenty years old. A good age for them to believe they're untouchable and they can get away with taking advantage of a couple drunk girls.

Well, these dirty *untouchable* dicks are about to find out just how *touchable* they are in this town.

In our motherfucking town.

Upon noticing there's now a third person joining the party, they pull their attention away from what Ace is saying and begin shuffling to reach for weapons or whatever shit they keep hidden in this dump.

Sterling immediately swings his right fist out, connecting his fancy-ass brass knuckles to the side of one of the assholes' face, while Ace takes his hammer and places it across another guy's neck, pinning him against the wall and lifting him up it.

That leaves the other two assholes coming at me.

One of them must have *some* brains, because he drops to the ground and surrenders when he notices the gun over my shoulder.

Now the other one. Yeah...he's stupid as shit.

Maybe this will knock some sense into him.

Reaching into my back pocket, I pull the bandana and swing it around, the padlock busting the idiot in the eye socket, blood splattering as his face splits open.

This has the guy on the ground thinking I'm too preoccupied to see his ass get up and come toward me with a knife.

That thought gets squashed the second I pull the shotgun from my shoulder and point it at his dick, stopping him two feet from me.

"Think again, motherfucker," I growl with a tilt of my head. "On your knees. And place your hands under them..." I nod toward Ace. "Unless you want my brother here to show you how good he is with that hammer. He may be pretty and shit, but he's the most twisted asshole you'll meet."

He shakes his head. "No. No. I'm listening. See. Here." His bloodshot eyes stay on me, watching my gun as he lowers to the ground and drops his knife, placing his hands under his knees. "There. Can you put that away now? No one needs to get shot, bro."

I turn to Sterling to see him leaning against the couch with a smirk, one of his arms wrapped around his guy's neck to keep him in place. "These sick fuckers aren't going anywhere, little brother. Put that away...for now."

"All right. I guess I can do that." I smile and place the gun over my shoulder before shoving my padlock back into my pocket and kicking the dude in front of me down to the ground. That padlock really did a number on his face. "Doesn't mean your ass gets to get up." I bend down and get in his bloodied face. "Those two girls you partied with last week didn't get the option of getting up when they wanted to. Why the hell should some sick fuck like you?"

With that I kick him over to his back and dig my foot into his throat, causing him to grab at my boot and choke for air.

He struggles for a few minutes before relaxing and giving up. "We won't do it again," he manages to get out through coughs. "You're crushing my throat, man. You're going to kill my ass. We're sorry. What else do you want from us?"

I smirk, placing my hand to my ear. "What was that? I can't fucking hear you."

"We're sorry. It won't happen again. Please..." He struggles with pushing at my boot again, his face turning blue now as he fights to breathe. "Please don't kill me. I'm fucking begging."

Dropping my shotgun, I remove my boot from his throat and replace it with my hand, dragging him over to the couch, where I slam his head into the arm repeatedly. I don't stop until the brown fabric is covered in blood and his body goes limp. "Do it again and I'll shoot you in the dick and then between the eyes. Got it?"

He nods his head, right before I throw him face-first down into the carpet, watching as he crawls away.

Feeling the anger completely take over me, I light up a cigarette, grab my gun, and walk outside, allowing my brothers to handle the other three assholes.

Standing here in the dark, with my hands covered in his blood, I lean against the SUV and close my eyes, attempting to calm myself down. It's not until I hear feet pounding against the sidewalk that I open my eyes and look across the street to see a woman with long black hair jogging up to the house straight across from this one.

Stopping in front of the door, she turns to face the street, her gaze landing on me.

I stand back and watch, my heart pounding like fucking mad, as she looks me over, stopping on my hands once she notices the blood.

Most people in this town would run by now. They'd

hide inside their houses, peeking out the damn windows to get a glimpse of us, but not this one.

Hell no. She's standing there, taking heavy breaths as her eyes move up to meet mine.

She doesn't say anything.

She doesn't scream.

She doesn't move.

She just stands there, looking curious, as if she's using this moment to take me all in. Every damn bit of me.

I can see in her expression she knows who we are.

"Come on, Aston," Sterling calls, getting my attention away from the beautiful stranger watching me. "Get the fuck in the vehicle."

By the time I look across the street again, the woman is gone and the light that was on in the house is now off.

That must've been her bedroom light.

"Did you get the money?" I ask while backing up and reaching for the door.

"Yeah," Ace says with a crazy-ass grin. "Those fuckers were quick to throw us all their dirty money the moment I nearly crushed one of their dicks with my baby." He holds up his hammer. "These little bitches won't even be thinking about their dicks for a long time."

"Good." I toss my cigarette at the ground and jump into the SUV, my eyes seeking out the house across the street one last time.

I can't quite tell, but it looks like I see the bedroom curtain move. Apparently she hasn't gotten enough of me yet. She's braver than most people in this town, and that shit definitely has my attention.

"Let's get the fuck out of here then."

2

Kadence

I suck in a surprised breath when Melissa yanks me into the house, slamming the door shut behind me.

"What are you doing?" She sounds worried as she rushes through the house to shut my bedroom light off. "I warned you about the Locke brothers the moment you moved into this town. Are you insane, Kadence? Hell, why am I even asking that? Of course you are."

Still fighting to catch my breath from my nightly jog, I meet my roommate in my bedroom and reach for the water bottle on my dresser. "You don't think *warning* me to stay away is going to make me curious? I've waited two months to get a glimpse of these brothers you're always going on about. I couldn't force myself to turn away even if I wanted to, Mel. You should know me by now."

She steps away from the window and tiredly runs a hand down her face. "They're dangerous, Kadence. Everyone in this town knows it. You may be new and all, but you should take my advice and never let them see you watching them. The last thing you want is for them to know you've seen what they've done. You just witnessed a crime. Do you get that?"

The sound of the SUV starting has me rushing over to the window, pushing the curtain aside to get another peek.

It's as if I'm drawn to him, needing to see the beautiful blond stranger one more time before he disappears.

I barely get a glimpse before Melissa pulls me away and yells at me for being so careless.

"Damn it, woman." She closes her eyes and shakes her head as if she's about to lose it. "You're going to get us both killed before we even get to see our twenty-third birthdays. Not only are you insane, but you have a death wish."

"How do you even know that?" I question. "Have they ever killed anyone before? You never once told me they're murderers. All you've told me is what you hear from others around town. But has anyone actually been killed by them? Who do you know that's been hurt because of the Locke brothers? I'm sure it's not just random violence."

"No, not that I know of. I don't know, but that doesn't mean they won't start with us. The youngest Locke saw what you look like. He saw you watching him like a damn nosy person. That whole family is bad news. Everyone knows to steer clear of them. Everyone but *you*, apparently."

"Don't you think he would've marched across the street and hurt me if he wanted to? It's late at night and the whole damn neighborhood is asleep. He could've done anything he wanted to me, but he didn't. All he did was look at me as if he was curious. It was like he expected me to run away, but I didn't."

"Probably because his hands were already covered in someone else's blood and he was trying to think of ways to catch you when you're alone at a later time, damn it." She stops to catch a breath. "I about died when I looked outside to see him staring this way. It wasn't until I looked closer that I saw you standing on the porch, looking back at him."

"Those guys that live across the street..." I pause to take another drink of water while gazing at the curtain. "Didn't you tell me they scare the shit out of you? That they're always trying to get you alone and one of them even tried slipping something into your drink once? How do you know they haven't done that to other women?"

"I don't," she says in aggravation. "And yes, they're fucking creepy as hell and I'm scared when I see them out at night. Every girl in their right mind is. I'm not denying that, but..."

"Maybe the Locke brothers were there to teach them a lesson," I say, cutting her off. "Maybe they're not as bad as you all think. From what I've seen, this town is full of judgmental gossipers."

"Listen...the youngest Locke might look like a beautiful blond angel, but I can assure you he's as sinful and dangerous as they come." She lets out a tired breath and stops in my doorway. "*Please* just promise me you'll stay away if you see them again? I'm trying to keep you safe. You're my friend, and you wouldn't even be in this shitty little town if it weren't for me. I'm responsible for you here. I've been keeping my eye out for you since we were eight. I'm not magically stopping now, no matter how hard you fight me."

I nod my head to make her happy and ease her worry as I jump onto my bed. "All right. I get it. You've always been persistent and overprotective. It's because I love your ass so much that I followed you to this small town. Well, that and my old life sucked anyway."

She smiles slightly before speaking. "Good," she says firmly, getting serious again. "Now, good night and lock your window. I know how you like to open it after your nightly jogs, but don't. Just don't..."

"All right, woman. On it. Good night."

After she walks out of my room and shuts the door behind her, I immediately rush back over to the window and look outside.

My mind knows he's not out there anymore, but apparently my body didn't get the memo, because I look hard in hopes of seeing him again.

I mean face smashed against the window hard.

My eyes immediately land on one of the residents of the house across the street instead.

His face is all busted up and he's pacing across the lawn, holding something in his hand, looking extremely angry and on edge. It may be a knife.

I can't quite tell what it is, but seeing that the Locke brothers didn't leave them for dead has me completely curious what their business was with them.

I've been here for a little over two months, and I have never seen them across the street before tonight.

There's obviously something that brought them there, but what?

It wasn't to kill the creeps, and I don't see or hear any sirens heading this way to check things out.

Maybe I'll never know, and that thought is driving me crazy and making me extremely curious.

This might be a dangerous game, but I want to know about the youngest Locke brother.

If I see him again, I'm not sure I'll be able to stay away like Melissa has warned me to.

3

Aston

My hands are shaky, my bare skin covered in sweat as I sit here in the darkness of the basement with a cigarette resting between my tight lips.

Ever since we left that house last night, I've been slammed with visions of what I witnessed over six years ago, getting me lost in my sick, twisted mind.

No one should've had to witness the fucked-up things I saw that night, let alone a kid of only fifteen.

Nothing about me has been the same since, and with every day I die a little more inside, feeling tormented and defeated about something I had no control over.

As time passes, I begin to realize I'm stuck in my own

personal hell I'll never break free of no matter how fucking hard I try.

One day, I'm afraid I'll give up altogether and just fade.

There's not much stopping that from happening.

Tensing, I step into the freezing, ice-filled water and lower myself to the bottom of the tub, hoping to chill my body temperature and distract myself from the hell in my head.

I need something else to pull me from my thoughts. Anything strong enough to keep me distracted. Something for me to fight for and remind myself I'm still alive.

My teeth chatter, my whole body shaking as I submerge deeper in the deep water, trying to imagine the life I had before my parents died.

Nothing comes to mind. No good memories. No happiness. Nothing. All that sits in the back of my mind is pain, suffering, and death.

Lying here in the ice water, I open my eyes and stare up at the emptiness that surrounds me. I'm completely numb in this moment, and I have no urge to *feel* anytime soon.

So I just stay here, shivering in the dark, not breathing.

I don't come up for air until my lungs feel as if they're on the verge of exploding and I know I have no other option but to breathe.

Sitting up, I lean over the bathtub and take in quick, deep breaths, every part of my body hurting as I fight to gain control.

Once I'm able to breathe without my lungs burning, I stand up and step out of the tub, making my way through the darkness to my room.

The warm temperature of the house has my body feeling as if it's on fire as I stare at my reflection in the mirror, taking in the damaged sight in front of me.

Slowly my hands run over the scars on my chest and abs, left there from six years ago. My numbness quickly turns into rage and hatred, taking me over until I'm grabbing for anything within my reach and shattering the mirror with it, until there's nothing left to look at.

Nothing there to show me how fucked up I truly am.

It's the first time in a long time that the blood covering my hands has been my own. Yet I still don't feel shit.

Taking slow, deep breaths, I wipe my cut-up hand off and throw on a pair of jeans and a white thermal shirt before heading out the back door, not bothering to inform my brothers that I'm leaving. Maybe they heard the glass shattering, but if they did they give no indication, don't come running to see what's wrong. They must be preoccupied which is perfect.

There's somewhere I want to go right now.

Somewhere I've been fighting to stay away from since last night, and I need to get out of this damn place before I lose it.

Walking fast, almost running as I leave my house behind, putting distance between my brothers and me I pull out a cigarette and turn down the alley that's a mile away from our property. I look straight ahead as I make my way toward my destination.

I make it ten blocks before I hear someone come up behind me. It's clear they want me to know they're following me, which means this dumb ass believes he has power over me.

The asshole follows me for two blocks, not speaking until he realizes I'm not attempting to run from him.

"What do you have in your back pocket, asshole? Show me. Now."

I keep walking just to piss him off.

"What the fuck is that bulge? I could use a new toy."

A small smirk takes over as I stop and toss my cigarette at the ground, ready to take on whatever this dick thinks he's going to do to me.

"I asked you a fucking question." The voice is closer now, almost right behind me. "Empty out your pocket. I want it, asshole. That and anything worth a shit."

Cracking my neck, I pull the lock from my pocket and slowly turn around, my gaze settling on a tall guy wearing clothes five times too big for his ass.

He gets ready to come at me, but recognition registers in his eyes when he sees the family symbol tattooed across my neck.

"Whoa, my bad. Didn't realize you were one of Locke brothers." He backs away, keeping his hands up so I can see them. “I don’t want any trouble, man. My mistake. I’ll just be on my way.”

Usually I wouldn’t let an asshole like that leave, knowing what he’s out here doing, but tonight is different. My mind is set on where I want to be, and nothing can change that.

He lucked out, but I have no doubt I’ll run into him again out here on the streets. He’ll get what’s owed to him.

Before I know it, I’m standing on the same street I was last night, looking over at the same small white house that had me distracted from my job.

My jaw flexes as I stand here and stare at the lit-up bedroom at the side of the house.

It was about this time yesterday that she got back from a run or whatever it was she was doing out on the streets so late.

If I timed it correctly, she should be coming down the street right about…

My attention gets pulled to the sidewalk when I hear the pounding of her feet hitting the pavement.

A strong urge to go to her hits me the moment her eyes land on me and she stops running.

It’s almost as if she’s luring me in with the way she looks me over, never turning her eyes from me as she unlocks her front door and opens it.

My heart races in my chest when she slowly shuts the door, her eyes staying on mine until she’s out of sight.

It's when I see the curtain in her room move that I hear her bedroom window opening, letting me know I was right.

She's just as curious about me as I am about her.

Maybe I'll feed her curiosity and give her a small taste of the youngest Locke.

I'm pretty sure this will be the last time she leaves her bedroom window unlocked and opened for me.

4

Kadence

I don't know what's come over me, asking this dangerous man, this stranger into my room. Even resorting to having him sneak through the bedroom window like a thief in the night, like I'm some teenager hiding him from my parents.

God, if my roommate finds out I have a Locke brother in the house, let alone my bedroom, she'll shit.

She's warned me, and I take that seriously, but the truth is ever since I saw him across the street the other night, he's all I've been able to think about.

Taking a deep breath, I step back and keep my gaze on the window, my heart speeding up when I hear rustling right outside.

He's not even in the house yet, and I'm already going crazy with anticipation of what's to come.

He pushes the curtain aside, braces a hand on the windowsill, and before I can warn him, remembering the jagged piece of metal sticking out from the frame, he's hoisting himself up and inside.

"Motherfucker," he says loud enough I know my roommate could have heard. The last thing I need is her in here acting crazy.

"Shit, I totally forgot about that," I say and find myself moving a step closer. It's as if I want to help him, like I can't stand to see him hurt. Of course, I know he's dangerous. That much is a fact, but I can't help myself.

He holds his hand out, and I see he has a nasty cut, blood welling up. "Let me grab a wet rag. Hold on."

It's an excuse as much as it is me wanting to see if Melissa has heard. Her door is shut, the light off.

I listen for just a second longer, making sure she's not getting up, then walk over to the sink, grab a clean rag, and run it under the water. We don't have a first-aid kit, not that I know of anyway, so I grab some paper towels, a roll of masking tape, and head back into my room.

I shut the door silently, staring at him, his focus on all my shit scattered around the room.

He starts running his uninjured hand over my stuff as if memorizing it, taking in the feel, the shape of everything.

This is grossly intimate in a way, like he isn't just touching my things ... but me.

But I don't say anything and instead stand here for a moment, letting him get to know me through those artifacts, as if he has every right to even be in here, sharing the same air as me.

"I'm gonna bleed all over your fucking floor," he says softly, his voice deep, serrated, like this knife moving over me, barely touching me but promising to break the skin and draw blood.

"Sorry," I say and walk over to him, handing the wet rag to him first.

He eyes me like he's surprised I'm willing to help him. Maybe he's not used to anyone not running from him. He doesn't say anything though, and instead takes the rag and cleans his hand off, and his arm where the blood has started dripping down the length. He tosses the rag into the small trash can by my bed.

"Here," I say and hand him the paper towel and masking tape.

"I'm good."

I look at his hand. It's already started to bleed again. Taking matters into my own hands, I grab his arm, wrap the paper towel around his cut, and tape it up.

When I look at him, it's to see him staring at me, this weird, almost frightening expression on his face. It's like this cold rush of air has moved over me, covering me in its icy touch, trying to suck the air from my very lungs.

And he's made me feel this way with just a look.

"Like you said, you'll bleed all over my fucking floor." The words just spill out.

I move a step back on instinct and take in the sight of him. Even now I have no idea why I've brought him into my room, invited the very devil himself into my life.

Yes you do. All it took was a look across the street for you to feel something. He made you feel like you're walking on this razor's edge, about to fall over, drop into the very bowels of hell itself.

His body is lean but muscular and hard. So damn sexy and tempting.

The air is thick, charged, alive. I feel the hair on my arms stand on end, as if they know the man in front of me is dangerous, someone I should get far away from.

With my body still damp from running, my clothes sticking to me, a part of me wants to go back out there and have my feet on the pavement. Running lets me be free, lets me feel alive. It's the only time I feel like I can be by myself, my thoughts my own.

Maybe that's how he feels when he's out doing what he does with his brothers.

I swallow, my throat tight, my mouth dry as his eyes stay on me. I don't know what to say. When I opened the bedroom window, it had been this automatic move.

My hands are twitchy, my mind replaying seeing him the other night, knowing he watched me, thinking about what he could do to me if he wanted to.

Dangerous, violent, no fucks given ... all those things and more have come up in the rumors. The Locke brothers keep to themselves because they don't do social hour. Yet here I was inviting one into my bedroom.

When it comes to Aston Locke, I'm flirting with danger, playing with fire right in the palm of my hand.

"You saw me last night," he growls, moving an inch closer to me. I find myself moving one back. We do this silent dance of me retreating because I know he's a predator and I am the prey.

"Yeah," I finally whisper, my voice soft, distant. I have no doubt he can see how scared I am, smell it on me. It isn't that I think he'll hurt me, which is foolish. This man could do that and I wouldn't be able to stop him. Hell, I invited him into my room like a crazy person.

"You see what we did to those motherfuckers across the street?"

I watch his sexy mouth as he speaks, then lift my gaze to his eyes. God, they are so blue. I don't know what it is about him, but I can tell the youngest Locke has seen some shit, lived through hell itself.

And when I retreat one more step, the door stops me. He places his tattoo-covered hands on the cheap wood beside my head, leans down, and I hold my breath.

"You know who I am?" he whispers against my lips, causing me to lose my breath for a quick second.

I can see in the way he appraises me that he knows who I am from last night. I have no doubt about that. "Yes."

He grins, but it's sadistic in nature, pleased that he made me admit it.

"You're about to learn who I really am soon enough."

5

Aston

I'm crowding her. She's nervous because of it, maybe even second-guessing letting me into her room.

I inhale. Fuck, she smells good, really damn good.

"I'm Aston Locke, a mean motherfucker that you just let all up in your space." I lower my gaze to her throat, see her swallow, watch the slight curve move up and down. "Tell me your name," I demand with a growl.

I could have said it a little nicer, tried to pretend and be sweet, gentle. But to hell with it; I'm not going to pretend to be someone I'm not.

"Kadence." Her voice is soft and so damn innocent. "Kadence King."

Kadence King.

God, how I want to defile her, make her see what all the hype is about concerning my brothers and me and how rough we are. I can imagine her naked, spread out for me, willing to do whatever the fuck I say. And she would submit to me, let me leave my marks on her, pretty purple and blue fingerprints that showed my ownership.

"What have you heard about the Lockes?" I want to hear her speak, want to know what she knows. Hell, I want to be pressed right up against her, her small body so soft where mine is hard.

I want to breathe the same air as her.

I want to fucking own her.

What the hell?

She swallows again, her breathing hard, fast.

She's nervous.

I lower my gaze to her chest, see the way her tits press against the stretchy material of her shirt. Her nipples are hard, and my fingers itch to touch them.

I might be a dangerous bastard, a violent fucker, but I don't touch a girl without her wanting me to. I'll wait until Kadence begs me, asks me to push my dick deep inside her, making her mine.

"I heard you guys aren't to be messed with." Her voice is low, really damn low. "I heard you keep to yourself, aren't social, and if someone crosses you guys..." She trails off, and I lift my brow, wanting more. "That you take care of it in the only way you know how."

"The only way we know how?"

She nods and licks her lips. "With guns and bats, hammers, or whatever else you can find to make it bloody."

I chuckle low. *That's about right.*

"And you thought it was a good idea to let one of us in your room, this close to you?"

She shrugs, and I see something shift over her face. She's trying to be strong.

Cute.

"Maybe not, but too late now."

I grin again. Yeah, it's too fucking late now.

There's something about her, something that grabs hold and won't let go. I don't want it to. I want to suffocate from it, need her to as well. I want her to feel the intensity, crave it, become addicted.

Would she really be scared knowing the depth, the lengths I go with my brothers to make any fucker who crosses us pay? Does she really understand exactly what I'd do to anyone that even so much as breathes wrong in my direction?

No, I don't think she really understands.

For her own good I should walk away, leave her alone so she doesn't have to deal with my shit.

But I'm not.

"Do you want to know more about me?" I stare into her green eyes. She's expressive but also cautious. I wait a heartbeat for her answer, already knowing what she'll say.

"Yeah."

God, that's really fucking good.

"You'll know more about me soon enough." I grin and lean in just an inch, so close our lips are almost touching. It takes a hell of a lot of self-control not to just kiss her, take her, knowing she'd love it. "Until then."

I turn and leave her there shaking, going out the window and feeling more juiced up than I ever have before.

6

Aston

Leaning my head back, I close my eyes and press my hands against the shower wall as the water beats against my sore muscles, relaxing me just a small bit after tonight's shit storm.

Truthfully, nothing ever fully relaxes me. Nothing has for a long fucking time now.

This lifestyle keeps me tense as hell, ready to take on whatever the fuck is thrown at me. But when you've seen what I have—lived through what I have—on edge is the only way to survive.

I'm doing everything I can not to take that next step that sends me falling into complete blackness that'll swallow me up whole.

Hurting motherfuckers who have hurt others has been my only way of doing that so far. My only way of feeling just a little bit alive.

Swallowing, I run my hands through my wet hair, my mind trailing back to last night when my body was so fucking close to Kadence's.

Fuck, how I wanted to feel her under my fingertips. How I wanted to taste every inch of her fucking body, leaving my mark on her.

I wanted to own her, make her scream my damn name as if she needs me inside her to survive.

The only problem with that is that I'm dark as shit. I need to know for sure she's ready to let me into her light.

There's nothing gentle about me. Not the way I talk. Not the way I handle others, and definitely not the way I fuck.

I feel myself becoming hard. I imagine my hand wrapped tightly around her sexy little throat as I bury myself deep between those slender thighs of hers, making her scream my name until it hurts.

Her roommate would definitely hear, and probably even the neighbors.

"Mmm... fuck," I growl while taking my length in my hand and stroking it to thoughts of her.

I don't remember the last time I've wanted a woman as badly as I want her right now. One look across the street two nights ago, and I knew right away I needed to touch her. To feel her shake beneath me as she comes undone.

I've still yet to do that.

I bite down on my lip, moaning as my strokes become fast and hard, bringing me close to losing my shit.

Fuck, I bet her pussy is nice and tight for me. It'd be a struggle to fit my thickness inside her, but I crave the challenge like I crave the darkness.

With just a few more strokes I feel my balls tighten. I release my load down the shower drain, gripping the wall with one hand as I slowly come down from my temporary high.

This isn't enough for me, imagining being inside her. I want more. I need more.

Stepping out of the shower, I quickly dry off and slip my jeans over my naked body before throwing on an old shirt and reaching for my leather jacket.

I barely make it to the top of the basement stairs before Sterling calls out my name, asking me to meet them in the living room.

"You going to tell us what the fuck happened to your hand last night?" He nods down at my wound that's still bandaged up, the dressing soaked from the shower. I could tell he wanted to ask me about it all night, but I knew he'd wait until our job was done first. "And why the hell you didn't answer your phone when we called ten motherfucking times."

"I cut it on the mirror downstairs." It's not a lie. It's just not the full truth. “Then I went for a damn walk to clear my head. I needed to be alone.”

Ever since my parents were murdered and I walked in at the end, getting stabbed three times and left for dead, you can say my brothers have been overprotective.

If it weren’t for them, I’d be dead and those murderous motherfuckers who took our parents’ lives would be alive, roaming the streets, looking for some other drug addicts to take from.

My parents weren’t good. They were fucked in the head. Consumed by their habits. The Locke family name is tainted as shit, and my brothers and I are the only ones left other than my uncle, Killian.

My brothers don’t realize, though, that I can take care of my damn self now. I’m not that helpless fifteen-year-old that couldn’t defend himself anymore. I’ve been through hell and back many times that they don’t know of.

And I’ve walked out, unscathed every single time, except that one.

“Don’t make me remind your ass what happened to our parents,” Sterling says over his whiskey glass. “Everyone in this town paints us as the bad guys, the ones to be feared, but we know more than anyone there’s fucks out there a lot more dangerous and twisted than us, little brother.” His jaw flexes as he tilts back his glass, emptying it. “We’ve witnessed it.”

“Don’t worry.” I slip my jacket on and pet King’s head as

he comes to sit at my feet. He's one of the most loyal pit bulls you'll ever meet. He's a mean fucker, you better believe that, but only when we tell him to be. "I'm always prepared."

"Good." Ace nods down at his hammer, sitting next to his feet. "I'm ready to play anytime."

I smirk and head for the door. "Because you're the most twisted Locke of us all."

As soon as the cool night air hits my face, I place a cigarette between my lips and light it, leaning my head back as I inhale.

It's a little earlier than last night, but I have a feeling I know where to find her.

Exhaling, I make my way toward the trails close to Kadence's house.

There's not one person brave enough in this town to run those trails at night, but I have a feeling Kadence isn't as fragile as she looks.

She obviously can't be that scared if she let a damn Locke into her room in the middle of the night.

Before long I find myself standing off in the darkness, watching Kadence from afar as she slowly jogs between the trees, stopping occasionally to catch her breath.

She seems unaware of anything around her, making me nervous that she chooses to run these paths alone, so late at night.

What if it wasn't a Locke brother lurking in the night,

watching her? What if someone far more dark and twisted than me decides they want her just as badly as I do?

Then what?

I'll be around to find out what. That I'm making sure of now.

7

Kadence

Being out here, alone, in the middle of the night, feels freeing after being stuck in a stuffy coffee shop, taking orders all day.

The cool air hitting my face calms me, making me feel alive as I take these trails each night, knowing I'm the only one around for miles.

At least so far.

In the two months I've been running at night, I haven't once seen anyone else out here. It's as if everyone's afraid to come out after dark in this little town.

As if everyone expects the Locke brothers to be lurking around every corner, ready to get their hands bloody.

Even though I've heard the stories of how dangerous

they are, a part of me has always been curious about the brothers, wanting to know why they are that way.

What drives them into the darkness they seem to survive in.

When the youngest Locke, Aston, looked at me from across the street for the second night in a row, I was quick to let him in, wanting a chance to get to know about him.

It was as if my body had a mind of its own, going right for the one thing that was keeping us apart.

Having him in my room, so close, his breath against my lips, had me going crazy inside.

My heart has never beat so damn fast in my life. Not even during my nightly runs, and if I have to be honest, I haven't stopped thinking about him since.

There's no denying I hope he comes back.

The sound of leaves crunching behind me has me stopping and turning around to see if someone's following me.

My heart is racing like crazy as my gaze scans the darkness around me.

I don't see anyone, so I take off running again, going faster this time.

Of course, the moment I begin to think I'm always out here alone, some crazy person might just pop out of nowhere, proving my ass wrong.

I run for a good three minutes before I hear someone come up behind me, right before I'm yanked back by a hand grabbing my mouth.

I scream, but it's muffled, his hand covering my mouth and nearly my nose.

My lungs start burning, the need to suck in a breath strong, making me fight for survival. I lash out, swinging my arms around, trying to hit him, hurt him.

I make contact with his face, my nails digging into his skin.

He grunts, and the pleasure fills me. I got the fucker. Good. But still he drags me back, farther into the darkness, away from the pseudo-protection of the park lights.

I know if I don't stop this, he'll rape me, hurt me. He'll make me his victim, and that I won't stand for. I won't allow him to dig into my soul, crushing me, making me afraid for the rest of my life.

"You stupid fucking cunt," he grits out. His voice is deep, but it sounds fake, like he's trying too hard to disguise it.

He's a coward.

Before I know what's going on, he has me pushed up against a tree. The side of my face connects with the bark, scraping the skin, causing a burn and pain to take root.

I try to turn around, to fight, even if he is stronger. But he has a forearm on my back, pressing me harder against the trunk, making me stationary for the violence he is about to deliver.

I scream, knowing it won't do a hell of a lot of good. It's late, and that's one of the reasons I come out here. I want to be alone with my thoughts, but it's clear that was a foolish mistake.

"I'm going to make you pay for that."

I know he's talking about the scrape across his face. Good, I hope it bleeds, hope it leaves a mark forever.

Then I hear his zipper being pulled down, and my survival mode kicks in. I fight harder, trying to be strong.

Then, out of nowhere, the weight on my back is gone, and there's a grunt behind me, a sound of flesh hitting flesh. I should run, leave, but my morbid curiosity has me turning and watching the scene unfold before me.

Relief rushes through me, my heart rate slowing down a bit when my eyes lock on *him*.

Aston is beating the shit out of my attacker, and as much as I should feel disgusted by the act of violence, all I can do is watch in awe.

8

Aston

All I can feel is my fist going into this motherfucker's face. Over and over I slam my knuckles into this bastard's body, hearing him grunt in pain, smelling his blood coat the air.

The metallic scent that fills my nose tingles, and makes me hungry for more violence.

This prick thought he could touch Kadence. He's about to learn the hard truth that she's mine, and anyone who fucks with her deals with me.

"God."

I hear her whisper, but I'm in my own world, the need to cause more pain, give more violence, rushing through my veins.

My heart is pumping wildly, my head exploding with the power, strength, with the degrading things I still want to do.

"You think you can fucking touch her, hurt her?" I say and pound my fist into his face again. We're on the ground now, me straddling him, wailing on his ass. "You fucked with the wrong girl, asshole." Blood coats my knuckles, splattered on my shirt, but I don't stop.

I can't.

"Enough," she says softly.

But I'm in my own world, wanting to hurt this fucker as badly as I can.

"You'll kill him," she says again, and when I feel her hand on my shoulder, I make myself slow. I look at her, the shocked expression on her face piercing me deep.

I'm breathing hard, my chest rising and falling, blood covering my hands, sweat coating my body. I stand, look down, and see the bastard still breathing. I would have much preferred to kill him, making him suffer.

"He's not worth it," she whispers.

She's wrong about that, but I find myself turning toward her, wanting to touch her, make sure she's okay.

I take a step closer, and she moves one back. We do this several times until she is pressed to a tree trunk, her chest now rising fast and hard.

"He's not worth it," she says again.

I shake my head. "He deserves to be six feet under the fucking ground for even thinking he can mess with you."

I may have stopped, but I have no intention of letting this fucker pass. If she doesn't want to see me take vengeance, fine. But I'll find this prick later, and then real damage will be done.

I lift my bloodied hand up, smooth a finger along her cheek, and stare at the smear of red on her flesh. I need her right now, want to combat this violence running in me with the feeling of her under me.

She's shaking, her breath moving in and out of her parted lips fast. Fuck, I can't help myself, don't even want to at this point.

I wrap my hand around her neck, the hold loose, but letting her know I'm serious. I stare into her eyes for long seconds, seeing her pupils dilate, seeing she is equal parts aroused and frightened.

I'm a bastard, wanting her after what almost went down. But I can't help myself.

Feeling the need claim me, I kiss her, just slam my mouth down on hers and take her lips like I own her.

I do fucking own her. She's mine.

I tighten my hand on her throat, press my body to hers, and feel my dick get hard. Fuck, I want her right now, want to part her thighs and slide my cock into her tight little pussy.

I bet she's tighter than a fucking fist wrapped around my

cock. Once I have her, I know she'll be wet for me too, so damn juicy my dick will be soaked, the sheets damp beneath her.

I groan against her mouth, sliding my tongue deeper between her lips, making her take it all, knowing she loves it.

But she breaks away, panting, her lips red, swollen. We stare at each other for long seconds, and finally I take a step back.

"Come on," she's the one to say, and I let her take my hand.

I know where we are going. Tonight I'll show her exactly how much I want her.

Tonight she'll see that she *is* mine.

9

Aston

The room is filled with silence. Kadence is moving around slowly to clean my hands, as if she's worried her roommate will wake up and find me here.

She can be quiet all she wants while she works on my busted-up hands, taking care of me, but there's no way she'll be able to be quiet once I take care of her and make her mine.

I'm going to make her scream so loud I'll feel it in my fucking soul, overpowering all the darkness around me, allowing me to get lost in *her* for a short time and forget about this hell.

"Thank you for doing that." She lifts her green eyes up

to meet mine, her lips slightly curving into a thankful smile as she wraps the last of the bandage around my hand. "There's no doubt he would've hurt me badly if you hadn't been out there tonight. I'm glad you were there, Aston."

Tightly clenching my jaw, I stand over her small frame, allowing her to take me in. She gazes up and down my sweaty body as if she wants to reach out and run her fingers over every dip and curve.

Anger is still swarming through me at the thought that that piece of shit believed he had the right to hurt her and take her without permission.

Fuck that shit.

I'll rip that fucker's throat out before he ever has the chance of that happening.

I can hear her breathing pick up, see the fast rise and fall of her chest as I back her to the door and brush my lips against her smooth neck. "No motherfucker will ever touch you without your permission," I growl. "Not as long as I'm around."

But what I don't say, at least not just yet, is that the only motherfucker who will ever touch her is me.

She lets out a small breath of air as I move my mouth around to the front of her neck then brush up to her lips. "You want me to touch you? You want my hands all over this tight little body of yours, Kadence?"

I hear her swallow before she lets out a quiet, "Yes,"

across my lips, confirming what I already knew from the first moment our eyes met.

As soon as the word leaves her mouth, my hands are gripping her waist and flipping her around to press her front against the door.

Before she has a moment to catch her breath, I quickly rip her pants down her legs and slam my body against hers from behind, letting her feel my roughness.

A small, needy moan escapes her pretty little lips once she feels my hardness pressed against her ass, ready to take her.

Pressing her harder into the door with my hips, I lift her shirt over her arms before pinning them to the door and grazing my teeth over her throbbing neck, tasting her sweaty flesh. The salt on my tongue has my cock jerking.

"Nothing is gentle about me," I grit out. "You're about to find out just how fucking *hard* I am."

"God, yes."

That's all I need to hear.

Reaching between our bodies, I quickly undo my jeans and slide them down my hips before yanking her panties down her thighs and thrusting into her tight little pussy, fast and deep.

I do it so fucking hard that she turns her head and bites into my arm, almost drawing blood, to keep from screaming.

Groaning against the back of her neck, I wrap my fingers

into her thick hair and pull as my other hand reaches around to grip the front of her neck and squeeze.

My thick cock fills her completely, easily sliding in and out from her wetness coating me, our sweaty bodies slapping together with force.

She's so much wetter than I imagined she'd be for me. I can feel her arousal dripping down to my balls.

Fuck, she likes my roughness...

This has me fucking her harder, being so rough that her body moves up the wooden door, her face smashing against the surface with each thrust.

"Aston," she pants while gripping at anything she can grab on to. "Keep going... don't stop."

I yank her hair back and smirk before running my tongue over her hot neck, all the way over to her ear. "I don't plan to."

Pulling out of her, I flip her around and crush my lips against hers, tugging and pulling with my teeth until her lips are red and swollen. "Not for a long fucking time."

A surprised breath escapes her lips as I pick her up and roughly toss her onto her bed before walking over to stand at the foot of it.

She's breathing heavily, gripping at the blankets as I grab the bottom of my shirt and rip it off over my head, tossing it aside.

I see the expression on her face change the second her

gaze scans my chest and abs, taking in the long, jagged scars.

Her focus stays there, examining them, but she doesn't say anything as I lower my jeans, stepping out of them.

I stand here in silence for a moment, my chest quickly rising and falling as she takes in the sight of me, naked, in front of her.

There's no mistaking she's completely turned on by what she sees, but also scared and concerned about what happened to me in the past.

If she knew half the shit I've been through, the suffering and pain I've endured, there's no doubt in my mind that she'd run and never fucking look back.

Now it's time for her to really *feel* me.

10

Kadence

I stare at Aston, my pussy sensitive from when he shoved all those hard inches into me, but my body still wants more.

I crave more.

I look at the inked-up skin he reveals, the scars I can see intersecting the art. What must he have gone through? What fucking horrors did he see to make him broken on the outside?

Sure, physically he's strong, powerful, but those scars had to have given him a lasting effect. They had to have chipped away at him.

I want to ask him about them, to comfort him, but a part

of me knows better than to pry. I don't want to push it, don't want to cross that line.

Maybe, given time, I'll open up and find the courage to ask him, to let him know I want to make sure he's okay.

But I can see right now talking is not in the plan. It's clear in his eyes that he wants to fuck me, and do it hard.

"Take off the bra. Now," he demands.

I rise up slightly, remove my bra, and once naked I rest on the bed again. He looks me up and down as if he's doing it to get his fill. Goose bumps pop out along my flesh, and I feel myself getting wetter.

"How primed are you for me?"

I don't answer, just brace my feet on the bed and spread my thighs wide, showing him I'm ready for him to take me, to claim me.

He makes this deep rumble in his chest and grabs his huge, thick cock and starts stroking himself. God, the sight of him jerking off while he looks at me is so damn hot I can barely handle it.

And then he's on me, pushing my legs wider apart, settling between them. He doesn't wait to shove back into my body, stretching me, making the pain and pleasure rise to this burn, this high.

The grunt he gives when he's to the hilt inside me, his balls pressed to my ass, has me gasping. I arch my back, thrust my breasts out, and ride the wave of pleasure as he starts fucking me.

In and out. Faster, harder, no fucks given.

He has his hand on my throat, cutting off my breathing slightly, making the intensity wash through my body.

I feel myself go higher, the root of his cock stroking my clit, the weight of his hand on my neck getting me off.

And then he's gently biting my shoulder, soft at first, but with more force the faster his thrusts become. Just when I think I'm going to climax, he pulls out, flips me over, and smacks my ass.

At this point I don't care if Melissa can hear me.

He spanks me hard, the blood rushing to the surface, no doubt my skin becoming ruby red. And then he's pushing my thighs apart, thrusting back into me, and fucking me like a madman.

I grab the sheets, curl my hands around the material, and let myself feel it all.

God, he's so big, so fierce. He thrusts in and out, hard and fast, hitting this deep part of me that has my toes curling and my body feeling as if it's on fire.

Grunting, he presses his hand on the center of my back, making me take all of him.

I feel myself going higher, know I'm going to come. Then it hits me almost like a distant memory, like a dream. He isn't wearing a condom. But in this moment I can't even find it in myself to care.

The youngest Locke brother is inside of me, proving just

how fucking rough and raw he is, and it feels too damn good.

"Come on, baby, fucking come for me. I want to fucking hear it." He thrusts deep inside me. "Let me feel this tight little cunt clenching around me, sucking at my cock, needing that cum."

His hand on my back hurts, but it also feels incredible.

And just like that, because he demands I let go, I get off, my body shaking as I dig my nails into his arm, most likely drawing blood.

This doesn't make him stop though.

He pumps harder and faster, his balls slapping my clit, his dominance making me wetter, needier with each thrust.

"That's it. Fuck." He gives my ass a hard smack. "This is only the fucking beginning. You're mine. Only mine."

He buries his cock in me, and I know he's coming. I can feel him filling me up, sense it slipping out from where we are connected.

My thighs are sticky with his cum, the sheet damp below me. I know I'll have bruises come morning, bite marks to prove he claimed me.

And all I can think is that I want more.

I *need* more.

11

Aston

Fuck, how I love watching my cum drip from her tight little pussy and cover the bed below her, showing her she's mine.

Nothing has ever even come close to feeling this damn good, making me feel *alive*. And I know the moment I leave here, that all I will feel is the emptiness that swallows me whole.

But that's what I'm used to. That dark, empty feeling that consumes me.

It's how I live, how I survive.

It's how I stay alive ... feel alive.

It's not something that can be changed so damn easily, no matter how fucking badly I wish it was so.

Standing from the bed, I look down at Kadence's naked, flushed body. I watch the rapid rise and fall of her chest as she looks up at me while fighting to catch her breath.

Her legs are still spread for me, her sweaty body on display for my viewing as if she's letting me know she's mine.

The cum dripping from between her beautiful legs already confirmed that, and we both know it.

Walking over to the window, I open it and pull out a cigarette, lighting it and inhaling a long drag as the night air hits my naked flesh.

Her gaze roams over my body as I stand here, taking in every hard inch of me as if she can't believe I just took her. It's like she can't believe that I just fucked her so good that the neighbors no doubt heard her cries of pleasure.

No doubt her roommate heard, as well.

I know I should be leaving now. Should be walking out that damn door and hiding in the solitude of my basement, but I don't want to.

Not tonight. Not while her body is covered with my scent... my sweat mixed with hers.

Taking one last drag, I snub it on the ledge and toss the cigarette out the window and close it.

I tilt my head when she gets ready to reach for something to clean off with. "Don't."

Locking eyes with her, I crawl back into her bed and roughly pull her body against mine.

Fuck, she smells like me. That has the possessive side rising up in me.

The little moan that escapes her lips is enough to let me know she wants me here just as badly as I want to be here.

"I want me all over your fucking body till morning." I drag my teeth over her sweaty neck and growl before whispering in her ear. "I want my cum inside you, Kadence. I want you to remember the way I fucked you and claimed you while you sleep."

She doesn't say anything.

She doesn't have to.

Kadence

I WONDER how long Aston will stay. I don't want him to go, but I also know that maybe this won't last.

Maybe what I feel isn't what he feels?

He pulls me close, this possessiveness coming from him.

"What happened?" I find myself asking, wanting to know about the scars, wanting to know his truth. I reach out and touch the closest scar to me, one that's across his tight abs.

He pulls away, lying on his back, staring at the ceiling. His jaw is clenched, his focus seeming intense.

"I'm sorry," I whisper, knowing I probably crossed a line.

"It's good." He looks at me. "I don't know if telling you about all this shit is the right thing. I'll scare the shit out of you, if I haven't done so already."

I push myself up, not caring that I'm naked. I don't care about anything but this moment.

He turns and faces me, pulls me in tightly, and I know that no matter what he says, I'm not going anywhere.

I want Aston.

I want to be owned by him completely.

12

Aston

Shit, she wants to know about my scars, about how I got them. I am one cruel motherfucker to anyone who crosses me, but a part of me wants to be ... gentle with her.

A part of me wants to tread lightly. I've never felt like that before. I've never given two fucks about what anyone thought.

If they are stupid enough to ask about us, they get the cold, brutal truth. They find out the hard way who we are.

"My parents were worthless. They were druggies, and we'd have dealers come to the house frequently." I run my hand along one of the stab wounds I got that night. The one across my abs. "My parents pissed a dealer off. It was a deal gone wrong, and he killed them." I exhale, that night flashing through my mind. I stare at her and look into her eyes, wondering what she's thinking right now. "Then the dealer turned that knife on me, meant to kill me."

I have to give her credit; she doesn't look shocked or scared.

"And that's why the Lockes are this way?"

I don't speak for a few seconds, not giving a fuck that my parents are in the ground.

"That's why my brothers are so protective of me. That's why we are so tight with each other and don't let anyone fuck with us."

"Do you miss them?"

How will she feel when I tell her I don't give a shit about my parents? "Our parents were worthless pieces of shit. They deserved what they got and more. Them being dead doesn't even begin to make up for the damage they did to me and my brothers. All the physical and mental hurt they caused us growing up." I feel rage and darkness creep up on me, transforming me, making me feel whole.

I feel its icy fingers stroke my skin, taking hold of my black heart, and squeezing. This is what I live for, and I will never back down from it.

I'll never let it leave me.

If Kadence wants to be in my life, she needs to see every cruel, heartless, and black part of my fucking soul.

"If they were assholes and hurt you and didn't care for

you the way they should, good, they deserved what they got."

I'm pretty fucking stunned by her words.

"But I'm sorry you went through that, had to deal with it all."

"It made us stronger." I sit up and start grabbing my clothes. I don't want to go, but I remember I have to go help my brothers.

They'll track my ass down if they have to, and it won't be pretty for anyone.

As much as I want to stay here and fuck Kadence until she can't walk straight, I have to go.

Just as I get the last of my clothes on, there's a knock on the bedroom door.

I see Kadence immediately stiffen.

"Kadence?" the roommate calls out. "Are you okay?"

"Shit," Kadence says under her breath. "I'm good." She goes to get up, gets tangled in the sheets, and falls to the ground, cursing loudly.

"Are you okay?" the roommate says as she opens the bedroom door.

The roommate and I lock gazes, and I watch her terrified eyes grow wide.

I turn and help Kadence off the ground, pull her in close, and kiss her, letting her roommate know she's mine.

I hear the soft moan come from her, and pride fills me. My cock also starts to get hard again.

Damn, I want her.

I pull away from Kadence, sure as fuck not wanting to, but needing to go.

I walk toward the roommate, grinning, not caring that she clearly knows what we just did.

Hell, I'm pretty fucking proud that I claimed my girl.

She moves to the side, allows me to walk by her without any issues. She's afraid, scared as fuck of my reputation, clearly.

I look at Kadence, feeling all kinds of possessiveness slam into me.

My girl.

Then I turn to the roommate again, give a wink, and leave the room.

If Kadence thinks this is the last time I'll see her, she really doesn't understand what it means to be mine.

13

Kadence

My heart sinks the moment Aston walks out the door. Realization hits me that I have no idea if I'll see him again.

That thought has me feeling sick to my stomach. Worry washes through me, and I wrap the sheet around my body and walk through the living room to watch him out the window as he walks away.

This feeling I have is foreign, strange in the best of ways. I want to see him again, want to feel him on me ... *in* me.

Melissa standing next to me with her hard, icy glare, making clear how damn angry she is with me, isn't even enough to make me forget about the man who just took me like no other man has before.

The way he handled me and made me feel like I was his and only his has me wanting and needing more of him.

"You have to be insane," Melissa whispers.

Maybe I am, but if feeling this way for Aston makes me crazy, I don't want to be sane.

Aston has me completely wrapped up in him, and I barely even know him yet.

But what I do know... is that he's been hurt far worse than he's probably ever hurt someone else before, and I *hate* the thought of him being hurt.

It makes me angry.

"You just had sex with a Locke brother?" Melissa says, pulling my attention away from the empty street. She phrases it like a question, but she knows the truth.

I didn't even get a chance to see him walk away. He must've taken a different route, disappearing between the houses.

"You let one of those dangerous brothers into your bed and into your body? Kadence, what the hell were you thinking?" The panic in her voice is real. She looks me over, standing here naked, still holding the sheet to my body. "He was in our damn house. That's not cool."

"He saved me tonight, Melissa." I let out a breath and walk past her, making my way back to my room. I just want to be alone right now. The last thing I want to do is listen to Melissa put Aston down. "He's not as bad as you think. He makes me feel... safe."

"Ha!" She runs her hand over her face and gives me a funny look, showing me again that she thinks I'm crazy.

And maybe I am.

"That's hysterical. A sadistic man makes you feel safe. Did you forget that you just saw him across the street the other night with blood on his hands?"

"Of course not." I place my hand on my bedroom door and look her right in the eyes. "And tonight, there was someone else's blood on his hands. Due to him protecting me. That leaves a bigger impression in my book."

She gets ready to speak but then stops as if she's trying to think of how to respond. "What almost happened? Are you okay?"

My heart speeds up when I feel Aston's cum slowly dripping between my thighs. I'm surprised I'm just now noticing it.

I was so wrapped up in him leaving that I forgot I never went to the bathroom after we had sex.

He wanted me full of his cum, and that thought has excitement moving over me again.

I squeeze my legs shut and answer her. "I'm fine. If it wasn't for Aston showing up when he did, then who knows what would've happened to me. I might not even be here right now."

She gives me a weird look, noticing the way I'm standing. It takes her a few seconds before her eyes go wide as if she's just figured it out. "Oh God. Please tell me his semen is not dripping down your legs right now? He did wear a condom, right?"

My whole body ignites from her question, sending my heart into overdrive. I feel my face heat, the embarrassment of her being so blunt filling me.

I know we should have used protection, but in the heat of the moment all I wanted was to have him inside of me, feeling him between my legs as he claimed me as his.

He's the first man I've let inside of me without protection, but the way he thrust himself into me bare, knowing without question that I'd want it, only seemed to turn me on more in some sick, twisted way.

I know being on the pill can only do so much, but something tells me he doesn't just randomly sleep around with women. He seemed surprised that I was even willing to let him within breathing distance of me.

The Locke brothers have a reputation that I'm sure doesn't have many women knocking down their door for sex.

My silence has her eyes widening even more.

"Holy shit." She throws her hand over her mouth and takes in the bite marks and redness covering my exposed skin as I stand here smiling at her expression. "Looks like he's just as rough in the bedroom as he is outside of it." She appears curious now and less afraid. "Was the sex at least enjoyable?"

"Honestly… I've never come so hard in my life."

I can't believe I told her that, but the words spilled from my mouth and it's the absolute truth. There's no hiding that even if I wanted to.

She stares at me, but I don't feel like justifying myself.

I've never felt this way before, and I don't want it to end. I don't want to pretend that I can let this go, just let Aston go. I've spent too much of my life sticking up for someone that no one else understood, someone that the whole town tore down, little by little until there was nothing left of her to save.

I will not step back now and judge Aston, especially understanding some of what he's been through.

Without knowing what that pained expression behind his ice-blue eyes is all about, I have no right to judge his actions.

Melissa may never understand, and that's because she didn't grow up with my mother. She didn't have kids laughing in her face her whole life because her mother was severely depressed and the talk of the damn town.

All because no one took the chance to ask what my mother had been through.

I will never be one of those people to let others' opinions get in the way and blind me from my own emotions.

Aston Locke is misunderstood.

He's feared by the whole town.

And I want nothing more than to see the real him.

The one that somehow has a way of making me feel safe around him.

14

Aston

I'm shaken awake in the middle of the night by one of my asshole brothers pushing me around, not giving a fuck that I'm dead asleep.

I left Kadence's place, not wanting to be without her, but fuck if things hadn't gotten weird with her roommate.

I figure they had shit to talk about since I got caught in her room, and me not being there was probably for the best. Not to mention I had a feeling this would happen and my brothers would've flipped their shit if I was gone.

"Wake your sleeping beauty ass up," Sterling says above me before slapping me across the face to irritate me. "We've got a job to handle."

Pissed off, I wait until he walks away, then I toss a knife

at the wall. It skims right past his grinning face and sticks in the old wood.

"Asshole," he mutters, but I hear him chuckle, clearly amused by my angry outburst of violence.

Grunting, I pull my tired ass out of bed and run a hand over my face while exhaling. I glance at the clock. It's still late as hell, but the sun will be rising in a few hours.

Whatever the fuck my brothers want to do will have to be finished while we still have the cover of darkness on our side.

I get ready, head to where my brothers are, and together we leave, ready to take on whatever needs to be handled so damn badly that some fucker is willing to pay us five grand to get the job done.

The atmosphere is pretty fucking somber, and although I don't know exactly what's going down, I know it's a dirty job. They always are.

I let my older brothers handle planning this shit. I just follow along and take care of business. I have been ever since they saved my ass that night.

With grim expressions we climb into the vehicle and head down the road. I pull out my knife and start running my finger over the blade.

It's a habit, one that calms me, one that lets me know I'm in control. I'm the one who holds the fucking power.

We drive for about twenty minutes before pulling into the driveway of an old-as-fuck, falling-apart house.

This is a meet-up spot, no doubt. No one lives here, not unless they are crackheads, or maybe a teenager looking for a spot to get his dick wet.

A few minutes later and another car pulls up beside us, setting my ass on high alert.

You never know what to expect at one of these, so you always need to come prepared.

Once we are all out of the vehicle, we head inside. The stench of mold, age, and decay surround me. I take in the waste, the despair and toxicity.

It's exactly the kind of place a person with a black heart —and one cold motherfucker—would live.

Guess that's why I feel so at home right now.

The guy in front of us looks shifty as fuck. He has two other guys with him, maybe scared being in our presence.

Good, he needs the backup if he decides to fuck us over.

"You can do this?" the guy asks, shifting on his feet, looking around the room, maybe thinking the cops will bust in or some shit.

"Yeah, you want the guy who fucked your sister up real good to get the message," Sterling says, cocking his head to the side. "That's our fucking specialty. But you already know that shit, so don't question it."

"You can't fuck him up yourself?" I'm never one to keep my mouth shut, but then again, all the Locke boys are this way.

We get it from our uncle. There's no doubt about that.

"We don't want our hands dirty in this, and I don't want my sister in danger anymore. If they know it's us, it'll be an all-out war. I just need this prick to walk away from her. I need him to know there's someone out there that has the ability to fuck him up and hurt him worse than he's hurt her."

"It's not a problem," Sterling says and looks at me. I can see in his expression he wants me to shut the fuck up.

Nothing new there.

Hell, it doesn't matter to me, so I shrug. I want this asshole to pay as much as the dick hiring us does.

"You know where to find him?"

Sterling nods. "We got all the information already."

"We'll handle it," Ace adds with a wicked grin.

Yeah, we'd handle it all right. I have some aggression to let out, and a motherfucker who doesn't know how to treat a woman seems like the perfect outlet.

Without another word Ace snatches the envelope from the dude's hand and shoves it in the front of his ripped-up jeans. "Let's go show these motherfuckers who they're dealing with so little brother here can get some damn beauty rest."

"Fuck you," I say with a grin while twirling my knife around. "I'm always down; let's just do this shit."

Really, I just want to get back to Kadence.

My brothers and I pile into the SUV again and head toward the address Sterling was provided with.

I'm surprised as hell to see this asshole lives in the rich part of town. Hell, he probably lives in his parents' basement and gets off on beating his woman, knowing she won't run because he has money and connections to keep her around.

That's some twisted-ass shit.

Sterling slows the vehicle down, creeping in front of the house as we scope it out.

There's no doubt the residents in his neighborhood are nosy as dick and will call the cops the second we step foot out of this thing, looking as rough as we do.

"Well fuck..." Sterling punches the steering wheel and turns the SUV around. "We can't do this shit here. That asshole should've known that before he wasted our motherfucking time by sending us to a damn subdivision."

Feeling the frustration and anger beginning to creep in, I pull out a cigarette and take a long drag before slowly exhaling.

It's shit like this that makes me want to go after the idiot that hired us for the job.

I close my eyes and lean my head back on the seat, getting lost in thoughts as we head to the house.

The thought of Kadence instantly gets my cock hard, which considering I'm in the SUV with my brothers, makes me feel awkward as hell. But I don't give a shit when it's all said and done.

What I want to do is get out of the vehicle now, go to her place, and fuck her so she knows that she's mine.

But I'd be an asshole to show up at her house at four in the damn morning, not knowing if she has to be up soon for work.

I have no doubt in my mind I already wore her out for the night. She's going to need as much sleep as she can get to make it through today.

And all the strength she can get for when I claim her again.

Once we pull into the long-as shit driveway leading to the middle of nowhere we call home, my gaze immediately sets on an old Buick parked in the grass.

My brothers must notice it too, because it has Sterling speeding up, now in a hurry to make it to the house.

Whoever the hell is stupid enough to be creeping around our property in the middle of night must not know shit about who we are and what we're capable of.

I'm guessing the asshole never made it inside to break in before we pulled up because King, that big bastard of a dog, would be tearing at the front door right now, ready for a late-night snack.

"I got this fucker." Before Sterling can stop the vehicle, I jump out the back and chase down the stranger who's now running and weaving his way through the trees behind the house.

He has another thing coming if he thinks this little hunt is something he'll get away from unscathed.

Fuck that. Not happening.

The adrenaline pumping through my veins has me catching up with the guy and dragging his ass over to the river.

With force, I throw his body down into the dirt and drag him down to the dirty water. "I guess you don't know what happens to assholes who think they can fuck us over." Growling out, I push his head down into the water and hold it for a few seconds, feeling the darkness consume me as he struggles in my arms.

He sucks in a burst of air the second I yank him up by his hair. "You gonna tell me what the fuck you're doing here, or are you still thirsty?"

"Fuck you," he coughs out. "Not telling you shit."

I tilt my head and smile. "All right, your choice."

Before my words can even register, I have the dick's head back under water, holding it there as I pull out a cigarette and light it, which is harder than hell seeing as the asshole is struggling.

I have all night to do this shit.

"What ya doing, little brother?" Ace walks fast down the hill, grinning like a maniac when he sees the scene before him. "You get more and more like me every day. That shit is scary as fuck. Leave the twisted shit for me. It's all I have left."

Exhaling, I release the back of the guy's hair and give Ace what he wants. We all know he needs this twisted shit to survive more than we do.

"I'll go find Sterling," I say stiffly.

"Don't bother. He found out where the boyfriend was and took off before I could stop him."

I toss down my cigarette and punch the tree, the skin breaking open, the pain lacing up my arm.

"He's alone. Sterling can handle it." He smiles down at the asshole crawling his way out of the water. "And I'll play with my new friend here."

I have no doubt about that.

These two assholes will be lucky if they survive my brothers tonight.

15

Kadence

The coffee shop I work at is small, family owned, and older than I am. But I like the owners and feel like I'm part of the family.

They also work with my schedule and allow me to make up my own hours because I take some classes at the community college.

The pay might not be the best, but it allows me to help Melissa with rent and all that shit, and makes me feel like I'm at least contributing.

"Can you clean off the corner table, honey?" Cheryl, the wife of Bryon, and the other owner of this place, calls out from the back room, pulling me from my thoughts.

"Sure," I say, grabbing a rag and heading to the table she's referring to.

All I can think about is Aston, what he's doing right now, if he's thinking of me...

God, I am still sore in the best of ways. His passion is unlike anything I've ever experienced, unlike anything I can even think about.

Even my thigh muscles protest as I lean over the table to clean it off. A flash steals over me, the images of what we did last night, of how he fucked me...and that's exactly what he did.

Another hour passes, and I clock out, anxious to get out of here. I don't know if I'll see Aston tonight, or again really. He was vague about it all, just up and leaving, making me wonder.

I need a run, need to get this anxious energy out of me. It's still light outside, and I'm not stupid enough to go running at night after what happened.

Once I'm back home, changed into my running gear and my phone shoved into my pocket, I take off. I have no particular place to go, no destination in mind. I just need to run as far and as fast as my feet will take me.

I need to be covered in sweat, my heart racing, the blood pumping through my veins. I need a distraction to keep my mind from being stuck on Aston.

I don't know how long I run, but I end up finding myself

at the edge of town, the dirt road that leads to the Locke brothers' house in front of me.

I only know of this place because Melissa made me very aware, when I moved into town, that this is the road I needed to avoid at all cost.

My heart is thundering, and as much as I know I should leave, go back home before it's dark, I still stand here, wanting nothing more than to take the forbidden trail.

It's the sound of tires on gravel that have me glancing over my shoulder to see a dark SUV, the windows tinted, coming right toward me. I move to the side, unable to run back home, knowing this is fucking stupid. Melissa was right; I'm insane.

And when the SUV comes to a stop right beside me, the window rolling down, my heart jumps into my throat.

I know the man in the driver's seat...Sterling Locke. The middle brother.

He stares at me, his gaze unwavering, his dark eyes and hair making him seem ominous, dangerous. Hell, he can look like an angel and still be known as the devil himself.

I take note of the tattoos covering his neck, his chest, arms, and hands. But that's not the only thing I notice.

Blood on his knuckles, splattered on his shirt, his skin.

And then he grins at me, this demonic-looking expression that has my blood going cold.

"I've seen you," he says. "Get in." That smile is gone, his voice hard, sharp.

I should go, could probably lose him in the woods. But I'm not that stupid. They live out here alone, away from everyone for a reason.

To think he can't find me, that he probably doesn't know where I live, is fucking dumb to even contemplate.

"I don't hurt women," he finally says. "Besides, I know Aston saw you last night."

This surprises me. Maybe that realization flickers over my face, because he laughs, low, amused.

"If you think my brother and I don't know what the fuck is going on with our youngest, you must not know us very well." He unlocks the passenger-side door. "Get in. Aston is at the house, and I'd like to know what the fuck is really going on with you two."

And I find myself walking over to the door, opening it, and climbing in.

God, did I just accept an invitation into hell?

16

Aston

Fuck. I wish my asshole brother would hurry the hell up and get his ass back home.

All I want to do is go see Kadence, to put my hands on her sexy little body and possess her. I've been itching to since the moment I left her alone, but there's no way I'm leaving this property until I know Sterling is safe, until I know the job is done.

He hasn't been back since he left last night to take care of that douchebag, and apparently his phone is dead because it's been going straight to voice mail since early this morning.

I don't like this shit. Not one bit.

It has Ace's crazy coming out as he paces around the

porch with his precious hammer, randomly slamming it into anything within its vicinity.

He's going to bust the whole damn house down soon if Sterling doesn't show his ass.

Hell, I'm even anxious as fuck right now, playing my damn guitar as a distraction, something to keep the demons at bay before I lose it like our eldest brother.

"I'm going to kill that asshole myself," Ace grits out while practice swinging his toy. "Hope he likes the taste of titanium, because if he *does* make it home, I'm knocking his motherfucking teeth out for making us worry."

"It's not the first time he's left us sitting around with our thumbs up our ass," I say stiffly while carefully setting down my vintage guitar. "If it were me out there, you fuckers would be searching the streets for my ass, knocking down doors to find me. Hell, I wouldn't be surprised if your crazy ass burned down every house just to get to me."

Ace swings his hammer around and then leans against the old porch railing, his dark eyes landing on me. "Damn straight. We almost lost your ass once already. You don't know what kind of fear that puts in a man. It makes killing an easy fucking decision, little brother."

Headlights coming down the dirt road have both me and Ace standing tall, anxious to see if it's Sterling pulling up and not another idiot who thinks he can pull one over on us.

King's silence as he watches the vehicle get closer lets us

know that it's Sterling and not a stranger approaching. If it was anyone but one of us, King would be barking and ready to attack.

"Lucky bastard." Ace growls and jumps over the railing, walking to stand in front of the vehicle, not giving two shits if he gets run over.

The tinted-out SUV gets within a few inches of hitting Ace before Sterling stops it and kills the engine.

I stand back with a smirk and watch as Ace swings out, punching Sterling in the face the moment he steps out of the vehicle.

"Calm the fuck down, big brother." After wiping his thumb over his bloody lip, Sterling cracks his neck before head butting Ace, sending him stumbling back a bit. "I had a rough damn night, brother. It took longer than I expected. Had to make sure that motherfucker knew to never lay his hands on a woman again." He holds up his bloodied, broken-up fists. "He got the message loud and clear."

Blood covers his shirt and neck, a testament to the violence that he delivered, the violence that runs in all of us.

Everything goes silent, every one of us Locke brothers freezing the moment the passenger-side door opens and Kadence steps out, looking unsure.

I feel King move beside me, but I quickly put my hand out, silently commanding him to stay.

He won't hurt Kadence—hell, he'd hurt us before going

after a woman—but I'm doing this for her peace of mind. To let her know she's safe.

Closing the door behind her, Kadence leans against the Expedition and takes her time looking us over before speaking. "Hi." I can tell she's trying to be strong, act brave even. But the tiny signs of her nervousness are clear. "I don't know what I'm doing here. I should leave. I... I should go..."

"Stay," I command as I watch her chest quickly rise and fall. "Don't fucking move." The sight of her has my damn heart pounding out of my chest, eager to get to her and claim her before one of these assholes get the idea that she's available.

"Well fuck me..." Ace says while looking her over with a side smirk. The asshole has charm when it comes to women, with his clean pretty-boy looks, but the dick is the most twisted of us all.

And that's pretty fucking twisted.

Before Kadence can even react to my brother's gaze on her, I'm coming up beside her, pulling her tight little body against me to let my brothers and her know she's *mine.*

This has my brothers smiling, reminding me how much they love a challenge.

Too bad for them, because after the way I *fucked* her hard last night, filling her tight little pussy with my cum, there's no way they're going to touch her.

Or that she's going to want them to.

Kadence is mine in every fucking way, and we both know it.

I just need my brothers to know that shit.

As much as I was wanting to see Kadence tonight, to feel her fucking skin all over mine as I claim her, having her here at the Locke house was the last thing I expected or wanted.

Not this damn soon.

Kadence

Every single one of the Locke brothers has their eyes on me, taking me all in. I can't hide the fact that it has my legs shaking below me, about ready to give out and send me to my knees before them.

Not from fear but from the raw intensity these brothers possess. They have the ability to bring any girl to their knees with just one look, and to be honest, I can barely handle Aston looking at me that way, let alone all three of them.

Holy hell... what have I gotten myself into?

"If one of you motherfuckers so much as breathes on what is mine, I'll cut your little peckers off without batting a damn eye." Aston's harsh tone has his brothers looking surprised.

As if they're not used to him staking his claim on something—or better yet, *someone.*

I look over at Aston, my heart beating wildly in my chest, my palms sweating. I was so nervous when I got in the car with Sterling, and even more so when I got out, not knowing what to expect.

I hope like hell I'm at least playing my calm well enough, so I'm not standing here looking like a terrified little girl in front of the three bad wolves.

Aston has me partially behind him now, his hard body blocking me from his older brothers as he stares them down, standing tall and firm.

The possessiveness is coming from him like a damn wrecking ball, about to tear down any asshole who gets in his way, family or not.

I can't help but feel this thrill rush through me at that.

I'm not exactly sure what's going on, but I have a feeling that trying to exert my independence, maybe making everyone know I can handle myself, can take care of myself, is not the best route to go.

These men are a breed of their own, dangerous and powerful, dominating and territorial.

I need to tread lightly.

"Shit, little brother." Sterling leans against the dark vehicle, looking amused as he takes in Aston's body in front of mine. "It looked like your girl needed a ride, so I gave her one. That's all. I didn't touch her, so calm your dick."

"Well damn," the oldest Locke adds with a twisted grin. "Since when the fuck did you get all possessive over a girl and shit?"

"Since I made one mine," Aston says with a confident smirk. "So back the fuck off. I'm taking her downstairs and away from you horny assholes."

I find myself swallowing as Aston grabs my hand and begins pulling me along with him toward the back of the house.

When you first step inside there's a set of stairs that leads right down to the basement, to where I assume Aston's room is.

The thought of what could possibly happen down here, alone with the youngest Locke, has my whole body buzzing with need, ready to feel him on my fucking skin again.

17

Aston

I take Kadence to my bedroom, away from the prying eyes of my fucking brothers.

Although I know they won't mess with her because I made it clear she's mine, I'm not taking any chances on them eye fucking her.

"That was...intense," she says, her voice soft, her focus on my room.

It's pretty fucking sparse, only the essentials, but it's one of the only places I can think if I need my space.

And all I can think about right now is being with her, fucking the hell out of her, really making my claim known. I want my brothers to hear, to know she's mine, that her screams are for me only.

“I’m sorry,” she says. “I needed a run and I somehow ended up... here. Your brother saw me and told me to get in the vehicle. I can leave if it makes you uncomfortable.”

I hear what she’s saying, but she doesn’t need to explain herself to me. The fact that she somehow found her way to me only turns me on more, making my need to be inside her grow.

“Come here,” I say, my voice deep, my cock hard. She has this little running outfit on, the clothes tight as hell, her tits on display.

Her nipples are hard, and the scent of her clean sweat fills my nose. She’ll be even sweatier once I’m done with her.

She comes close to me, her breathing ragged her desire clear.

“How wet are you for me?” I reach behind and grab her hair, yanking her head back until our eyes meet.

I kiss her, making her take my tongue, suck on it, want more of it. I grow harder from Kadence’s flavor, the way she feels against me, the fact that she wants this just as badly as I do.

“I’m going to fuck you so hard you can’t walk straight tomorrow.”

She gasps against my lips, and I kiss her harder, grazing my teeth over her mouth and drawing blood.

“God, Aston.”

I turn us around, lay her on the bed, and take a step

back, admiring her sexy little body that's meant just for me. "No, not God, but you'll be screaming his name once I'm done with you."

Kadence

I'M SO LOST in Aston I can't think straight, can't even breathe. He has our clothes off before I can even contemplate what's happening.

I don't care though because I want this so badly I can taste it.

"Get on your hands and knees," he grits out.

I obey, because it turns me on to do what he says, to know he likes it when I am good and obedient. I can see it in his eyes, in the way his breathing changes.

When I'm in the position he wants, I glance over my shoulder, seeing him grabbing his huge cock, stroking it from root to tip.

"You want this in you, stretching you, making you feel good?"

All I can do is nod. I'm so wet, my thighs damp, my clit tingling. I need him in me, showing me know what it feels like to be possessed, to be owned.

"I want you screaming, want your cries to fill this fucking house." He's on the bed, his hands on my hips, his hard cock right between my legs, so damn close. "If you're going to be in this motherfucking house, I want my brothers to hear you, to know that you're mine."

I'm breathing so hard now, so fast.

I feel him reach between us, place the tip of his dick at my entrance, and in one thrust he's buried in me, making me take all of his huge, thick inches.

I gasp, my eyes watering from the intrusion, from how damn good it feels.

And then he's fucking me, shoving into me and retreating, over and over. I cry out, the feeling of pleasure and pain too much to handle, too much to bear.

His hand reaches around to grip my throat, him squeezing as he buries himself deep, showing me and everyone within hearing distance that I'm his.

It turns me on more than he could ever fucking know.

The sheets are tangled between my fingers, my nails aching from how hard I dig them into the mattress. I'm going to come and he's just started, just filled me.

And then he grabs hold of my hair with his other hand and yanks my head back hard. I do come them, crying out how good it feels to have him take me. To have Aston all over my fucking skin.

Before my body can come down from its orgasm, Aston has me lifted off the bed and my back slammed against the wall, taking me hard and deep again.

The wall shakes from our weight against it, my body

moving up and down the surface as he fucks me hard. So fucking hard that I'm screaming again, no doubt his brothers hearing every last second of my pleasure as the youngest Locke stakes his claim on me.

I can barely breathe, his strong hand tight against my throat, his body pressed so hard against mine. And I love it. I want more of it.

Screaming, I dig my nails into his muscled back, feeling his flesh under my fingernails as he continues to pound his cock into me. Our mouths are so damn close it's like we're both fighting for air.

Leaning in, I bite his lip and tug, causing him to shove inside of me and stop. When he doesn't move for a few seconds, I bite him again, but harder, feeling him smirk against my lips.

"You want more. Good, because I'm not done yet."

With that he tosses me back down onto the mattress and flips me over before slamming into me and cupping my breasts in his hands.

"God, Aston." I yell that repeatedly, not sure if I'm saying it in my head or the words are spilling from my lips.

"Yes, so fucking good," he grunts, smacks my ass in a bruising sting, and makes me get off again. I know there will be a bruise in the morning.

I want it. I crave it.

And when I feel him tense behind me, I know he's

getting off, know he's filling me up with his cum. He has a tight hold on my hips, a painful grip.

I want those black and purple fingerprints on my flesh, a mark of his passion, of his need.

I collapse on the bed, not able to breathe, not able to even move. He only fucked me for a short time, but God, I can't even feel my legs.

I guess he got that right.

18

Aston

I don't know what the fuck Kadence was thinking, coming to the Locke house like she did, but damn, I'm glad she's here and in my bed.

I'm glad my brothers now know she's mine, and that I'm not letting her go.

She fell asleep shortly after we had sex for the second time tonight, her body worn out from mine claiming hers.

I'm just hoping like hell my brothers and I don't get a call to take care of a job tonight, because sitting here, playing my guitar softly as she sleeps is the only thing relaxing me and keeping me calm.

I haven't felt this kind of peace in a long fucking time,

and I don't want to let it go. With the darkness that was eating me up earlier today, I need this right now.

I need *her* right now.

But I should've known it wouldn't last for long, because her roommate no doubt has no idea where she's at. And she'd freak out knowing that she's here, with me, in this house.

Which is exactly why her phone is now vibrating across the floor.

The sound of her cell has Kadence sitting up quickly looking panicked as she searches for her phone.

She looks good sleepy and well fucked.

"Oh shit!" She scrambles across the bed and bends over me to get to her phone. "Melissa is going to have a heart attack because I'm not home yet."

By the time she goes to answer the phone, it's already stopped ringing.

"Come here," I say while setting my guitar down and pulling her naked body over to straddle my lap. "I'll drive you home if you want." I grip the back of her hair and graze my teeth over her neck. "Or you can sleep in my bed."

She lets out a small gasp as if she's surprised by my offer. I've already claimed her as mine, so you better fucking believe I want her sleeping in my bed.

Just as she gets ready to say something, her phone goes off in her hand again, causing her to lean back and exhale in annoyance. "I should probably go home before Melissa loses it even more and sends out a search party. I hate that she worries." She eyes me. "But then again she probably has good reason to if she thinks I'm with you." She smirks.

Damn right.

Tilting her head to the side, I run my tongue up her neck, stopping below her ear. "Fuck, I could do this all night with you if we had the time." I grip her ass and pick her up to set her on the ground. "Get dressed. I'll throw on some jeans."

Once I get my jeans on, I reach behind me and slide my pistol into my waistband—a normal thing for us Lockes to do when leaving the house so late at night and by ourselves.

I'm surprised when I feel Kadence slowly run her hand across the handle before her lips come down to gently kiss my shoulder.

"Have you ever had to use this thing?"

I nod my head and clench my jaw at the memories. "I've put a bullet in a few motherfuckers that deserved it, yes. But I haven't killed anyone."

I hear her swallow from behind me. Her breathing picks up as if me having this pistol is a turn on. "You should get me home."

After we're fully dressed, we make it upstairs to the back porch to find my brothers smoking a joint in front of a small fire.

Ace immediately rushes over to stand in front of us

while taking a hit. "Well shit. I think our baby brother needs a few hits after all that hard-core fucking downstairs."

"Not now, asshole. Gotta get Kadence home."

"I'll take a few hits." Kadence snatches the joint from Ace's hand, surprising us all.

"She's a keeper," Sterling yells over at us with a laugh. "Hell, she hasn't run off yet. She's braver than most we know."

"I've been through more than you might think. If I learned one thing throughout my childhood, it's that you can't judge others just by what you hear. There's a reason everyone is the way they are." Kadence's gaze meets mine as she takes a hit off the joint and then slowly exhales. "Being scared isn't something I want to do anymore. I refuse to. After losing my mother last year, I fought too hard to be brave just to give up now and wither in a fucking corner."

On instinct my arm wraps around Kadence's waist and I pull her against me as if to protect her from anything she might fear. "And you'll never have to be fucking scared again. I will tear down any fear that ever threatens to haunt you."

I grab the joint from her hand and take a few quick hits before tossing it back to Ace. "I'm driving her home and I'll be right back."

Kadence

I GLANCE OVER AT ASTON, wondering what in the hell I've gotten myself into.

I'm head over heels for this guy, and I don't even know how it happened, but ever since the first night I laid my eyes on him, he's consumed my thoughts.

I don't know why I took those hits when Ace offered me his joint. I'm not even a pot smoker, but I needed something to mellow me out, and it seemed like the perfect time.

The images of what we did in Aston's room play through my head, making my want and need for him grow again. This man has a way of making me crave him, like my darkest desire.

As it is my thighs are sore, the slight stickiness of Aston's cum on the inside of my panties, making me acutely aware that he claimed me.

I shift on the seat and notice he glances at me.

"You okay?"

I nod, my face heating.

"I bet your panties are wet with my cum, aren't they?"

I find myself gasping, the shock of hearing him so blunt still unusual for me.

He smirks, and the sight of the corner of his mouth kicking up has my inner muscles clenching.

That wicked smile always gets me. It's so unbelievably sexy in every way.

God, I can't believe I want him right now again. I am still sore from the other two times we had sex, and that wasn't even that long ago.

"Go on, admit it," he says. "Tell me how wet your panties are from my cum."

My face burns as I grip the seat, needing something to dig my fingers into.

I contemplate lying, but in all honesty I don't want to.

"You know they are wet."

He groans, this deep, rough sound that makes me tingle all over.

Before long we are pulling up to my place, and I'm disappointed our little sex conversation can't go on.

The living room light is on, and I know Melissa is waiting up for me, so sitting out here too long will have her blowing up my phone again.

Before we left his place, I called her, listening to her ranting about how worried she was. But the thing is, I didn't tell her I was with Aston.

Of course I have to. I have to admit that I am with him… that I am his.

And as crazy as it is, I look forward to admitting that. I'm not ashamed one bit that Aston has claimed me as his own.

"Good." Aston's voice is deep and full of need as he reaches between my legs and cups me. "Remember that if any fucker tries touching what is mine."

I close my eyes and suck in a breath as he wraps his

hands into the back of my hair and leans in to bite my bottom lip. "Fuck, I need you, Kadence. I need us. Tell me you want the same."

"Yes," I admit. "I want this... us."

"Fuck... I could listen to those words leave your lips all damn night."

My breathing picks up as his tongue swipes across my lips before slipping between them.

I'm not sure I'll ever get used to the sinful taste of Aston's mouth.

Once our lips separate, he releases the grip on my hair to place his hands on my face.

I find myself swallowing as his eyes meet mine and hold my gaze. "I'm sorry about your mother." My eyes close as his thumb gently brushes my cheek, comforting me. "I want to know what you've been through, Kadence. And if you didn't need to get home right now, then I would've stayed up all fucking night learning about your life and everything that hurts you. I'm fighting really fucking hard to let you go right now."

I'm not really sure what to say, so I just nod and offer him a small smile.

I haven't really gotten to see this softer side of Aston yet, and I have a feeling it'll only make me fall for him more.

19

Aston

We climb out of the vehicle, and I want to immediately pull Kadence against me again, keeping her as close to me as possible.

I should stay in the car, go home, and let her deal with this. But a part of me wants to protect her, wants to be there for her.

Always.

But there's something in the air, something thick, almost ominous. I look around, not knowing what it is but understanding this sensation, this pull on my skin.

We're not alone. I know this feeling well. It's something I've become used to over the years.

I instantly bring Kadence closer, and I can see she's worried, not sure what the fuck is going on.

"What's wrong?" she asks, her voice raised, her worry clear.

"Shhh, baby." I scan the area, and that's when I notice the guy standing across the street, right in front of the house.

I can't see him clearly, just a dark figure in the shadows, but I know he's one of the fuckers from the other night, the night my brothers and me fucked them up.

He's probably been waiting for his chance to get back at one of us, and this asshole would be smart if he ran inside and told his little friends about me being here alone.

I push Kadence behind me, this protective instinct rising up. The need to protect her is the only thing running through my fucking head right now, consuming me.

Once I see that he's not moving from his spot, I grab Kadence's hand and quickly begin guiding her to the house, needing to get her inside so I can relax a little. "Come on," I demand. "Let's go. Now."

Without question she speeds up in front of me, allowing me to walk behind her, my body protecting hers, all the way to the door. I don't even wait for her to look for her house key before I reach out and turn the knob, hoping like hell that it's unlocked already.

Relief washes through me as the handle turns, allowing me to push it open and get her inside.

"Make sure you lock this door as soon as I walk away. Got it?"

She nods her head and turns the lock. "There. It's already locked..."

Before she can finish what she's saying, I grip her face and crush my lips against her, feeling a rush of air leave her lips as I pull away and look her over.

"I'll be out here for a while. Get some sleep."

"Do you really think he's going to try something?" she asks, sounding a bit nervous. "I don't want anyone to hurt you."

My lips turn up into a small smile as I take a step back. It's fucking cute that she's worried about that asshole hurting me. "Don't worry about me, babe. He'd be stupid to try."

Once the door is closed and I see the light turn on in Kadence's bedroom, I head back out to the SUV, lean against the back and pull out a cigarette.

I need something, anything, to calm my nerves right now. Even the slightest idea that Kadence could possibly be in danger has me feeling like a fucking madman, ready to explode at any second.

Placing the cigarette to my lips, I take a long drag and slowly release the smoke as I scan the area once more, to see that motherfucker just standing there, staring, trying to be intimidating.

After the hell I've been through, he's gonna have to try a lot fucking harder than that.

Still... it angers me to have him out here and so close to her.

I don't go after him though, not with the bastard just staring, although I want to. I'll leave him be right now, watch him, make sure he doesn't fuck things up or mess with Kadence.

Tossing down my cigarette, I get in my vehicle and watch him. I'll stay out here all damn night if it means I'm going to make sure she's okay.

Hell, I'd prefer to have her at my place, where I know she'll be safe, where I know I can better protect her.

But I also know I can't smother her. She needs to be at her place, needs to feel at home. But I'm not gonna pretend that having this fucker just watching and waiting isn't working my ass up and making me want to kill him.

I'm so focused on the house across the street I don't even realize someone is beside my car until the sound of knocking on my window draws my attention. I turn to see Melissa standing there.

I roll down the window and immediately notice how nervous she is.

"I'm not going to hurt you," I say. "We don't fucking hurt women."

She glances away, her focus on the ground.

"Yeah, but I know how dangerous you guys are." She lifts her head and looks at me. "Everyone knows."

Well, yeah, that's the truth, but she should have also heard we protect women if it comes down to that.

"I just want to make sure Kadence is in good hands, that this isn't some random hookup for you. I can't just stand back and let my best friend get hurt."

I have to give the girl credit; for being afraid of us, she sure has some balls of steel.

I smile, not trying to be a bastard. "If I wanted her for a piece of ass, I wouldn't be here. I wouldn't still be seeing her after I've already had my cock in her pussy, nor would I have made it known to everyone that she's mine."

Melissa's eyes widen, and I grin wider.

"She's mine." I say it harder, wanting Melissa to know I'm not going anywhere. "Now go inside and lock the door. I don't like you girls being outside when that asshole across the street is. Got it?"

After a second she nods and heads back inside.

I glance across the street again, and see the fucker is gone. But I'm going to hang out for a while, because leaving right now is not something I'm comfortable doing.

If shit is going to go down, I'm going to be here to handle it.

Even if that means sleeping in the damn Expedition.

20

Kadence

The next day

Melissa had an earful to give me the second I stepped into the house last night and shut the door behind me.

I understand where she's coming from. I do. We've been friends for as long as I can remember, and we've always had each other's back, no matter what.

Even when all the kids at school made fun of me because of my mother's mental instability, her sometimes not leaving bed for weeks, Melissa was the one who stood up for me and offered to ask her parents for permission for me to stay with them from time to time.

It's not surprising that she's still feeling the need to protect me after all these years.

When my mother decided to take her life last year, Melissa begged me to move closer to her and told me she'd be there for me always.

I hesitated at first, not wanting to leave the safety of my hometown, but after months of my mother being gone, moving in with Melissa seemed like the best thing for me.

Especially with all the judgment and whispers being thrown around behind my back. People believing one day I'll end up like my mother, allowing the whole world to cripple me and hold me down.

That's what my mother did. It started out with my grandparents beating her and abandoning her before she even turned sixteen. My mother met my father shortly after that, and he took care of her.

But after a while he couldn't take it anymore. Couldn't handle her waking up in the middle of the night, crying and popping pills. So...he left too.

Left the both of us, and after that everything went to shit, rumors being spread until there was nothing left of my mother, no strength or will to live.

Then one day I found her lying on her bedroom floor, not breathing.

She overdosed, looking for a way to escape. A way to run away from all the rumors and twisted facts about her and her life that people chose to believe because *no one* could understand the suffering she'd been through.

I guess you can say that's why I was drawn to Aston in the first place. I wanted to get to know the real him. To see and *feel* the scars that made him who he is today.

Sighing, I look down at my tea, the liquid swirling around, the steam rising above it.

"You know I just worry because I care about you."

I glance up at Melissa and smile, thankful that she's been such a good friend to me. "I know, and I care about you too, but I really do feel connected with him."

Melissa smiles, her mood toward him seeming different now for some reason. "Yeah, I spoke to him briefly last night when you got in the shower."

That surprises me, and I'm curious about what they said.

"Basically he said I have nothing to worry about because he's claimed you." She scoffs. "Sounds like a caveman."

I start to laugh, picturing what her face must've looked like when he told her this.

"But if you're happy, I'm happy for you."

I let her words play through my head. "I'm happy." I find myself grinning. "He makes me feel like there's something to look forward to. I haven't felt this way in... well... ever."

"Good, then I'm going to stop worrying so much, or try not to at least." She grabs her bag and stands. "I gotta head to work. Please, just text me or call me this time if you plan to stay out with him late."

I stand and give her a hug. "Sorry, I know. I should've done that, and I will from now on."

"Good. Enjoy the rest of your break and don't work too hard."

I watch her leave the coffee shop and sit back down to finish my break and drink my tea. My thoughts instantly go to Aston, about what he said to Melissa and how he makes me happy.

I want to know more about him, want to have him in my life, bond with him.

I want him to be mine as much as I'm his.

The future is still unknown, but that's part of the appeal, wanting to see where it leads me.

Aston

I PULL my Harley up at the coffee shop Melissa said Kadence works at, and kill the engine, my mind being made up about being seen in public.

Feeling a bit anxious, I slide my helmet off and jump off my bike, setting it on the seat.

I flex my jaw, feeling gazes on me as I run my hand

through my messy hair, smoothing it back while placing a cigarette between my lips and lighting.

It's been a while since I've been out during the daylight, around the prying eyes of this nosy-ass town, judging me. It's something I try to stay away from.

But after spending all of last night and most of this morning sitting outside Kadence's house, I woke up and instantly wanted to go back to her.

This need taking over, wanting to make sure that fucker didn't try anything after I left.

Although Melissa told me Kadence was safe, I couldn't help but want to witness it for myself.

Which is exactly why I'm here, standing in the open, with gazes all over me.

Standing tall, I take a few drags off my cigarette, keeping my focus straight ahead as the whispers surround me, everyone taking this moment to try to figure out what I'm doing in town.

I know they are all afraid of me, of the things I've done with my brothers to exact revenge. But if they don't fuck with me, I won't bother them.

Everything in this damn town is so close together that it's not just the people at the coffee shop getting this very rare glimpse of me, but everyone at the convenient store next door and the hair salon on the other side.

I can still feel their gazes on me, their curiosity making

it impossible to turn away as I toss my cigarette down and make my way to the door.

If it was dark out, I guarantee each and every one of these people would be running fast and locking their damn doors, afraid of what I'd do to them.

Smirking, I turn around and give them all a good view of my face before I open the door and step into the coffee shop.

The scent of coffee and baked goods slams into my nose, surrounding me, momentarily making me feel like I've stepped off a damn cliff and entered a different world.

The amount of times I've actually been in a coffee shop, diner, or hell, anywhere that had a group of fucking people in it, equals zero.

And I sure as fuck wanted to keep it that way, but for Kadence I'd do anything.

That realization slams into me, and I falter in my steps. Fuck, she's so embedded in me it's hard to even fucking think straight.

I don't see Kadence right away, so I take a seat at one of the back tables, away from everyone, the shadows partially obscuring me.

And then I see her walking out from the back, her bag over her shoulder, her focus on her phone. God, she's so fucking hot, so mine.

I rise, walk over to her, and in front of everyone pull her

close. She gasps and looks up at me with wide eyes, her surprise clear.

Keeping her body flush against mine, I cup the back of her head, aware everyone is watching us, their scrutiny clear, potent.

I don't give a fuck.

And when I lean in and claim her mouth, press my tongue between her lips, make her taste me, take me, I hear her moan.

"Kiss me back, baby." I pull her in closer, harder. "Let's give these fuckers a show. Let them see you're mine."

I feel her smile against my mouth.

After a long minute I pull back, loving how her mouth is red, glossy, and so fucking lush.

"Let me take you out, show you off." I never do this shit, never wanted to go this route. But with Kadence I want to do a lot of fucking things I never thought I would.

She seems surprised again.

I grin. "Let me wine and dine your sweet ass."

She laughs, and I pull her in for a hug, loving the feel of her against me.

"So, what do you say, baby?"

She makes me wait for an answer, this sexy smile on her beautiful face.

"Yeah, wine and dine my sweet ass. Let the world know I belong to the youngest Locke brother and I don't care what the hell they think."

I grin. That's what I'm talking about.

21

Kadence

Being out in public, doing normal everyday activities is something I know Aston doesn't do very often. Maybe never. Which makes this moment so damn special, only making it that much easier to allow myself to fall for him even deeper than I already have.

I'm lost in this man, and I don't care who knows.

When we walked in the door over thirty minutes ago and asked for a table, I could see the way people looked at him. I could see in their eyes how much they feared him.

Could see the judgment.

Didn't matter to him though. All that seemed to matter

was him taking me out and treating me to the night he believes I deserve.

He's barely taken his eyes off me since we sat down, and I love it.

But truthfully I don't need these kinds of things from him. I don't need a nice dinner out in public for him to show me how much he cares.

I realized that the second we walked inside and all I wanted to do was get him alone again.

All I need is for him to touch me the way he does.

For him to kiss me and take me like no other man ever has or ever will.

As much as I love us being here right now, showing everyone that he's mine and I'm his, I want to do something for *him*. I want to show him that I don't need this nor want it.

He's what I want. *We're* what I want.

"Let's get out of here." I toss my napkin on the table and walk over to him, leaning down to wrap my arms around his neck. "Take me to your place. I'd rather be alone with you. There are too many eyes on my man, and I don't feel like sharing you... ever."

His lips curve into a small smirk as he stands up and yanks me to him. "You don't want to finish your food first?"

I smile and shake my head. "We'll take it to go and eat it for a late-night snack. I don't have anywhere to be tonight now that Melissa knows I'm yours."

With a small growl he leans in and bites my bottom lip, pulling it into his mouth. Goose bumps cover my flesh as I feel the tip of his tongue swipe across where he just bit me.

He doesn't bother pulling his mouth away from mine as he digs into his pocket with his free hand and tosses some cash onto the table.

"Fuck, baby. I love the sound of that." He possessively grabs my hip and begins walking us to the door. "Let's get the fuck out of here so I can have you to myself. Forget the food. There's plenty at the house."

WE'VE BEEN STRETCHED out on Aston's couch for the last hour, the house empty, his brothers gone. Although I didn't finish my dinner, I'm feeling full, content. As if being here with Aston in the comfort of his arms is all I need.

But what makes me feel even better is the fact that Aston went out of his way earlier, went against his comfort, and took me out. I still haven't stopped thinking about how he did that for me. He may be a hard-ass who thinks he has no heart, that his soul is black, but he's proved to me more than once that that isn't the case.

My heart goes crazy the moment Aston sits up and kisses my forehead, before he stands to his feet.

"How about we get some fresh air, talk out on the porch?"

I sit up and smile. "Yeah, okay." I want to talk to Aston, want to get to know him more, to have him know more about me.

I get off the couch, and we head toward the back of the house. I notice he grabs his guitar one the way out.

Once we're sitting down, he looks over at me, this intensity on his face, but this softness comes through when our eyes meet.

"Tell me what makes you happy," he says the sincerity in his voice not masked by the harshness that is all Aston.

I glance up at the sky, the stars so bright among the darkness.

"I've never really thought about it," I answer honestly. I think about his question, about when I was truly, really happy. "Melissa has always made me happy. She's my best friend, but you know who really makes me happy?" I glance at him.

He's picking at his guitar, but I can tell he's listening to me.

"You make me happy. So happy, Aston, and that kind of scares me."

He sets his guitar down, and before I know what he's doing, he's pulling me onto his lap.

I rest against his chest, his body big and warm, hard and masculine.

"You make me fucking happy too, more than I ever thought possible in my life."

I smile at that, knowing how he feels. It's how I feel, too.

"Tell me about your mom? Tell me what happened to her." He squeezes me tighter to him, his warm lips brushing against my neck as he speaks again. "Tell me everything I should know about you. I want to learn every fucking thing."

Closing my eyes, I lean my head back and rest it against his shoulder. "My mother was mentally ill. Severe depression and anxiety that no pills seemed to fully control. She'd been through a lot in her life that no one understood, and when you live in a small town... people talk." I stop to release a small breath, thinking about how damn much I miss her. "It got so bad that my father up and left her with barely even a good-bye. Left us both as if we were nothing, and eventually she realized she couldn't handle being here any longer. She couldn't handle being in her own head, and she took her own life."

A tear slides down my cheek the moment Aston's lips gently press against my neck to comfort me. "I'm sorry, baby. Sometimes a person's own mind is their worst enemy. I know that feeling all too well, and it can consume you, making it so damn hard to breathe."

"It's been over a year now," I continue. "I stayed in town at first, trying my best to move on with everyday activities, but it became overwhelming with everyone around me always bringing her up and making snide remarks about her death." A small breath escapes me when I feel Aston's thumb run across my cheek, swiping the tear away.

I take a few seconds to regain my composure before I attempt to go on. "Melissa kept telling me to move in with her and forget about our hometown. Finally, I found my way here. So here I am. Here with you under the stars."

"I'm so fucking happy you listened to Melissa." He kisses my neck again and buries his face in it, his arms holding me protectively. "Remind me to thank that roommate of yours one day. Fuck, I owe her for bringing you here."

For long moments we stay this way, the remembrance of the soft tune he'd been strumming filling my head and the stillness of the night surrounding me as he holds me.

But as I feel myself drifting off, feeling so comfortable in his arms, the sound of tires crunching on the gravel driveway rouses me.

"What the fuck?" Aston says, his voice harsh, dangerous.

We rise and walk around the house when we hear what sounds like a truck approaching. By the way Aston pushes me behind his back and how tense he's become, I'm going to assume this is some bad shit.

22

Aston

The truck comes to a stop in front of the house, and I know that this isn't going to be a good fucking night.

I recognize the truck from the house across from where Melissa lives, and know the fuckers we offered a beat down to have decided to come back for a little vengeance.

I had a feeling they'd want to retaliate, especially when I noticed that fucker watching Kadence's house. I just had no idea they'd actually have the balls to do it.

But only one guy gets out of the car—at first, anyway. The tinted windows make it hard to see if there's more inside, but this fucker would have to have a death wish to come alone.

It's the same prick who'd been mean-mugging me the whole time I fucking watched his ass at Kadence's house.

It's the same fucker who I beat the shit out of and smashed his face into the arm of the couch.

I might need to call my brothers. I can handle this prick, even his asshole friends if one chooses to join him. But any more and there will be trouble, a lot of fucking trouble.

That's when I'll need my sadistic brothers.

"Hey, remember me, you fucking asshole?"

"Go inside, Kadence." I hope she actually fucking listens to me.

I'm thankful as hell when I hear her close the door behind her.

I stare at the asshole in front of me and notice the gun he's got in his hand. It's close to his body, and from the way he's tense, his finger twitching on the side of the gun, I'm almost positive he's never actually fired the thing in his life.

That makes for a pretty dangerous situation. He's working on emotion, and although that might make him sloppy, it might also make him unstable ... even more so than he was.

"You made a huge fucking mistake by coming here. You know that, right, motherfucker?"

He grins, trying to keep his grip on the pistol firm, but I can see his hand shaking. This kid doesn't want to use that thing.

Hell, maybe he doesn't have to.

Reaching for my guitar, I grin and walk down the steps, keeping my eyes steady on his, knowing that I'm intimidating him.

It's then that I hear one of his asshole friends coming at me from the side. The prick tried to be slick by walking the property instead of arriving in the truck.

Too bad for them King is out walking the property and will hunt them down real fucking soon. This one got lucky to get past him unnoticed.

Knowing this could possibly be a huge fucking mistake, I take my eyes off the kid with the gun and slam my guitar into the other guy's face, knocking him down into the dirt.

I take my anger out on his face, slamming my broken guitar into him repeatedly until his face is covered in blood and the knife he was holding slips out of his hand, allowing me to kick it away.

Turning back around, I toss the guitar down and come at pistol kid before he can get brave enough to use that thing.

I hear the sound go off right before I feel the bullet slam into my shoulder, pain spreading throughout my arm, stunning me for a short moment.

This has Kadence rushing out of the house to make sure I'm not dead. I immediately push her behind me to keep her out of his shooting range, but before I can react, she's holding out the pistol I had sitting downstairs on my bed, and aiming it at the guy.

I don't know what in the fuck is going on, but my girl is fierce as fuck. Maybe a little too fierce.

"Put the gun down, or I won't hesitate to use this thing." She takes a step closer to him, but I quickly throw my uninjured arm out, keeping her back. I can feel her body shaking, but I can tell by the tone of her voice that she means business. "I mean it. Do it! Don't even think for one second that I would hesitate to put a bullet in your chest."

As much as I love the fact that she's just as willing to protect me as I am her, I couldn't let her pull that trigger even if she wanted to.

This is my life. It's the life me and my brothers chose. There's no way in hell I'm letting her get her hands dirty to save my ass.

Holding my shoulder, I keep my eye on the fucker, taking in every movement he makes, waiting for just the right time to make my move.

"Nah-ah. Nope." He waves the gun at us while talking. "This motherfucker and his brothers came into *my* house, roughed us up, took our money, and broke fucking bones. No one does that shit and gets away with it. Locke brothers or not. Well tell me, motherfucker..." He cocks back the hammer and begins walking toward us. "Where are your brothers to fight now?"

The closer he gets, I can see the sweat trickling down his forehead, this asshole clearly not confident with that pistol he's aiming at me. Maybe worried that even that won't be enough to save him.

And if his friends don't come out to help him soon, worrying is what he *should* be doing.

"Stop walking!" Kadence shouts. "Right now, damn it!"

This has the asshole laughing, throwing him off his game. If you're going to use a gun, you should know to never take your eye off the enemy, not even for a split fucking second.

He made a mistake with that, giving me just the time I need to take charge of this situation before he can put another bullet in me or, hell, Kadence.

Quickly, I snatch the pistol from Kadence's hand and stalk toward him, pressing the barrel right between his eyes.

I push past the pain, ignore it as I focus on this bastard.

"Who said I need my brothers?"

Truth is I wish I had my brothers here, but if this fucker thinks I can't handle him on my own, I'm about to show him exactly how fucking crazy I am.

"Kadence," I growl. "Get back inside and lock the fucking doors. Now."

She says no at first, but finally takes a few steps back toward the house once she hears King's bark coming from somewhere down by the river.

Ace comes from out of nowhere, dragging another one of the assholes by his neck as if he's a rag doll.

Once she sees that one of my brothers have now joined me, she rushes into the house and locks the door as told.

I warned this motherfucker that coming here was a huge mistake.

He's about to see just how fucking huge.

Now it's time to push that point home.

23

Kadence

I don't know what the hell came over me, but when I heard that gunshot, fear of losing Aston took over and before I knew it, I was rushing outside with Aston's pistol in my hand.

As soon as he sent me inside the first time, I ran down to his room, knowing there'd be a gun on his bed. I remembered seeing it before we got comfortable on the couch earlier.

Melissa would kill me if she knew I'd risked my life for Aston tonight—risked my life in general—and that I'm hiding out in the Locke house while there's a possible war breaking loose just outside.

I'm not going to lie; I'm terrified. Terrified for Aston and his brothers, although I have a feeling I shouldn't be.

The whole town knows how dangerous the Locke brothers are. They can handle themselves, and I'm pretty sure this can't be the worst situation they've been in.

Still, I can't stop my body from shaking as I think of the worst possible scenario. The thought of losing Aston has my stomach rolling, feeling as if I'm about to lose my dinner.

It's quiet outside. Too quiet, as if they've somehow managed to take this situation away from the house. Possibly into the woods, where I know their pit bull got ahold of one of those assholes attempting to sneak around the property.

Who knows how many more are out there. They're most likely outnumbered.

Twenty minutes go by. Then forty, before I finally hear someone yanking on the door handle, trying to pry it open.

My heart sinks, my stomach twisting into nervous knots until I hear Sterling's voice, telling me to unlock the door.

Before I know it, I'm standing in front of the door, pulling it open to see Sterling and Ace looking back at me, both of them splattered with blood and looking a bit roughed up.

Panic immediately starts to kick in, my worry for Aston taking over until he rounds the corner, smiling up at me as if to tell me not to worry.

On instinct I rush over to him and throw my arms around his neck, crushing my lips to his.

He kisses me back hard, so fucking hard that I somehow end up biting my bottom lip.

Once we pull away from the kiss, he cups my face, his gaze meeting mine. "Don't ever risk your life for me again, Kadence. Yours is worth so much more than mine ever could be. Got it?"

"You might have the whole world fooled," I say while keeping my eyes locked with his beautiful blue ones, "but not me. I see the real you. I *feel* the real you, and it's so much better than you think. Don't ever tell me you're not worth it."

"All right, time to break this mushy shit up and get this damn bullet out of your arm, little brother." Sterling slaps him on the back and flashes me a smile. "You're one badass chick. Looks like you're more than capable of handling a Locke. Just do us all a favor and don't get yourself killed." He winks and calls for Ace to join him in a different room, where I'm guessing they plan to take care of Aston's shoulder.

What in the hell have I gotten myself into?

But even thinking that, I can't help but smile.

Aston

I HEAR the sound of the bullet hitting the sink, smell the blood filling the air, and feel the tugging as Ace bandages the wound up.

"All right, you're good, little brother." Ace secures the bandage and steps back with a smirk, proud of his handiwork.

"You're not going to the hospital?" Kadence says with shock in her voice, looking between the three of us.

Sterling is the one to speak. "It's a gunshot wound. That would draw too much attention. It went in clean, and we'll watch it. He'll be fine. You're both lucky as fuck we pulled up when we did, but just remember our job is to protect *you*. You're one of us now, Kadence, but that doesn't mean you fight for us. When things get dirty, you run, got it? Plain and simple."

Kadence nods her head, offering a small smile, seeming pleased to be called one of us.

"Good. We'll leave you."

Ace and Sterling leave, and I stare at Kadence, taking in her expression.

"I'm fine, baby." I can see she's worried, so I pull her in and hold her, wanting nothing more than to comfort her. This woman that was willing to risk her fucking life for me.

"That was insane," she whispers.

"Yeah, it was. I wish you hadn't been involved." I pull her back and look into her eyes. "Sterling was right. You may be one of us, but I never want to see you out there on the battlefield again. Let *us* protect you and never the other way around. Promise me." My voice is hard, wanting her to know how damn serious I am. "Fucking promise me now."

"I promise," she says, a little breathless as her eyes search mine.

I might be wounded, but I need her right now, need to touch her, hold her, feel her. I need to know this is real, that she's not going anywhere.

Maybe she needs this moment as much as I do. It sure as hell feels like it, and when it comes to Kadence, I haven't been wrong yet.

A second later we're kissing, my tongue between her lips, my body pressed to hers.

A small noise leaves her, this one of want, of need...of being here with me.

Has me so fucking hard.

I can't help the small noise that leaves me. She just feels too fucking good.

She breaks the kiss, panting.

"No, you're injured. Let's just rest, talk."

But the way she looks at me after I grin tells me she knows I'm not about to let this end.

Kadence

We need to stop this because Aston needs to rest. But he's alive and I want him. I want to feel him, to know he's here with me.

He's on me, pulling me closer, kissing me again until we're somehow making our way downstairs, our mouths barely leaving each other's.

I'm lost in the sensations, making it impossible for me to resist him, wounded or not. Doesn't matter; I will *always* want this man.

We go to the bed, he lays me on it, his big body over mine, and I just absorb the feelings.

He starts to kiss and suck the side of my neck, completely ignoring the pain in his shoulder as if I'm all he cares about. Aston is thorough with his tongue and lips, making me squirm beneath him, ready to beg for his cock in me.

I try not to touch his shoulder, but I want to feel his heat, his strength. I want to know that this moment is happening.

The hot, hard length of him is between my thighs. He starts moving his hips back and forth, rubbing himself against me.

"I need you out of these fucking clothes," he growls next to my ear. "Get them off."

I don't wait for him to ask twice.

Sitting up, I strip myself of my shirt and pants before

reaching over and gently pulling Aston's shirt up his body, until I'm tossing it on the floor next to mine.

I reach for his pants, to undo them, but Aston makes it hard, his mouth capturing mine and biting as I struggle to undress us both, until we're both finally free of our clothing and panting into each other's mouths.

I look down as much as I can, and with the way Aston hovers over me, I can see his cock sliding through my cleft. It's so damn arousing, and I know I can get off from this alone.

His cockhead moves against my clit every time he presses his dick upward. I groan at how good it feels, wanting and needing it inside of me before I go crazy with this need.

"How much do you want me?" he whispers against my lips while wrapping his hand around my throat. He gives it a gentle squeeze and moves his cock against me again. "How fucking much?"

I want to feel him stretching me, pushing into me hard. I want to feel like what happened, him getting hurt, nearly dying, was a dream.

A nightmare.

He starts to swirl his tongue around the shell of my ear, causing my lips to part and my eyes to close.

"I need you in me, now."

Without breaking away, Aston releases my throat and

reaches between our bodies, grabs his cock, and places the tip at the entrance of my pussy.

Everything inside of me stills, my hands gripping his back, preparing for his intrusion. For his thickness to fill me, to consume me.

"I can't go slow. The thought of you getting hurt or killed because of me makes me fucking insane. I'm about to show you just how much I need you."

All I can do is nod and hold on tight, more than ready to take him, to feel him. Everything he has to give me.

In one deep, hard thrust he shoves his thickness into me, causing me to scream and dig my nails into his muscular back. His balls are pressed right up against my body once he buries himself all the way inside me. I am stretched to the max, the pain mixing with the pleasure, making me hungry for more.

"Fuck," he says harshly. He pushes in and out, over and over, groaning with every thrust and retreat.

I scream against his sweaty neck, holding on for dear life as he takes me hard. Fast and hard, as if he needs to be inside me to survive. As if we need each other to breathe. And in this moment, I do.

I lift my gaze to his abdomen, seeing his six-pack clench and relax with every thrust. He slams his pelvis against mine, the sound of sloppy sex so arousing.

With just a few more hard thrusts from Aston, I'm

coming around his cock, scraping my nails down his back, most likely drawing blood.

This has Aston growling into my neck, his hands gripping me anywhere he can as he continues to pound into me until I feel his cum filling me once again.

"You're so fucking perfect, Kadence." He slams into me and stops. "And you're mine."

24

Kadence

We spend the next couple of hours alternating between fucking and catching our breath, until we finally find ourselves lying in his bed, him holding me as he talks about his old life.

The one he had before his parents got murdered.

Hearing all the stories of how his parents hurt their children rips my heart out, only giving me more of an understanding of the lives of the Locke boys.

I can't even imagine going my whole childhood afraid of what my parents might do next. Afraid of what new way they might find to physically hurt or torture me.

It wasn't until their uncle Killian, found out and stepped in that the boys moved into the safety of his home.

The boys should've been safe then, but their parents always found some way to manipulate the boys out of their uncle's house and back with them, until the process started all over again.

Aston was just moving of his parents' house for the fourth and final time when he stopped at home late at night to pack his belongings. He found his parents murdered and two dealers robbing them of anything of worth.

The dealers assumed he was alone and stabbed him three times, leaving him for dead, but Sterling and Ace were just outside, smoking a joint and waiting for him.

As soon as they saw the dealers running from the front door, they rushed into the house to find Aston on the floor, bleeding to death.

Sterling took care of Aston until the ambulance arrived, while Ace tracked down the dealers and made them pay.

He killed them both without question, and I have a feeling that when it comes to protecting each other, that they'd kill every single time.

The Locke brothers have been hard and cold ever since, not letting fear cripple them anymore.

"I don't know what to say," I whisper into Aston's neck. "I hate that you almost died. That you could've died tonight too. The thought kills me, Aston. I can't lose you. I won't."

He pulls me onto his hard chest and kisses my forehead, giving me the reassurance I need right now. "That shit ain't going to happen. Nothing is going to fucking keep me from you. Ever. Never forget that. I don't give a shit what it takes. I'll never stop fighting when it comes to being with you."

His words relax me, causing me to fall further into him, allowing his embrace to comfort me. "I hope so," I say gently. "I'm in too deep with you now."

"Me too, baby. Me too."

I practically jump out of Aston's arms when there's a loud bang on his bedroom door.

"Holy shit!" I grab my chest and bury myself under the sheet.

I feel Aston laugh against my arm before he pulls me back to him and yells to whoever's knocking on the door. "What do you want, asshole?"

"We need to discuss some shit," Sterling yells back. "Get dressed and come upstairs. You've got five minutes or we're coming to you."

"Fuck." Aston sits up and runs his hands through his slick hair. "He's right. Even though we roughed these motherfuckers up and showed them we're not to be messed with, we need to come up with a solution for you and your roommate. These guys weren't playing. They came here ready to take us out and hurt us in any way possible. It nearly took Ace drowning a motherfucker to get them to finally back off and leave, agreeing to our terms if we took it easy on them. Still, I don't trust them."

We both crawl out of bed and begin getting dressed. I

can see how tense Aston is, as if he's busy thinking about me getting hurt.

"We're gonna need to find you guys somewhere else to live. It needs to be somewhere safe and closer to us so we can keep an eye out on you two better. Even though we made it clear we wanted those fuckers out of town by tonight, you can never be too safe."

Aston grabs my hand, keeping me close. I follow him upstairs to where his brothers are eating a pizza and chilling on the couch as if they hadn't just almost killed or gotten killed.

Aston didn't go into detail about what happened out there, besides Ace almost drowning someone, and honestly I don't want to know. Their enemies were out for blood when they arrived, but the three Locke brothers are still breathing. All I care about is that the boys took care of them before they were able to take care of the Locke brothers.

Ace pats the seat next to him and gives me a sexy little wink. "Sit. Have some pizza."

I get ready to sit down, but Aston sits first, pulling me into his lap and wrapping his strong arms around me. "All right. Let's discuss this shit so I can get my girl back to bed. It's late."

Sterling shakes his head and hands me a slice of pizza, which I take and begin eating. It's well past two now, and suddenly my stomach is growling.

"I called Uncle Killian, and he's looking into a few properties nearby that we can get our hands on. Said he might have some connections. We should have word within a few days." Sterling tosses his pizza down and gives me a stern look. "I'm sure Aston already told you the plan. It's better to be safe than sorry. Being sorry isn't something us Lockes do very well. We need you to do this for us. Got it?"

I nod my head and lean into Aston as he holds me tighter to him to comfort me and let me know that I'm safe in the hands of him and his brothers.

My safety isn't something I'm concerned about when it comes to the Lockes. It's getting Melissa to agree that worries me.

She already hates the idea of the Lockes even coming close to our house. I can't imagine how she's going to take us needing to move next to them and into their safety.

"I'll talk to my roommate tomorrow and let her know what the plan is. It's going to take some convincing to get her to agree, but I'm down for anything that you guys feel is safe for us. I trust you guys, and I'm going to do my best to get her to as well."

"Good." Sterling stands up and hands me a beer. "Welcome to the circle."

I feel Aston smile against my neck before he kisses his way up it. A small moan escapes me, causing him to growl into my ear.

"Finish that beer so I can take you back to my bed. I'm not done with you yet. I won't be for a long fucking time."

Holy fuck... I don't want him to be. Ever.

Aston

One week later

I STARE at Melissa and Kadence as they argue over what they need to keep and what needs to get trashed.

They've been doing this for the last three hours, and I have to admit that it's been quite amusing.

Her roommate wasn't comfortable with us helping them move at first, but after I made it clear that there was no way in hell we weren't helping, she calmed down a bit, allowing us to touch her things.

Doesn't mean she hasn't been watching our every move from the corner of her eye as if she expects us to bite her or some shit.

I am a possessive bastard when it comes to Kadence.

I don't fucking deny that.

Her friend Melissa is important in her life, and although I don't want Kadence staying right across the street from the assholes we sent away, I'm not going to leave her friend high and dry and put her in potential danger.

So we helped them find a place closer to us with the

assistance of Killian. It's nicer, not near where those fuckers lived, and I'm five damn minutes from Kadence.

Sterling and I are helping them move, and Ace is setting up some security shit at their new place. Can never be too cautious when it comes to the safety of my girl. Even with having her close, you never know what the fuck could happen.

There's some pretty fucked-up people in this town.

I assumed Melissa would have been totally against this whole idea, but once we told her what had gone down with those fuckers, me getting shot, and Kadence in danger, she was more than willing to pack up and move where it was safe. Apparently she just wasn't expecting us to physically be here helping.

"One last time, ladies." Sterling holds up an ugly old lamp that looks like it was salvaged from the dumpster. "Is this shit coming with or staying? Please tell me this ugly fucker is going in the trash."

"Staying," Kadence says quickly before Melissa can respond. "Staying."

"I like it, but fine." Melissa rolls her eyes at Kadence. "Toss the damn thing. Less junk to unpack."

Sterling grins and throws his cigarette down. "Good fucking choice. This is the most hideous thing I've ever seen." He kicks the lamp across the yard and jumps up to close the back of the truck. "I'm gonna do one more sweep to make sure those assholes are really gone and not just hiding out. I'll meet you at the girls'."

I nod my head and turn to the girls. "You two ready to roll?"

Kadence and Melissa stop by the moving truck, look back at the house, and then glance at me.

"As ready as we will be," Kadence says, and I pull her into the hardness of my body, reminding her that I'll do anything to protect her.

She's one of us now. She's mine and I protect what is mine, no matter the consequences.

"Then let's roll."

EPILOGUE

Kadence

Six months later

I stare at the bonfire in the center of the Locke brothers' property and smile. Aston is beside me, his new guitar in hand as he strums on it.

The sound is peaceful, lulling almost.

I've gotten so used to this that I'm not sure what it would feel like not to be here right now, under the stars with the Locke brothers.

It's something we've been doing every Saturday for the last six months. Even on the colder nights, we still find our way out here in the stillness of the night sitting around a fire having drinks and just giving each other hell.

The boys have been doing this for years now. It's their way of letting each other know that they're a family and nothing will ever break them apart.

It's their short moment of peace in the chaos of their lives. If it weren't for these moments, then I'm more than positive they'd lose their shit.

"You fucker," Ace says to Sterling while elbowing him hard in the chest. "Get your own beer. You saw my ass just grab that one and set it down."

Sterling holds up the bottle with a cocky grin. "You know what happens when you leave shit sitting around. Becomes available to the first motherfucker to grab it."

Ace reaches under his chair for another beer. "It's cool." He pops the top and sits back. "Good thing I'm always prepared."

I start to laugh because this is pretty typical of these guys. And to be honest I'm loving it. I feel like I'm at home, like they are my family.

It's a damn good feeling.

I glance at Melissa, who over the last few months has actually warmed up to the idea of hanging out with them. This is the eighth bonfire she's joined us for, and she seems to fight less and less with each time I ask her to come.

She was still hesitant at first. But she saw how much Aston cared about me, and how much I do for him. She realized this is my life now.

Aston is the man I love. He's where I feel the safest.

"Beer?" Aston hands me one, and I smile and grab it. Before I can take a drink, he grabs my face and kisses me hard, reminding me, just like every day, that I'm his.

I love that about Aston. He's not afraid to show me every single day that I'm his and he'll do anything for me. It doesn't matter what it is, anything I ever fucking ask—although I try not to ask for much.

Truthfully all I want is for him to be there for me, and that's something I know he'll always be. He's proved that every day for over six months, and I've done everything I can to do the same for him.

Leaning against him, I tilt my beer back, taking a small sip. It's cold and runs down my throat, this hoppy, bitter taste that covers my tongue.

I watch the flames again, wondering how my life ended up here. I love it, I really do. I feel like I've finally found my family, like what I was given in life led up to this moment.

"Chug, little sister," Sterling says with a grin.

I smile, the endearment hitting my heart. They welcome me, see me as their family, too.

I glance at Melissa, and see she's grinning. I'm glad she came around and is happy hanging with us, being around them.

She's my family too, my sister, and without her in my life I would be lost.

"Come here, baby," Aston says and pulls me into his lap, his strong arms holding me protectively.

"Come on, chug, Kadence. There are a lot more beers to go around, and this night isn't over until they're all fucking gone." Ace tilts back his beer right before he falls to the ground from Sterling kicking his chair over. "Fucker," he growls before placing the beer back to his lips and taking a drink anyways. "I can drink from here just fine."

"Ignore them and kiss me," Aston says, and before I can do or say anything, he's kissing me, making everything else around us disappear. His mouth on mine always seems to do that. Makes me feel as if it's just the two of us. No one has ever been able to make me feel this happy, and I know from the way he treats me, like I'm his fucking everything, that no one has ever made him feel this happy either.

"I love you," he whispers against my lips. "Do you fucking know that?"

My breath hitches in my throat from his confession, and heat swarms throughout my whole body, making me feel as if I've just burst into flames.

I can hardly breathe, to be honest.

Aston Locke loves me, and I have a feeling that's something he doesn't feel for many people other than his brothers and uncle.

I've known I loved him for a while, but hearing him say it first has my heart beating straight out of my chest.

I love this man so fucking much that it hurts. Belonging to Aston is everything I could've ever asked for.

Aston

KADENCE'S BREATHING picks up against my lips, letting me know that my confession has her heart and body reacting.

Good. That's real fucking good.

It lets me know that she loves me too. Even if she doesn't say it back. She doesn't need to.

I feel it with every moment we spend together.

Every touch.

Every kiss.

Every time I'm inside her.

Kadence is mine, and I've known it from the moment our eyes first locked that night across from her house.

Smiling, she leans into me, gently brushing her lips over mine. "Guess what?"

"What?" I whisper while running my thumb over her cheekbone. "Tell me."

"I love you too, Aston."

Feeling overwhelmed with emotions, I grip the back of her head and kiss her so fucking hard that it hurts.

I kiss her until we're both fighting for air and one of my brothers is throwing something at us to break it up.

Doesn't matter.

They can throw shit at me all night, and I'd kiss this

woman until I can't breathe. I wouldn't stop until I knew she needed to come up for air.

"Holy shit, little brother."

I glance at Ace.

He jumps up from his spot on the ground. "Did I just hear you say love?"

"Hell yeah, you did," Sterling says with a smile. "Our littlest Locke has found his woman."

"Well, I know that shit. But that dipshit has barely even said he loves us. This calls for a cele-fucking-bration."

Ace disappears into the house and comes out a few seconds later with some guns and moonshine.

This motherfucker...

"You don't have to drink that shit." I laugh against Kadence's lips. "Even I think that crap taste like shit."

She leans in and bites my lip. I love it when she does that.

It reminds me that she doesn't give a shit who's around us. She wants me and she's not afraid to show it.

Standing up, I grab Kadence and throw her over my shoulder, giving her ass a hard smack.

"Oh come on!" Melissa laughs while holding up a beer. "You're going to leave me out here with the two craziest Lockes?"

I smirk. "She'll be back... in a few hours."

I'm just about to escape inside with Kadence so we can

get a little time alone when a set of headlights has us all looking down the driveway.

I instantly set Kadence down and stand in front of her, while Ace pushes Melissa behind him. None of us know what to expect.

But from his expression, Sterling recognizes the little white car the second it pulls up and the engine cuts off.

We all watch as a petite brunette steps out and closes the door behind her. It's not until she walks closer to the fire that I realize it's Sterling's old crush from high school... a girl I know Sterling has still kept in contact with. A girl Sterling still cares about.

Wynter's face is busted up, causing Sterling to immediately throw his bottle of beer at the house and walk over to her, pulling her into his chest as she cries into him.

Looks like some whole new shit is about to happen.

There's no way my brother will allow the asshole that hurt her to get away with it.

I love Kadence, and I'd do anything for my girl. Same goes for my brothers, and I know Wynter is the one that got away for Sterling.

The one girl he always wanted but never quite got.

And so it continues.

The dark, twisted ways of the fucking Locke brothers.

The End

SAVAGE LOCKE

LOCKE BROTHERS, 2

Cover model: Jonny James

Photographer: Wander Aguiar

Cover Designer: Dana Leah, Designs by Dana

Editor: Kasi Alexander

Sterling Locke

They say us Locke brothers are savage and that we'll take care of any motherfucker who steps out of line without even batting an eye.

They're right as shit.

The last thing you want to do is get on the bad side of a Locke.

There's no fucks given when it comes to protecting the people we care about. We'll fight to the motherfucking death if it comes down to it.

So when Wynter shows up on our property with a busted up face, looking for protection, you better believe that's what she'll get.

It may have been three years since I've seen her, but I instantly feel the need to protect her. It consumes me, turning me into a monster that even the devil himself doesn't want to fuck with.

I know she's here because she's certain I'll go to great lengths to protect her, but I'm going to show her that she's gonna want me for a hell of a lot more than just that.

I can take care of her, not just making sure she's protected, but by showing her with my body how good I can make her feel.

I'm going to show her that sometimes savage… can be good.

Winter Lowe

I don't know what I was thinking when I showed up at Sterling's house. I guess knowing that only he could protect me made me do this pretty stupid thing.

The Locke brothers are dangerous, and have been since long before I really knew them.

Coming here beaten won't just humiliate me and make me feel weak, but I know it will get the Locke's worked up. And hurting the person who did this to me runs strong in my veins.

But maybe that's the reason I came here… because I knew they'd help me no matter what.

All it takes is one look at Sterling for me to realize my feelings for him are still there… and strong as hell. I want to hold onto these emotions because after what I've gone through they make me feel safe, protected, and like nothing can touch me.

Sterling makes me feel like all of that and more. I want to be his and this time, the dark rumors around town, won't keep me from letting that happen.

WARNING: Savage Locke is a short co-written, kind of twisted love story from NYT Bestselling Author Victoria Ashley and USA Today Bestselling Author Jenika Snow. If you like it hot and a little rough... this is the book for you. 18+

1

Sterling

I feel a rush of adrenaline take over, heightening my need to punish this asshole, and hyping me up about what we're going to do next.

This motherfucker has no idea how much I'm going to enjoy pounding his face into a bloody pulp and leaving him here on this filthy fucking floor to rot if he doesn't talk soon.

"Where's the kid, huh?" Tightening my hold on the collar of the asshole's shirt, I pull him up so we're face to face, not giving a shit about the blood that is dripping onto my jeans. "Tell me where you took him. I won't ask you again."

My brass knuckles are blood-covered, and I make sure

to keep them in his view, reminding him of what it felt like to have them embedded into his face.

"Just tell him, Paul," Ace says from the doorway, swinging his hammer around with a wicked grin. "We've already broken two fingers and that pretty little pinky toe of yours. Want it to be your face next? Not sure how much more of a pounding it can take before those bones begin to shatter."

Paul shakes his head violently back and forth, blood splattering all over me as he fights to catch his breath enough to talk. "I didn't kidnap anyone. He's my fucking nephew. He wanted to work for me so I gave him a job."

His words make me angrier, causing me to lose it on this piece of shit.

Growling out, I slam my forehead into his hard as fuck, and make sure to keep my hold on his shirt. I want it to hurt more for him. "You know that *shit* doesn't matter, now does it, motherfucker? Family or not, he's fifteen and selling fucking crack."

"How the hell did you guys even know about Abel?" the little fucker wheezes out.

"You took off with Camille's son in the middle of the damn night and you didn't think she'd call us to handle your junkie ass?" Ace tosses his hammer down and snatches Paul out of my reach, dragging him across the ground by his neck.

He doesn't stop pulling him, not until he's shoving his body halfway out the fifth-floor window.

This shithole warehouse is so abandoned that I'm not worried about anyone hearing his screams. Other than cracked-up fiends that are so used to this sort of violence that it won't even faze them, the surrounding area is pretty much barren of life.

"If I were Killian, your body would already be smashed against the pavement below and I'd be home happy and peaceful, getting my motherfucking cock sucked while throwing back a bottle of whiskey. But since Abel is like a son to him, here the fuck we are dealing with your dirty ass. You're lucky Killian isn't here himself." Ace grins as if he's just now thinking about what he said. "Oh, wait... did I say lucky?"

With that, he releases Paul's body, catching his feet right before he falls to his death.

This has the asshole so shaken up that all I hear is him crying and pleading through snot bubbles to not let go of him.

"All right, brother." I laugh and put out the cigarette I just barely lit. "I can deal with blood but I'm not dealing with the stench of this fucker's shit if he loses control of his bowels. Pull his ass back in."

Ace shrugs and pulls him back inside. He kicks him to the floor and pins his neck down with his boot.

Then he pulls out a cigarette and lights it as if he's got all night to chill and torture this asshole. "You have until I'm done with this smoke to give me a fucking address or your ass is mine for the rest of the night. We'll be having a motherfucking sleepover, except instead of jumping on the bed and pillow fights..." He stops to take a drag from his cigarette, speaking as he blows out the smoke. "There'll be breaking bones and losing body parts."

"Okay!" Paul screams, prying at Ace's big-ass boot. "Okay! I'll tell you where he's at."

Ace grins at me before flicking his cigarette at Paul's head and kicking him over to his back. "Write that shit down."

I laugh and toss the pad of paper and pen at his busted-up face. "You could've just told us this shit an hour ago and saved us the fucking hassle of beating the shit out of you."

He grunts and rolls over, fighting to open his swollen eyes far enough to see what he's writing. When he's done, he tosses it at my boot. "You'll find him at this address unless Benny has him working the block. Fucking assholes." He whispers the last part.

I look down at my boot and crack my neck before reaching down and wrapping my hand around his throat. "Want to say that shit louder and see if you're still breathing afterward?"

He shakes his head.

"That's what I thought." I release his neck and stand up.

"Let his friends out of the closet so they can see what'll happen to them if they ever attempt to fuck with us."

"Gladly." Ace reaches for his hammer and walks over to the closet door. He swings it around as if practicing for impact. "Might want to stand back, nut sacks."

"Well, fuck. Here we go..." I mutter.

I stand back and watch as Ace swings his hammer through the door, taking the shit down with four swings.

He doesn't even wait to make sure he didn't kill one of the two assholes inside before he turns and walks away. "Let's go pick up this kid and get him home where he belongs."

Paul must've sent word ahead because Benny is nowhere to be found when we arrive at the address thirty minutes later.

Abel is sitting on the couch, high out of his mind and seconds away from losing consciousness.

"Fucking shit." Rushing inside, I pick him up and get him into the SUV as quickly as possible, slamming the door behind me. "Drive fast. I'll call Camille and let her know we're headed to the hospital."

Paul better hope on his motherfucking life that this kid doesn't lose his or he won't just be hearing from us.

And if they think we're bad... they should meet Killian.

2

Sterling

I slam back the third beer of the night, my knuckles burning from the beating I gave that little prick earlier, but my fucking adrenaline still going strong.

I stare at my youngest brother, his girl Kadence on his lap, the affection he has for her clear. I know Aston would fucking die for her, as it should be when you love someone.

I instantly think of the one girl I wanted, but never had. I think about her so fucking much it's damn pathetic.

Wynter Lowe.

Fuck, even thinking her name gets me hard.

I shift on the seat, not really caring if my brothers see how hard I've become, but wanting to be comfortable.

Flexing my jaw, I reach for another beer, pop the cap and down half of it before taking another breath.

There's a flash of headlights coming up the gravel drive, and everyone straightens, already at attention, wondering who would be stupid enough to come out here. Wanting to be prepared, I set the bottle down, reach in my pocket for my brass knuckles, and get ready to beat some motherfucker's ass.

But when I see the little white car come to a stop a few feet from the bonfire, I feel my entire body stiffen with attention.

Fuck.

I'd recognize that car from anywhere. Even if it has been years since I've seen it.

She cuts the engine and climbs out of the car. Wynter looks the same: small, petite, her hair seeming darker now that it's dark as hell outside.

And I still fucking want her.

When she comes closer, her nerves clear, the shadows covering her face partially, my damn cock jerks to attention even more.

But it's when she comes more into the light that I see her face is all busted up. She's got a swollen purple and blue eye. Her lip is split, and there's a nasty fucking scrape along the side of her face.

I toss the half-empty bottle of beer aside, my anger, rage,

burning so damn badly I wish there was some little asshole here for me to beat the fuck out of.

I walk over to her, see she's on the verge of crying, and pull her against my chest instantly. I hold her, telling her things will be okay, and feel myself soften for her.

Only her.

She starts to cry and I grow pissed, not that she's broken in this moment, but because I want to hurt whoever the fuck did this to her.

And I will hurt whoever did this. I'll make sure to work them over so much that not even a dental record can identify them.

"Come with me." I keep her head held against my chest and guide her across the yard and into the house, where she can feel comfortable and safe, out of everyone's view.

I know my brothers are on fucking edge, just as anxious to find out who did this to her as I am.

But this is something I need to handle by myself first.

Wynter

I LET Sterling take me into the house, up the stairs to a bedroom, and set me on the bed.

I feel like I'm unraveling, like what I've been through doesn't compare to the fact I am actually here with him.

It's been a long time since I've seen Sterling, since I left this fucking town and tried to start my life elsewhere.

Should've known that someday I'd be back. This town has a way of keeping people here and my reason is Sterling Locke.

The bed dips beside me when he sits down, causing my heart to race with anticipation of his closeness.

So many times in the past I have wondered what it would feel like to be touched by the middle Locke brother.

He turns me to face him, tips my head back with his finger under my chin, and stares at me, looking at the fucking disaster that is my face.

His anger is tangible. I feel it surround me, coating the air. But it's clear he's trying to stay calm, maybe for my benefit, maybe because he thinks I'm broken.

I'm not wrecked, not yet anyway.

"Tell me what the fuck happened so I can destroy whoever did this to you."

I turn away from him, staring at presumably his bedroom. It's sparse, lacking anything warm, inviting... just like Sterling.

He turns my head so I'm looking at him, his gaze fierce, strong, frightening. "Tell me who did this, and I promise they'll pay."

I knew coming here would be dangerous, not for me, but deadly for the asshole who'd put his hands on me. But when Kevin had started hitting me all I could think about was Sterling.

"Tell me, baby."

In all the years I've known Sterling, known the Locke brothers, never have I heard him sound so… gentle.

"I was dating this guy… Kevin." I swallow the lump in my throat. "At first, he was nice, sweet. But when he started getting verbally abusive I knew I couldn't stay. I knew I had to get out before it escalated."

Sterling's body is tight. I can see the way his muscles are bunched under his shirt, how tense his jaw is.

"But when I went to break it off the escalation was already there." I touch the side of my face, wincing at how tender the whole thing is. "I ended up knocking him over the head with the first thing I could grab, which was a lamp." I can see the scene in my head, fresh, brutal. "He'd just gone crazy, hitting me, cursing at me. It was so bad that I even passed out once and close to a second time. Finally, once I got enough strength to fight back, I reached for the lamp and knocked it over his head as hard as I could manage." I know my eyes are wide when I look at Sterling again. "What if I killed him?"

I'd seen blood, knew I'd cut him pretty good when the ceramic had broken.

Sterling starts grinding his teeth in anger. "I hope not, because what I have planned for that asshole is far worse than death."

He pulls me against his chest again and I close my eyes instantly. I just absorb the feeling of being here, in his arms, knowing everything will be okay.

Yeah, it'll be okay, with a dose of blood and violence that only a Locke brother can deliver.

But somehow... I'm okay with that.

3

Wynter

Without a word, Sterling begins searching through his dresser, pulling out items of clothing before walking back over to the bed and handing them to me.

"The shower is down the hall. You'll sleep in my room tonight. No one will fuck with you here, I fucking promise you that." His voice is deep, rough, as if he's finding it hard to be gentle.

"Thank you, Sterling." I stand up and walk over to him, stopping just inches before him. I know reaching out and touching him, especially his face, without permission might be stupid, but I do it anyway, wanting him to look me in the eyes when I say this next part. "I trust you. I know no one will touch me with you around." *It's why I came here.* "You're the only person I wanted to come to when he hurt me. No one else..."

His jaw tenses beneath my fingertips and a small growl leaves his lips, causing goosebumps to cover my flesh. If Sterling Locke growled at anyone else this way, they'd go running. And they'd have good reason to.

"Clean up and I'll bring you something warm to drink and eat." His amber gaze locks on mine with an intensity that makes my knees go weak. He wasn't asking. He was telling me. "If you weren't covered in bruises, I'd offer to help, but my touch is anything but gentle. When I lay my hands on things... they get broken."

With that he turns and walks away as if he has no other choice.

I take a deep breath and slowly release it, while gripping the pile of clothes in my left hand. His words shouldn't turn me on right now, but I'd be lying if I said the idea of him helping me in the shower doesn't have my body burning with need.

I've always wondered how rough and savage Sterling would be in the bedroom. How much it would hurt when he slammed deep inside me. I've fantasized about his big, strong body taking me far too many times to remember.

And just as I expected... he'd break me. He just said so himself.

The very knowledge that Sterling is so brutal makes me

feel this heat inside. I shouldn't feel anything but pain, disgust, and fear over what happened, but there are buried feelings—strong ones—that can't be ignored.

When I get to the bathroom, the shower water is already on for me, a towel draped over the sink for when I get out.

In the years I was with Kevin, he'd never once taken care of me in the way Sterling has in just the last twenty minutes.

Sterling may be dangerous, but I know without a doubt that he has a gentle side. I know from when we used to talk at school that he believes any gentleness is long gone from the years of abuse he suffered at his parents' hands.

He's wrong.

I moved to Rookeland just after my fourteenth birthday, over eleven years ago, and I still remember the day I laid eyes on Sterling.

His biceps were covered in bruises and scars, and it was clear he fought to keep them hidden, even though his shirt-sleeves were too short for him and kept riding up his long arms.

I remember thinking he was the biggest fourteen-year-old I had ever laid eyes on. He was even taller than our teacher, Mr. Hannagan, by a few inches.

Then by our junior year he finally stopped growing, after reaching just over six feet and four inches. At least that's what everyone said. I'm pretty positive no one was ever brave enough to get close to check.

But by that year, the bruises had spread to his face. The

abuse had shifted from his parents delivering it to Sterling causing fights with other students. I paid attention to him each and every day and wished I was brave enough to at least talk to him about his family and see if he needed a friend.

He watched me every day too. I could never figure out if it was only because he knew I watched him and he wanted to make sure I stayed out of his business, or if it was because he was protecting me.

After Bobbie Mason came to school one day with his face beat to hell and back—the day after causing a scene with me in the hallway—I knew then the real reason that Sterling watched me.

He was protecting me. Just like I *wanted* to protect him.

By the time we graduated, Sterling had moved on to bigger, more dangerous things, causing the whole town to fear not only him, but all the Locke brothers.

All of that seems like another life now, so long ago.

When I step out of the shower, I jump back a few inches, not expecting Sterling to be standing there, holding the towel out for me.

"Holy shit. You scared me." My heart races as I look him over, standing there tall and stern. I have the shower curtain covering me, and although him seeing me partially naked should embarrass me, it doesn't. I'm more embarrassed by what Kevin did to me—by what I feel I *let* him do to me—than anything.

Sterling's gaze hardens as he looks me over, taking in the bruises covering the parts of my body he can see. "I'm going to kill this fucker for laying his hands on you. But I'm going to do far worse than that first. By the time I'm through with his ass he'll be begging me to put him out of his misery."

I close my eyes as he gestures me forward and wraps the towel around me. I don't miss how he presses his face into my wet hair.

Having him so close gives me a feeling of peace and safety I haven't felt in a while, but when his hands grip my waist and his body moves in close to mine, it gives me a whole other feeling I haven't felt in a while.

This is crazy. I'm crazy for feeling these things in this moment.

"I've always wondered what it'd feel like to have you touch me..." I lean my head back, feeling his hard chest against it. "What your strong hands could do to my body. If they would hurt or feel good."

I hear him swallow next to my ear. "How do they fucking feel right now?"

I swallow too, knowing that at any moment his hands will be gone and I'll be left with the memory for the night. "Good. Safe."

"That's really fucking good." He removes his hands from my waist and takes a step back. "Get dressed and I'll come check on you in a bit. I made you something to eat."

Once I'm dressed and back in Sterling's room, I look

over at the bedside table to see a mug of hot chocolate and a sandwich waiting for me.

I grab it and take a seat on his bed, placing the warm ceramic to my lips. I'm not hungry, but I know he'll insist I eat something.

I sit here for long moments, finishing the hot chocolate and eating half of the sandwich. I instantly grow tired, the stress of the night and the three-hour drive hitting me hard, now that my stomach is filled with something warm and comforting... now that I feel safe.

My father doesn't even know I'm back in town yet and if he knew I was here with a Locke brother, he'd send one of his squad cars to pick me up and lock me away just to keep me from Sterling.

I could've sent my father after Kevin. Could've let the law handle him, but after the way he hurt me and treated me like some kind of prisoner for the last few days, scared and helpless as he tortured me... spending a couple days behind bars won't be enough.

He needs to *feel* what I felt. He needs to *hurt* and *bleed* as I did.

I want him to suffer at the hands of the one guy that I know will protect me. The one guy I wish I would've known how to protect when I had the chance.

The guy everyone calls the *Savage Locke.*

4

Sterling

I stand here for a second and just watch Wynter sleeping. She fell asleep about ten minutes ago, and although I'm furious, in a blood-boiling rage over that fucker hurting her, having her here calms me.

I walk over to her and place the blanket on her fragile little body. She's gorgeous, even though she has bruises all over.

God, I'll kill that fucker.

I lift my hand and run my finger along her arm, which hangs out from under the blanket. Her flesh is so smooth, so warm. God, I hate that this is happening with her, but she'll be avenged.

No way in hell am I going to let some asshole hurt her and get away with it.

I force myself to leave her in the room sleeping, and shut the door. I stand here for a second, controlling my breathing, knowing I need to speak with my brothers.

I need to get shit sorted out and a plan made on how we are going to handle the motherfucker that hurt Wynter.

Even though the door is shut I turn and look at it, wanting to go back inside and just hold her and comfort her, letting her know she's damn safe in my arms. My feelings for her have never lessened over the years.

In fact, having her here makes them heightened, makes them rise tenfold.

I head back downstairs and go outside to the bonfire. Aston and Kadence are the only ones not there, and I have to assume that they went inside, probably so he could fuck her.

I'm actually surprised to see Melissa still here, her chair now sitting close to Ace's as if he pulled it there to talk to her while Kadence is gone.

Flexing my jaw, I walk over to Ace and sit down, my anger so fierce it's like a living entity in me. Ace turns his attention from Melissa to me, but doesn't say anything, and honestly it is probably because he knows better.

Talking about it right now is only going to piss me off more.

A few minutes later the front door opens and I lift my

head to see Aston coming toward us. He sits down across from me, his expression guarded, serious.

"Kadence wants to talk to you inside," he says to Melissa, while keeping his hard gaze on me. He waits until she disappears inside before speaking again. "So, what the fuck is going on?"

I don't say a thing for long seconds, just stare at the fire, watching the flames dance and lick at the logs.

"Well, who are we going to go fuck up?" Ace asks.

I look at each of my brothers, knowing they have my back, knowing that they will kill and die for me.

I'd do the same for them.

"Wynter's ex-boyfriend beat her." I have to clench my jaw and curl my fingers into my palm or I'd go out and beat the first motherfucker to cross me.

The pain claims me, and I breathe out slowly. Just saying those words out loud makes me so damn pissed I want to go hunt the fucker down right now and slice his throat open.

"Motherfucker," Ace says under his breath.

"Yeah, that about sums it up," I say.

"Wynter's old man know?" Aston asks.

I shake my head before responding. "I didn't ask her and she didn't tell me. But her coming here tells me that she probably didn't let him know."

I have a feeling she didn't tell her father what happened. Him being involved with law enforcement would've probably made the situation even worse, drawing attention to her.

I know she probably didn't want that.

No, she came to me because she knew I'd handle it old school, real dirty and brutal.

And I will. Hell, I'll make the prick hurt so damn badly he'll never be able to hurt another person again. He won't even be breathing when I am done with him.

Ace hands me a beer and I pop the cap, chug half of it in one go, and stare at my bedroom window. She's up there right now, sleeping in my bed, hurt, scared, but not broken.

I'll make sure she is avenged, make sure she knows I'll always protect her. For her I'd level the fucking world.

"So how do we go about getting to this asshole?" Aston asks, and I glance at him.

"She'll tell me where he's at, because that's why she came here." I look at Aston again, and then glance at Ace. "I'll make sure she doesn't regret coming here."

My brothers grunt in agreement.

Blood will cover our hands, faces, the very ground beneath us. I'll make sure he pays with his life. I'll watch the life fade from his eyes.

I'll be so fucking savage with him he'll beg me for death, for a reprieve.

And all the while I'll have a fucking grin on my face.

I take one last chug off the bottle in my hand before

standing and tossing it into the flames. "I'm going upstairs in case she wakes up and needs me."

"Got it, brother," Aston says. "Let us know if there's anything we can do to make her comfortable here."

"Yeah," Ace adds. "She's welcome here for as long as she likes. The closer she is, the better we can fucking protect her."

"Appreciate it." I turn to leave. "Good night, motherfuckers."

When I get back upstairs, she's still sleeping, lying there looking completely peaceful and at ease.

Good. I'm glad her being here can make her feel that way.

Grabbing the extra pillow, I take a seat in the chair beside the bed and get comfortable.

It'll be hours before I'm able to fall asleep, but I'll stay here anyway, making myself as available to her as possible.

I'm not fucking leaving this spot tonight.

5

Wynter

I wake up in the middle of the night to see Sterling sleeping in the chair. He looks so uncomfortable. My first instinct is to want to make him comfortable, just as he was so quick to do for me.

I crawl to the edge of the bed and grab his hand, running my fingers over the light scars that cover them.

You can tell he uses his fists a lot more than the average man.

He opens his eyes as I tug on his hand, letting him know that I'm giving him permission to join me in his bed.

In fact, I'd feel better if he did: safer.

This isn't about sex, isn't about pleasure. This is about

keeping him close and making both of us feel a little better about the world. Or maybe that's just me.

"Are you sure?" he questions, his voice deep and full of sleep. "You've had a rough night. I want you to be comfortable."

"Yes," I whisper. "Please..."

The bed dips beside me the moment his knees hit the mattress, his body towering over mine as I look up at him, watching his heavy breathing.

But even though I don't think this is about pleasure or sex, I can't help how he makes me feel.

He makes me feel wanted, heated. He makes me feel pleasure after the traumatic event I just went through.

He's hot. I can tell by the sweat that covers his neck and the part of his chest that is exposed by his shirt collar dipping low. I reach out and grab the bottom of his shirt, slowly pulling it up.

He sits tall, his body flexing as I pull it higher, my gaze taking in the scars that cover his tattooed chest. Scars I know were left there by his piece of shit parents.

I fucking hate it. Hate that I wasn't there for him.

God, I shouldn't feel this way... wanting him the way I do. This is fucked up, me being wet and needy. He helped me, didn't try to make a move on me when I was so vulnerable. But here I am touching him... wanting him.

I toss his sweaty shirt aside and suck in a breath. I carefully run my fingertips over the marks that look as if they were left by many beatings from a belt buckle or something really hard.

My arousal instantly vanishes. I feel his pain as if it's my own.

He allows me to do this for a few seconds, his eyes closed tightly as I touch him. Then he reaches for my hand and stops it from roaming over what I know are painful reminders of his past. "It happened many years ago. None of it matters now. They're both six feet under." With a small growl, he grabs my hips and lays back, pulling me down with him and into the safety of his strong arms. "Go back to sleep, Wynter. You need to rest."

My heart beats wildly in my chest at the feeling of being surrounded by Sterling Locke. His hard, sweaty body—a weapon most people fear—is pressed against me, tucking my body into him as if to protect me from everything bad in the world.

And just like that, my arousal raises its head like a vicious beast.

The urge to touch him... to have him touch me overwhelms me, making it hard not to focus on his cock, which is hard as stone, pressed against my backside. He's breathing so heavy, and those hot, humid pants hit my ear.

I almost think he's about to say something when he just squeezes my hip and lets out a small, seemingly frustrated growl instead.

It has my entire body on fire with need, something inside of me feeling alive for the first time in years.

This is wrong, right? Me wanting this, needing it after all that happened?

But I want to continue to *feel* this.

I don't want to sleep, but I know I should. I'm both mentally and physically exhausted, drained from everything Kevin put me through over the last few days.

I've never been so damn scared in my life. When he dragged me down those stairs by my hair, I thought I would die. I was sure he'd beat me until there was nothing left, holding me in his arms until he knew I'd taken my last breath.

I'll never forget the lies I told to keep myself safe while he kept me captive with him in the basement of our home. How I had to convince him of my love for him and that we'd be together forever.

He'd be fine for a little while. He'd calm down and believe the bullshit that was coming from my lips. Then out of nowhere he would freak out again and hit me, telling me he knew I'd leave him as soon as I left the house.

And I did.

I didn't tell Sterling all of this, didn't know where to start. Although I wanted to be honest, I also knew it would just upset him more.

And then I'd gotten free.

I had jumped in my car and headed back home to the

town I had told myself I'd never return to. To the place my father always controlled me, giving me reason to want to get away as soon as possible… to feel free for the first time in my life.

But I knew I needed to get back to Sterling, because Kevin won't stop. His love for me is sick; an obsession he can't control.

Obsessions are dangerous and sometimes deadly.

I know that because that's how my mother died. At the hands of my piece of shit father while he was drinking. He thinks I was too young to remember, but I'll never forget that day. Not for as long as I live.

He denied to himself that it was his fault, covered it up with a lie that I think even he grew to believe himself, and if I had stayed with Kevin, I have no doubt, from the possessive look in his eyes, that Kevin would have done the same to me.

6

Wynter

I try to go back to sleep, but as the heavy, deep and even breathing of Sterling almost lulls me to rest, all I can think about is my past.

I feel like I've fucked up so much in my life.

There is so much I wanted to do, wanted to see. The love I have in my heart is big, strong, and I almost wasted it on that piece of shit Kevin.

I sit up and bring the blanket around my body, this slight chill racing over me. Sterling shifts on the bed slightly, but he still seems asleep.

I stare at him for long seconds, wondering what he's thinking, what he's dreaming about.

Does he wonder about the life he could've had if he'd

had a different childhood? Does he wonder where he would be right now if he'd left this town?

I stand and walk over to the bathroom, the blanket still wrapped tightly around me. I turn the light on and stare at myself in the mirror, the person looking back at me a reflection of what I've let myself become.

Dark messy hair is scattered around my face. My eyes look wide, the bags under them noticeable.

Taking a small breath, I drop the blanket and grab the hem of my shirt, pulling it up so my stomach is exposed. There are bruises along my pale flesh, a reminder of what Kevin did.

They'll heal, the physical memory gone, but I'll always remember. I'll have that scar inside of me forever.

I don't know how Sterling or the other brothers have gone through it, or lived their lives. They have gone through so much, worse than I have in these last three days, but they are still surviving.

Closing my eyes, I let the shirt drop back down and brace my hands on the counter, breathing out roughly. Can I actually go through with this? Can I actually have Sterling go find Kevin and hurt him the way he hurt me?

The more I think about it, the more dangerous—maybe even petty—it sounds. But there's a part of me that wants revenge, wants Kevin to know that there are bigger, stronger people out there who won't let him hurt people, hurt women.

There's a part of me that wants blood drawn, wants Kevin to feel what I felt.

"Are you okay?"

I glance over at Sterling, who is leaning against the doorframe. He's still shirtless, his big arms crossed over his chest. His biceps are bulging, his tattoos on display. I stare at the scars, wanting to ask him about how he feels, but knowing better.

Sterling is not the type of man who will open up easily, if at all.

"Yeah, I'm okay." It's partially a lie, but the truth is I think I will be fine.

Even if I hadn't come here and asked Sterling for help, this part of me, deep down, knows that I'll get through this.

I have no choice but to survive.

Sterling

I LET her walk past me and back to my bed. I can't sleep, haven't been able to once I was lying beside her. I listened to her sleep, listened to the steady breathing of her respirations.

She calms me, whether she ever knows that or not.

She sits on the edge of the bed and I move next to her. I

reach out and stroke her back with my hand, wanting to comfort her, to fucking *feel* her.

"You don't seem okay," I say stiffly.

She shakes her head, but glances at me.

"I'm fine, just tired on the inside and out." She smiles at me and it lights up my fucking life.

It's the most beautiful fucking thing I've seen in a long damn time in this dark and fucked-up life I've been living.

"We'll handle that motherfucker. Don't worry. He won't ever hurt you again." I feel my anger start to rise again at the thought of that prick. "That's a fucking promise I don't intend to break, no matter what hell I have to face."

She swallows, keeping her gaze down at her lap. "A part of me thinks maybe I'm selfish for coming here, for asking for you to help me. I hate that I'm doing this to you. Maybe I…"

"Don't." I pull her in for a hug, holding her close, keeping her against my chest. She smells like me, and that has the possessive side of me rising up like a violent fucking beast.

I don't say anything else, because truth is I can't just let this go. I will go after that bastard. I will make him pay.

I will avenge the woman I love.

Wynter is far from selfish for wanting to hurt that prick back. For wanting me to hurt him for her.

The fact that she came here in the first place makes me happy as shit. It means she trusts me to protect her. It means she's thought about me over the years—and that's all the push I need.

"I need something from you, Wynter."

She tilts her head up to look at me. "I'll give you anything you need, Sterling."

A savage smile tugs at my lips. "I need you to tell me where that motherfucker lays his head at night. My brother and I have a little trip to plan."

"It's about three hours from here. In Gaylin."

Grinding my jaw, I look up at the old clock on the wall. It's just past two. "Ace and I can make it there in just over two." I stand up and start packing a bag of shit I'll need. "Aston will stay here with you. If you need anything, let him know and he'll take care of you while I'm gone. Got it?"

Her gaze stays on me as she reaches over and into her purse and pulls out a key, holding it out to me. "You're gonna need this. It unlocks the back door."

I grab the key and shove it into my pocket before crawling above her, covering her small body with my big one. "Tell me you feel safe here, Wynter." I place my hand around her neck and give it a light squeeze. "Tell me this doesn't scare you."

I feel her swallow as her gaze meets mine. "I feel safe here and you don't scare me, Sterling. You never really have." She closes her eyes and lets out a small moan as my body moves to settle between her legs. "Still not scared," she breathes.

I move my lips down to press just below her ear. “Good. That’s all I needed to hear.”

With that, I crawl out of bed and finish packing my bag, happy as hell to hear she’s not afraid of me.

‘Cause I’m anything but gentle.

My family is anything but gentle and I need her to realize that and still feel safe here.

Ace better be ready for a motherfucking road trip, because this shit is happening tonight.

7

Sterling

After throwing our shit into the back of the SUV, Ace jumps into the passenger seat and yells out the window for me to hurry my ass up.

As *if* I'm not in as much of a hurry as he is.

That motherfucker is lucky he's family because it's not going to take much to set my ass off right now.

Good thing his hammer's in the back, because I have a feeling he's gonna want to use it on me by the time we reach our damn destination.

"Give me a fucking minute, asshole." I take one last drag from my cigarette before snubbing it out and jumping into the SUV. "When Wynter was writing down the address she told me he's got a few friends most likely staying with him now that she's gone. You ready for this, brother?"

Ace gives me that twisted grin he's known for. "I've been looking for another excuse to use my baby and you've just given me one, brother. Drive... fast," he demands.

His response gets me even more pumped up and ready to teach this prick a lesson.

Wynter may not have told me all the details of what Kevin did to her, but she didn't need to. I know he hurt her bad, not just physically, but pretty fucking badly in the emotional department too.

Seeing her in the bathroom with her head hung low showcased just how much damage he truly did, giving me every reason in the fucking world not to wait another day.

I smile and hit the gas.

"Let's get bloody."

Two hours and fifteen minutes later, we show up outside of a big brown house that has two cars and a motorcycle parked out front.

Unfortunately for these assholes, the house is at the end of the street, secluded from the other houses.

More room to allow things to get as messy and loud as needed.

I park the SUV and look over to see Ace grinning again. "Fuck, this is perfect."

"No. It'll be perfect after I smash that motherfucker's face in and teach him what true fear feels like."

We both jump out at the same time and walk around to the back of the Expedition. Ace reaches for his hammer, while I grab for the small bag in the back and unzip it.

Keeping my gaze on the big brown house, I slip my brass knuckles on before tossing the strap of the bag over my shoulder.

"It's going to be a long night for us, brother, so be sure not to bust the coffee pot with your ten pounds of titanium this time when we get back."

He shrugs and swings his hammer around a few times, before setting it atop his shoulder. "I can't make any promises. Let's go."

It's late as fuck, and the perfect time to do this. No need to have the fucking neighbors see all the heinous shit we are about to do.

We make our way up to the front of the house. The lights are off, but I can hear the steady thump of music coming from the back.

"Come on," I say, and we head around to the back. I see a light on from a basement window, and know the music is coming from there even though I'm not close enough to make sure.

Ace gets close to the window first, crouches, and peers inside. I do the same and see a group of guys sitting around a poker table, bottles of opened and half-drunk liquor sitting on the table.

I may not know what the fucker Kevin looks like, but I

don't need to, given the fact the only one with a nasty fucking bruise on the side of his head is the damn prick.

My rage comes alive even more as I stare at the motherfucker. I curl my hand into a tight fist, the brass knuckles digging into my skin.

I stand slowly and roll my head around my neck. I am feeling pumped, juiced up, ready to kick ass and take names. Hell, I hope his little friends jump in on the action.

The more violence the better.

We make our way to the back door, kick that fucker in, and head inside. This is going to be fun, like broken bones kind of fun.

I grin. Yeah, time to settle the fucking score.

Wynter

I WAKE UP WITH A START, my heart racing, my body covered in this light sheen of sweat. I glance around the room, not seeing Sterling and having this feeling in the pit of my stomach intensify.

I know where he is, know what he is doing right now. I'm scared, not for Sterling, because I know he can handle himself, but for the repercussions that might happen because of all of this.

I stand and make my way into the bathroom, turn on the

light and stare at myself in the mirror. Beads of sweat cover my forehead, and I turn the faucet on and splash water on my face.

I try to grapple with everything that's going on, with everything that will go on after this is all said and done. I freeze when I hear a knock on the door. Before I can see who it is, I hear the door opening.

I leave the bathroom and see a young woman standing in the doorway. I recognize her from when I first came to Sterling's place. She'd been sitting on Aston's lap, the love on her face as she looked at the Locke brother clear.

"Hey," she says softly, her smile making me feel a little easier. "I'm Kadence."

"Hi." A moment of silence passes. "You're Aston's girl?"

She nods but doesn't move any farther into the room.

"Come on in," I say.

She comes in and sits on the chair in the corner, looking nervous, or maybe she's worried about me. I have no doubt that she knows good and well why I'm here and what happened.

The Locke brothers don't keep anything from each other, and I made my presence known pretty strongly when I first arrived. I also had a nasty bruise covering my face.

"How are you feeling?"

I shrug, because honestly I don't know how to answer that.

We sit in silence for several long minutes. I know she's

probably trying to make me feel better, maybe letting me know I have somebody to talk to if I want, but there's nothing I really have to say.

"Everything will be okay," she finally says.

I nod, but to be honest I don't know really if that is the truth. Yes, Sterling will handle everything, take care of Kevin and make sure I am never hurt again. But what about after?

I care about Sterling so much, but I don't know if a man like him can ever really be with somebody. And even if he is with me, can I really stay in town, my own past tarnished and darkened?

I close my eyes and pinch the bridge of my nose, knowing that right now Sterling is probably destroying Kevin. But to be honest all I can feel is a mixture of emptiness, but also this spark of happiness over what is happening.

Maybe Sterling and I aren't so different after all?

8

Sterling

Keeping my jaw tightly clenched, I make my way down the basement steps, prepared to take out any motherfucker who gets in my way.

Ace is following at my heels, no doubt his face plastered with a wicked grin, the adrenaline rushing through his veins just as it's coursing through mine right now.

The thrill of destroying someone who hurt a woman I care about has completely taken over and transformed me into a beast ready to take out its prey. There will be no fucks given tonight, no matter how hard he begs.

As soon as we hit the bottom of the steps, the asshole

facing us jumps up from the table and tosses his cards down. "Who the fuck are you assholes?"

I smirk as everyone at the table turns to look at us. "You're about to find out if you don't sit the fuck down."

The first guy throws his hands up. "Look, we don't want any trouble. If you're looking for Kevin he's not here. He went looking for his girl around town."

"Not his fucking girl," I growl out, ready to rip this motherfucker's head off.

"Who's this little prick then?" Ace walks up behind the guy with a bruise covering the side of his face and places his hammer across this throat.

"James," he squeaks out. "My name is James. I swear I'm not Kevin. I'm telling the truth, he's not here."

This son of a bitch is testing my patience right now. "Throw me your fucking wallet." I hold my hand out and wait, but the asshole is moving so damn slow. "Now!" I yell.

"Okay... I'm getting it. It's kind of hard to function when there's a hammer across your throat." He pulls a black leather wallet from his back pocket and hands it to Ace, who tosses it to me.

Disappointment washes through me when I open it to see the fucker isn't lying. "What happened to your face, James?"

"Got into a fight a few days ago with my ex's new boyfriend."

"Kevin took off a few hours ago when Wynter never showed back up. My guess is he's either out getting laid or looking for her." The little guy gives us a confused look. "Why are you guys looking for Kevin, anyway? What did the dumbass do?"

Rage boils throughout me, making it hard not take my anger out on one of these innocent pricks just to let off some steam. "He hurt someone I care about. Now he's gonna hurt."

"Fuck." Some tall blond guy grabs for the bottle of whiskey and tilts it back, looking pissed off now. "That son of a bitch."

Looks like blondie has a thing for my girl.

I walk around the table and stop behind blondie's chair, getting all up in his ear. "Whatever the fuck feelings you have for *my* girl..." I growl, "I suggest you lose them real fucking fast. You wouldn't want that pretty face of yours getting all jacked up and unrecognizable."

He stiffens but doesn't say a word, so I squeeze his shoulder hard as fuck and grin. "Now enjoy the rest of your game as if we were never here." I grab a slip of paper and write my number on it before flicking it across the table. "If Kevin shows up you call. Don't tell the little bitch anything or you become our problem too. Got it?"

"Yeah," James says. "We've got it."

Ace finally removes his hammer from James' throat and throws it over his shoulder all casual-like and shit. "Fuck... I'm hungry. Let's go, brother."

I keep my eyes on blondie, reminding him of my warning, before I follow Ace up the stairs and into the kitchen, where he decides to begin digging through the fridge.

"Seriously?"

He pulls out some lunchmeat, cheese and lettuce, shrugging as he tosses it down on the counter and begins searching for bread. "Want a sandwich?"

"Fuck no," I say, annoyed. "I want to get back to Wynter. Hurry the fuck up with your sandwich before I take my rage out on you. Your hammer doesn't scare me, asshole."

Laughing, he slaps his sandwich together, reaches for his hammer and takes off out the front door as if we weren't just here on a damn mission, possibly to kill some asshole.

I shake my head and step outside, pulling a joint from my jacket pocket and lighting it.

I lean against the SUV, smoking and looking at the house, wondering what life could've been like if it were the two of us living here instead of that asshole Kevin.

What if I would've told her how I felt back in high school? Would it have been us getting a nice place together, living a happily ever after in some other town away from the hell we grew up in? Or am I even capable of living that sort of life?

Fuck, I can't see myself ever living the suburban life. I never have seen myself in that situation. But truth is with Wynter I do want that, even if a fucked-up asshole like me may not deserve it.

But I'm hoping to one day find out what being truly happy is really about...

Wynter

EVEN THOUGH I hadn't seen myself chatting with someone casually, talking about random things like I don't have my own problems, speaking with Kadence is really nice.

She starts talking about her life with her previous roommate, Melissa. Even in high school I didn't have a ton of friends, and certainly not any that would be considered close enough to tell my deepest secrets to.

But I wish I had known Kadence back in the day. I think we would have been good friends, real friends.

I listen to the funny stories she's telling me, no doubt to help keep my mind off things.

It's nice having someone to laugh with, and not worry about what's happening in my life right now.

It makes me feel, even for just a second, that I haven't dug myself into this big, shitty hole.

"So what's going on with you and Sterling?" She smiles right before she scoops a big helping of vanilla ice cream into a bowl.

I watch as she starts eating the ice cream right off the spoon.

She's a really sweet girl, maybe even a little naïve. Or maybe she's not. Maybe she knows what she wants, and I'm just so used to the darkness of the world that I mistake innocence for not giving a fuck what anyone thinks.

That has me laughing internally.

"Silence usually means there's something there."

I snap out of my thoughts and look at her again. "There's nothing there." I lie easily. Yeah, the sexual chemistry and tension is explosive, but aside from that there is nothing there.

Truth is I highly doubt Sterling would ever want anything more than a fuck with me. And on the heels of that I don't even know if he'd want that.

Maybe he sees me as someone he wants to take care of? Maybe that's where I am getting his affection from?

Hell, maybe my need to have him—to be with him—is making me see things that aren't really there.

You wanting what you can't have. Or maybe I can have Sterling but I don't have the courage to actually make that first move.

I start rubbing my head, this headache taking root right behind my eyes.

"There's nothing going on like that. He's helping me out because we knew each other in high school." I feel wrong saying that out loud, like there is something more there, like it isn't just because we are "friends" that he's helping me out with Kevin.

Kadence doesn't say anything, but I can see she senses I

don't want to talk about it. Or at least I hope she catches on. I don't want to bring up Sterling, and what may or may not be there between us.

Before anything else can be said by either of us, the flash of headlights through the kitchen window and the sound of gravel crunching under tires has us both looking toward the noise.

Kadence puts the ice cream away.

"I'll let you talk with him alone." She gives me a smile before heading downstairs to be with Aston.

I head outside at the same time Sterling and Ace climb out of the vehicle. I scan Sterling, but don't see any blood on him. This pressure leaves me, my chest heaving as if this weight has been lifted off.

I don't care if he hurt Kevin; I wanted him to even. But I am worried for Sterling, about him and what this could mean to him… to us.

Before I can say anything, if I was even going to, Ace leaves us alone. Sterling walks up to me, cups the back of my head, and for long seconds, just stares at me.

And then he kisses me, presses his mouth on mine and makes me gasp. I reach out and grip his bulging biceps, feeling warm and happy, relieved he's back here with me.

The way his tongue swipes out to taste my lips has me opening for him, my heart practically beating out of my chest as his mouth captures mine and completely owns it.

After a few seconds, he breaks away and we're both

panting. I want him, but I don't want to be forward, don't want to use this situation as a bandage because it feels good.

"Let's go upstairs and talk." The fierce look on his face softens and he smiles at me.

That sounds like the best idea, and something we both need right now.

9

Sterling

I couldn't stop myself from kissing her downstairs just a few moments ago.

After seeing how blondie had a thing for Wynter, it made the possessive side in me snap. I realized that even though my world is all kinds of fucked up and I may never be good enough for her, I want her anyway.

There's no way in hell I'm letting some douchebag frat-looking dude swoop in and snatch her up as if he's enough to take care of her needs.

The thought of him putting his hands on her, touching her in places I've wanted to since high school, had my blood boiling.

"Who's blondie?" I ask stiffly.

She takes a seat on the edge of my bed and looks up at me, confusion written across her perfect face. "Blondie?"

Walking over to her, I wrap my fists into the back of her hair. She gasps slightly, her legs spreading. I stand between them as I look down at her. "Blonde douche-looking guy that hangs out at your house."

It takes her a moment to answer, but I see the realization on her face. "His name is Zachary." She grips my arm and lets out a small moan when I pull back on her hair slightly, forcing her gaze to meet mine. "He's one of Kevin's friends. Sort of quiet, and has always given me the creeps if I'm honest. I think he's had a thing for me. He always would watch me."

My jaw tightens at the knowledge that he wants her. Creepy fucker. I'll pluck his motherfucking eyes out. "I have a feeling he won't be watching you anymore." I help her farther onto the bed so she's now slightly under me.

"Good," she whispers up at me. "It made my skin crawl and Kevin never seemed to give a shit. It was as if he enjoyed knowing that his friends wanted me."

Keeping my gaze on hers, I place an arm around her waist and pull her up the bed even more, allowing myself room to get on my knees between her thighs.

Her legs begin to tremble as I lay above her, holding myself up with my elbow. She swallows as I rub my thumb over her lip. "I'll make sure no one fucking watches you again. Not this douche and certainly not Kevin. Now tell me..."

She closes her eyes for a few short seconds before opening them, her gaze locking on my lips as I breathe above her. "Yes. I mean... I'll tell you whatever you want."

"Where would Kevin be looking for you at?"

She inhales a deep breath and slowly releases it. "I had a feeling he wouldn't be home, but I wasn't sure. Kind of figured he would've given up looking for me after the first hour."

"Where would he be?" I question again, but firmer this time, while leaning down to speak against her lips. "Don't be afraid to tell me, Wynter. You better fucking believe I'm going to see to it that you never have to fear anything or anyone again."

"He has a friend," she says, breathlessly. "Lives here in town. Huge asshole who was always trying to get him out to bars to get fucked up and hook up with women. But... they haven't spoken in almost two years. Not after Riley attempted to take advantage of me when we were all drinking one night. But I don't know if he'd go there or not. They could be hanging out now that shit has fallen apart between us."

Rage courses through me the moment the words *take advantage of me* leaves her lips. I reach out and grip the headboard, squeezing it so hard that the bones in my fingers feel like they could snap. "Where does he live? Tell me now," I bark out.

She swallows and hesitantly reaches up to touch my face, cupping it with both hands. "Do you think you can just stay here with me for now? I just want a day to feel safe so I can get some rest. Would that be okay? I'm pretty exhausted both mentally and physically. Please… just stay with me."

I find myself nodding, even though I want nothing more than to burn out of this damn property on my bike to kill that son of a bitch for trying to take her against her will.

My need to get revenge on both Riley and Kevin is strong as fuck but at the same time I want to be here for Wynter and show her that I'll do whatever she fucking wants me to.

I want her to know that I'll do everything to protect her, even if that means just waiting while she rests and recovers from all the stress Kevin put on her over the last few days.

"If you want me to, then I will. I won't leave your side until you tell me it's okay." I release the headboard and grab both of her wrists, pulling her hands down from my face gently. "You never have to fear me. You ask me to do something and it's done. Anything you want." I kiss her fingers, her skin soft, sweet smelling. "I'll never make you feel powerless like those sons of bitches did. The only power I need is in the bedroom." I don't know why I tell her that, but the words come out of me like this vicious beast, like this testament for her to know exactly what she's getting into with me.

I run my hands down her arms before gripping her waist and lowering my body to hers.

"When we're naked with my hard body above yours, I need to be in control, Wynter. I need to make you scream and tremble beneath me so you know I'm the only man you want buried inside you. Ever." I lower my face to hers and bite her bottom lip, tugging on it before releasing it. "Think you can handle that?"

I feel her heart pound against my chest as her breathing picks up against my lips. "For you..." She swallows. "I wouldn't want it any way but rough with you in control."

"Good. I fucking love that response." I run my lips up her neck before running my tongue over my mouth, tasting her skin on me. "I've been wanting to touch you this way for as long as I can remember, Wynter." I squeeze her hip and press my erection into the warm spot between her legs. "And I won't let go, not now that I have you." I inhale her scent, take it into my lungs so it's imprinted. "How long have you wanted me to own you, Wynter?"

She closes her eyes and digs her nails into my arm at the feel of my cock pressing against her pussy. "Since we were in high school and you used to watch me... as if you were protecting me, as if I was yours."

"Fuuuuck," I growl against her lips. "It should've been me and not Kevin. I'm going to make up for that mistake. Starting right now..."

10

Wynter

My heart has never beat as fast as it is right now and my body has never been as hot and needy.

The feel of Sterling's hard body between my legs, mixed with his alpha tendencies, has my entire being feeling as if it's about to burst into flames.

As exhausted as I am—as I have been for days—I shouldn't be craving his touch right now. I shouldn't be dying to feel his strong hands on me... to have him taste me and take me any way he wants.

I want him to be savage and in control. I want to *feel* everything that is Sterling Locke and what makes him who he is. The darkness and all.

The fact that I've wanted him for years has this ache in me, this need that has claimed me like a chain around my entire body.

"I want to make tonight about you, to make you feel good, focus on you." His voice is so low, so demanding yet gentle that I can't help but moan softly.

I don't know how tonight will play out, but I want this to last, want this to be the part that has us both coming undone.

Sterling

THERE IS nothing more that I want than the woman in front of me.

Wynter is mine. She'll always be mine and fuck anyone who thinks they can take her from me.

I should go slow, take my time, but I feel like a fiend right now. I push her top up, look at her big, round breasts, and my mouth waters.

My cock jerks at the sight.

Hell, I can jerk off and come from the very sight of her bared for me. But fuck no. When I come it'll be deep in her tight little body.

I'll have plenty of time to take in every part of her, to

make her mine in all the ways that count. Right now is about her. Only her.

I see the way her throat works when she swallows. She's nervous, but there's no need for that. Tonight is about making her come with my lips and tongue.

"I want—need—you unhinged for me, screaming out my name, clawing at my flesh."

"God, Sterling." She breathes the words out, her chest rising and falling as her arousal increases.

I can't help but growl low, this animal in me breaking free, coming undone. It wants out, wants to make Wynter feel so fucking good.

I move an inch closer. "I'm so fucking ready for you. I want to devour every part of you, want to see you break free and not worry about a thing." I can see how she trembles for me. "You want me to make you feel good, to make you come using my mouth?" I want to hear her say she *needs* me. That she craves for me to taste her just as badly as I do... "Tell me how much you want to be mine. Tell me how much you want my mouth all over your body, Wynter."

She closes her eyes and moans.

It's music to my fucking ears.

"Look at me." I need to see her expression, her eyes as I make her feel good.

She opens her eyes and I tip her chin slightly up with my fingers.

Jesus. She's gorgeous.

It takes all of my control not to just say fuck it and be with her, part those pretty thighs of hers and align my cock with her pussy. I want in her so damn badly, but I can wait. I can sure as fuck make this about her.

I watch as she licks her lips, and I can't take my focus off the sight. The dirty fucking images slamming into my head make me harder than a rock.

I'm a dirty bastard for imaging her on her knees, her mouth wrapped around my dick, her gaze trained right on me.

I find myself grinding my cock against her, the sweet little sound she makes in response making me groan.

Growling, I lean forward and run my tongue along the seam of her lips, loving that she tastes so damn sweet. I am already addicted to her. I grind myself on her again. "You see what you do to me, how hard you make me?"

She makes this needy, desperate noise for me and I love it. I slip my hand behind her nape, curl my fingers into her soft flesh, and tilt her head to the side. My mouth waters for her, for her flavor, her taste.

"More," she whispers.

I lean down and run my tongue along the side of her throat, feeling her pulse jack up higher, knowing she's wet between her thighs.

She digs her nails into my skin and my cock jerks at the pain and pleasure I feel.

"That's it, baby. I need that pain, need you to do that

over and over until you can't breathe." I push her shirt up even more, and let my fingers skim along the underside of her breasts. Her skin tightens slightly, goosebumps forming on her creamy flesh. "I wish I hadn't been an asshole, and would have claimed you all those years ago."

"I wish I would have told you how I felt too," she whispers.

I close my eyes, never having felt before like I can be broken in two by one person. I pull back then and go on my knees, staring down at her. Before anything else is said, I help her out of her pants and panties. "I want to see you, all of you. Show yourself to me, baby. Let me see how much you want this."

Once she's completely naked before me, my gaze slowly scans over her tight little body, taking in everything that is Wynter Lowe.

Fuck, I've waited so many damn years to see this beautiful sight right here in front of me.

I could take hours, even days just tasting and admiring her sexy as sin body, taking my time on each and every curve. I want to corrupt her with my tongue, make her feel all my fucking sins as she screams my name.

"Fuck yes, baby. I love you this way. Bared to me, ready for me to pleasure you." I run my hand over her hips before reaching up to gently grab her throat, running my thumb over the slender column. "Once I taste you... you'll know you're mine. No other man will get a taste again. Do you want that? Do you understand that?"

My words have her releasing a small gasp, her breasts quickly rising and falling.

"More than you know."

The savage beast inside me has me letting out a deep growl, showing her without words she's mine.

I'll protect her and take care of her in every fucking way possible.

But I need to know that she can handle my roughness in the bedroom. I need to know that she can handle all that I can give her because there's no changing me.

I'm Sterling Fucking Locke 'til the day I motherfucking die.

Her gaze locks with mine and stays there as I grip her thighs, roughly spreading them open even wider.

"Fuck me, Wynter..." I say to myself.

Seeing how wet her bare pussy is for me has me digging my fingers into her flesh as I lift her bottom half up to meet the tip of my tongue.

A moan escapes her lips the moment I run my tongue along her sensitive pussy, slowly tasting her arousal before sucking her clit into my mouth and growling against it.

Her hands immediately grip at the sheets, her body shaking below me from the vibration of my mouth against her pretty little pussy as I suck and lick it in ways I'm positive she's never experienced.

"No man has ever *licked* or *fucked* you the way I will, baby. That's a fucking promise."

I grip her ass tighter and swirl my tongue around her clit one last time, before I quickly flip her over and spread her ass cheeks, running my tongue along her pussy more.

The way her body jerks beneath me shows me I was right. No man has *ever* licked her the way I am.

"This pussy..." I run my tongue along her soaking wet pussy, causing her to moan out my name and bury her face into the bed. "This is mine. And this sweet little asshole..." I reach up with one hand and run my thumb over her tight asshole. "Is mine too. I'll take every inch of your body once I'm sure you can handle me."

Panting, she sticks her ass further out for me, her body beginning to shake as I circle my thumb around her asshole, while tasting her pussy at the same time.

My cock is so fucking stiff from the sweet taste of her on my tongue that I can feel it practically ready to burst from my jeans.

I've never been harder in my damn life.

After a few minutes of making her squirm below me, I grip her hips with both hands and slip my tongue inside her pussy, slowly pumping it in and out of her.

Me fucking her with my tongue has her body collapsing from pleasure, but I hold her up and continue to pleasure her.

If her body has this kind of reaction from my tongue

alone, fuck me, I can't wait to see how it reacts to my cock taking her.

"Sterling..." she moans.

I roughly suck her clit into my mouth and growl again, knowing her body will thrash out, needing release.

"Holy... ahhhh... fuck... keep going," she pants. "Just... don't stop."

Knowing that she's close, I swirl my tongue around her clit then move up to lick her ass before shoving my tongue into her pussy again.

The combination has her body jerking below me as her sweet release coats my tongue.

I take my time licking her cunt one last time. She buries her face into my bed and pants my name over and over again as her orgasm washes through her.

Before she has time to catch her breath, I'm gripping her waist, flipping her back over, and pulling her on top of me so she's lying on my chest.

Now that I've taken care of her sexually, I want to take care of her emotionally.

I've never cared about a woman's emotional needs until Wynter. I'm not gonna lie; I've been a fucking dick when it comes to women. Because none of them have been *her*.

"What now?" she asks, still sounding completely out of breath.

I run my fingers through her hair and kiss the top of her head. "Now I hold you while you rest. Tomorrow..." I tighten my hold on her. "I take care of the assholes who hurt you."

"What about your needs, Sterling?" She looks up at me, our gazes locking as she runs her fingertips over my chest. "I want to take care of you, too."

I close my eyes and suck in a deep breath, slowly releasing it. My cock may hate me later for this, but I know damn well that she's exhausted and just needs a day of rest. This isn't about me. "I'm a man. My needs can wait until after you're taken care of." I kiss her head again before looking up at the ceiling. I plan to take this time to think of all the savage ways I can hurt those motherfuckers for hurting her. "Just close your eyes and know that I'm here to take care of you. I'll wake you up when it's time to eat dinner."

She nods and yawns, while gripping me so damn tightly that it has my heart skipping a few beats.

Wynter is mine and in the way that she's holding me, I know without a doubt that she knows it too and wants it just as badly as I do.

11

Wynter

I wake up to the gentle pressure of fingers along my bare arm. I stretch, the sense of completeness filling me.

The first thing that comes to mind is how Sterling made me feel, how he brought me to pleasure over and over again, focusing solely on me. He hadn't even wanted me to take care of him, hadn't wanted me to finish him off.

That had to take strength and self-control on his part.

I roll over onto my back and see Sterling watching me, this intense expression on his face. He's focused right on me, his gaze locked on mine, his fingers still dancing across my flesh.

"I hated to wake you, but you need to eat."

I push myself up and move the hair out of my eyes. Just then my stomach growls and I can't help but chuckle. My cheeks heat, and I glance over at Sterling once more. He's wearing a small smile. It looks good on him.

"Ace is cooking, so we might actually get to eat properly tonight." He laughs harder and I can't help but smile wider.

"Let me just wash my face and get cleaned up." I get up and grab my clothes. I head into the bathroom, turn the faucet on, and splash the cool water on my face. It feels good, refreshing. But it doesn't get rid of the heat that is still a constant presence inside of me.

The truth is I always have this heat because of Sterling. And especially after what he did just hours ago, it feels like an inferno burning inside of me.

When I leave the bathroom he's leaning against the bedroom door, his focus on me, his arms crossed over his chest and causing his biceps to bulge. He's so big and strong, so powerful.

He's a man in all the ways that count.

When I get up to him he embraces me and pulls me in for a hug. For long seconds all he does is hold me, his big hand spanning my lower back, this feeling of security and safety filling me.

"Are you hungry?"

Before I can answer, my stomach growls again. I pull back and smile at him.

"I guess that's a yes," he says.

"I would've said no, but it looks like my body has other ideas."

He leans down and kisses me in the center of my forehead, and together we leave the room and head downstairs. Instantly I smell a savory aroma. Even though my stomach made it known I needed food, I hadn't realized until now how hungry I really was.

We reach the landing and round the corner to head into the kitchen. I can see Ace at the stove, the sound of something grilling filling the air. The scent is stronger in the kitchen, and my mouth starts to water.

Aston is sitting at the table with Kadence beside him. And even her friend, Melissa, is still here, sitting across from them. Everyone is focused on something else and they don't see us right away.

Sterling takes me over to the table and I have a seat. I like him taking care of me, and this warmth that fills me has nothing to do with the arousal consuming me.

Kadence glances up and smiles at me. "How are you feeling?"

Before I can answer, Ace is coming over to the table with a plate full of steaks, the aroma so appetizing my mouth waters again.

Sterling comes over with a plate full of corn on the cob and other side dishes. They place everything on top of the table.

For as rough and brutal as these men can be, they are just a family.

Sterling already has a plate made for me before I can even reach for an empty one. Maybe I should be embarrassed for as much as I want to eat the entire thing, but at this moment I really don't care. I start digging in and soon everyone is doing the same.

The sound of silverware clanking on ceramic fills the room. Aston and Kadence start joking with each other, and Ace starts bitching to Sterling about something that happened yesterday that pissed him off.

For just a second I don't think about Kevin or the shit storm I'm in.

Everyone starts laughing at how angry Ace is getting despite the fact whatever pissed him off initially isn't even a big deal.

I glance around the table at everyone, seeing that these men have their own lives, their own troubles. They protect each other in the most barbaric of ways at times, but at the end of the day they are blood, family. They would do anything to protect people who are not as strong as they are.

When I look at Sterling I can feel my love for him grow. I don't know what will happen with Kevin or this entire situation, but what I do know is I don't want to leave Sterling.

We've started something since I've been here, and although the situation hasn't been ideal, and is downright gritty, I am glad that I came.

I'll never regret what happened because it brought me to Sterling. And right now that's all that matters.

I feel Sterling's breath hit my ear before he speaks. "This here is my family and now that you're here, no one at this table will let any harm come to you ever again." He grabs my chair and pulls it closer to his, grunting across the table at Ace as he grins at us. "Just eat, brother."

Sterling

"Oh, I'm eating. Eating up the fact that my other little brother is in fucking love, too. Big fucking softies. Looks like I'll be calling in Killian for some backup soon."

Ace doesn't notice, but I catch him glancing over at Melissa, who is focused on cutting her steak.

He's always said he'll never fall for a woman, that he'll never allow an emotion as strong as love to make him weak and vulnerable. But I have a feeling he wants to fall in love more than either of his brothers.

Without saying a word, I allow my gaze to go on to Wynter. I see her face is completely red as she pretends to be focused on her food and not on what Ace just said about me being in love.

He's not wrong. A part of me has loved Wynter from the

day I laid eyes on her as she watched me from across the classroom, looking as if she wanted to help me.

"Don't mistake me for being a softie, big brother. I will still rip a man apart limb by fucking limb if I have to. Love doesn't make you weak; it makes you stronger. Now eat," I say stiffly.

I catch Wynter suck in a surprised breath, before she reaches for her glass of wine and chugs it, almost choking on it.

"You need another?" Kadence asks, standing up and reaching for the bottle. "Here, sweetie." She smiles and looks at Melissa, both the girls seeming to know she needs more wine.

"Thank you." Her gaze lands on mine and stays on me as she tilts back her glass for a drink before setting it down in front of her.

"Come here." I scoot my chair back and pull her into my lap, reaching around to wrap my hands into her long hair.

I'm not afraid to show everyone in this fucking house how much this woman means to me. But Ace is wrong. My love for her will only make me stronger, fiercer as I take out every motherfucker who has ever hurt her.

I pull her down to me until our lips are brushing, the softness of her skin barely touching mine. Shivers run along my body, causing a small growl to sound in my throat at just the feel of her heavy breath hitting my mouth as she waits for me to kiss her.

Digging my hands deeper into her hair, I press my lips against hers, kissing her hard until we're both fighting for air.

"I'll never hide the way I feel for you from anyone. When I finally find that piece of shit he'll know with the pain I inflict upon him just how I *feel* about you, too. He'll *feel* it in every part of his body."

Wynter places her forehead on mine and wraps her hands into my hair. "I've never felt safer than I do right here in your arms. But I just have one thing I need you to promise me."

"Anything," I say against her lips.

"Promise me you won't let Kevin and his friends hurt you. Promise me I won't lose you after this is all over."

I grab her hand and run my lips over her knuckles, before gently kissing them. "I promise there is *nothing* that son of a bitch can do to hurt me besides placing his hands on you. And that will never happen again. That's a promise."

"Fuck yeah, that's a promise." Aston stands up and reaches for another beer. "You're with the Lockes now. No one touches you *ever* again. If my brother here fails to keep you safe, you have two others as backup."

I grin and throw my steak bone at my little brother, hitting him on the lip. "Oh, what? You don't think I can keep my woman safe on my own? Fuck off, bitch. I'll take you and Ace both on at the same time and still win."

Aston and Ace both laugh.

"All right, little brother." Ace pushes his plate forward and finishes off his beer with a twisted grin. "We'll test that out someday, but trust me: I won't be needing Aston."

"All right, boys!" Melissa stands up and pours another glass of wine. "Maybe I need another glass, too. Does the bickering ever stop?"

Ace stands up and grabs the bottle from Melissa, leaning in until his mouth is against her ear. "Never. Welcome to the fucking Locke home."

I ignore everyone else in the house and turn my attention to Wynter on my lap. "Ace and I will be heading out late tonight to find Kevin. Aston will be staying behind to keep you safe just in case the fucker comes here looking for you before we manage to get to him. King, our big fucking dog, will sleep in my room once I leave."

King stands up at the sound of his name.

"I don't want you up worrying after I leave. Okay?" I say and look at her mouth.

She nods in understanding and gently kisses my lips. "I'll try my best not to."

"Good. I don't want you to have to worry about anything. Especially not me fucking getting hurt."

There's no way that son of a bitch is capable of physically hurting me. I just hope he's ready for a long ass night of pain.

12

Wynter

I wake up in a sweat, immediately sitting up and panicking as if something's wrong.

It takes King sitting across my legs and looking up at me to make me realize that I'm safe in Sterling's bed.

"Shit..." I say to myself while running a hand through my sweaty hair. I have no idea what time it is but I know for a fact that Sterling is out there looking for Kevin and I have no idea if he's found him or if he's hurt, in jail or... dead.

The thought has a whole new wave of panic taking over, causing me to run my hands over my face right before I toss the covers off and jump to my feet.

Aston must've heard me moving around because a few minutes later, he shows up in the doorway, gripping the frame above his head. “Sterling and Ace left a couple hours ago. If there was an issue I would’ve heard about it.”

I nod and stop pacing long enough to look him in the eyes. “Are you sure?”

He offers me a half-smile before releasing the frame, walking over to their huge Pitbull and petting him. “I’m positive, Wynter. My brothers and me have been dealing with assholes our whole lives. This isn’t new to us. This ex of yours is nothing compared to the shit we’ve been through. Now go back to sleep and I’ll let you know if something comes up. Got it?”

I let out a relieved breath and walk over to take a seat on the edge of the bed. “Yeah, okay. Just please make sure Sterling wakes me up as soon as he makes it back in. Please…”

“I’ll send him straight up. Now get some rest.”

After Aston leaves me alone in Sterling’s room, I lay back and close my eyes, hoping with everything in me that Aston is right.

I want to believe nothing bad will happen to Sterling. But I have a feeling that even if he takes care of Kevin, that after my father realizes I’m here and with Sterling, we’ll have a whole new situation to deal with that might be a bit more complicated than just my asshole ex.

I’m positive my father will find some way to control me again, even if it means arresting Sterling and threatening him to make sure he stays away from me.

He’s been controlling me—or trying to—my whole life

and he's the reason I left to begin with. I can't even count the times he had Kevin arrested in the beginning just to prove a point.

And now I wish that asshole had stayed locked up, or I'd been smart enough to leave his ass.

But in regard to Sterling... my dad has hated the Lockes for as long as I can remember. It all started with their uncle Killian, and I know for a fact that he'll do anything he can to hurt anyone associated with this family.

Especially if my father believes it'll get me back home so he can control me just like he did my mother.

Sterling

My heart is racing and my body is strung so tight it feels like it will snap in half. We're on our way to finally getting the revenge that is due.

It just pisses me off that we wasted time first by going to that asshole Riley's house just to come up empty of both those bitches. It wasn't in the plan to have to take a three-hour drive again to find Kevin, but I'll do whatever it takes to get my message across.

My blood is boiling, and all I can think about is the violence I will inflict upon Kevin. I don't care who is there, don't give a damn if there are twenty of his friends ready to throw down.

I am ready, and so is Ace.

We turn onto his street and I get even more juiced up. I start clenching my hands into tight fists before relaxing them, doing this over and over again. This light sweat starts to cover my body, and I know this will be a fight that will go down in Locke history.

"Dude, you're raring to go, aren't you?" Ace says as he continues driving toward the house. "I don't think I've ever seen you this ready to lay down and draw blood."

Truth is, I have never been this angry, never wanted violence this much before. But when it comes to Wynter, something in me has changed. I am like this feral, vicious beast, and I won't let anyone live that harms her.

Ace pulls the vehicle up to the curb, just a few feet from the front of the house where Kevin lives. We won't make this obvious. I won't give them a warning bell that we are here. They'll know that when I bust in the fucking door and beat the living shit out of anyone who stands in the way of me getting my vengeance.

"Ready for this, brother?" Ace glances over at me and the grin he gives me is primed for tonight, dangerous.

"I've been ready." I'm focusing on the house, envisioning all the things I will do to that motherfucker.

"Then let's get this party started."

Ace and I climb out of the vehicle and head toward the

house. We scope out the front, and when we see no lights on we make our way toward the back. If these fuckers are in the basement again I'm gonna lose my shit.

We stop right before we hit the backyard and I can see a large detached garage. The bay doors are closed but I can see light coming from the inside.

I gesture for Ace to stay put and I make my way toward the garage. Looking in the window, I can see three guys sitting around in a loose circle, a joint being passed between them.

Although I don't know what Kevin looks like, I can see all the guys. None of them have marks on their faces, so that tells me Kevin isn't one of them.

I turn around and go back to where Ace is standing. He's leaning against the side of the house, a cigarette perched between his lips.

"The fucker in there?" Ace gestures toward the garage.

I shake my head and move toward the basement windows. I crouch down and look in, seeing several guys sitting on the couch. There's a TV on across from them, a makeshift bar set up on the other side of the room, and a few girls giving lap dances.

Of course these dicks are in the same place they were last time.

I scan the room, trying to make out which one of these assholes is Kevin. And then I see him. I know in my gut, in the tightening of my muscles, that the prick who stands in the corner with a half empty bottle of Jack in his hand and a bruise covering his cheek, was the one who hurt my girl.

I feel my heart start to race as I think of all the things I'm going to do to him. They're going to be dirty, violent things. They're going to be acts that a sane person would never think of committing.

But in this instant I'm not sane.

In this very moment all I can think about is making him pay. And I will. I'll make him pay with broken bones and blood covering my hands.

And it'll feel fucking incredible.

I turn and look at Ace and gesture him over. He grins, this evil smile that I feel to my bones, that makes me know this is gonna be a good fucking night.

I grin in return, not able to help myself because I know what's about to happen.

Ace stops in front of me, smashes the butt of the cigarette out, and flicks it aside. He crouches down low and looks in the window. When he glances back up at me, I see the excitement in his eyes.

"Are you ready, brother?" I ask just as he stands.

"Let's show these motherfuckers what it means to mess with someone who's associated with the Lockes."

Together we make our way over to the back door. I'm tempted just to kick it in, but Ace reaches out before I can do that and twists the handle. It opens soundlessly, smoothly.

We make our way inside and step over empty beer bottles and cans. We reach the kitchen and see a door partially open, light spilling up from the stairs that descend. We can hear music and laughter, even a few female groans.

Both of us look at each other at the same time, matching smiles on our faces, violence surrounding us.

Yeah, this is what we've been waiting for, what *I've* been itching to do ever since Wynter showed up with her beat-to-hell face and the fear in her eyes.

No mercy will be shown tonight.

13

Sterling

The closer we get to the basement, the more prepared my body becomes. My muscles tighten and I'm ready to strike at the first motherfucker who stands in my way in getting to Kevin.

I'm smiling like a fucking madman on the inside at just the idea of hurting him, of placing my hands on him in ways that will scar him for life.

Once we reach the bottom of the stairs, my gaze immediately locks on my target. I clench my jaw in rage as I watch Kevin tilt back his bottle of whiskey, oblivious that we are standing right here.

With the music playing and women dancing, these fuckers haven't even noticed us yet. It's obvious Kevin doesn't believe he has any reason to fear his life even though we passed on a message to blondie the last time we were here.

That's a mistake on his part.

I turn to Ace and grab his long hammer, holding it my hands. A savage smile pulls at my lips as I walk over to the stereo system and swing out, causing shattered pieces of plastic and metal to fly across the room, getting the attention of everyone in the basement.

"The fuck?" I hear a bunch of assholes say.

"Who the fuck are you pricks?" Kevin sets his bottle down and pushes off the girl who was dancing against him when we first walked in. "And what the hell are you doing in my house? Don't make me call the cops."

I nod over to Ace with a lifted brow as he whistles and takes a step toward the middle of the room as if he owns the place. He motions toward the women, who are now reaching for their clothes in a panic. "Go. Now!"

It takes the females less than a minute to reach for whatever they believe is worth it and run up the stairs.

Tilting my head, I place Ace's hammer across my shoulders and growl out, keeping my gaze locked on Kevin,. "If you don't want to get bloody, now is your chance to leave. You've got ten fucking seconds before things get ugly." I point the hammer at Kevin when he moves toward the stairs. "Not you. I've got a long fucking night planned for you."

"Fuck you!" he yells, spit flying from his mouth. "Just take whatever the hell you want and get out of my house. Can't you see we're just some guys trying to have a good time? I don't want any beef. Things don't need to get ugly. I can even call the women back. They're down to fuck and we're good to share."

I toss Ace's hammer to him and stalk toward Kevin with a fierceness behind each step, stopping once I'm within inches of him. Before he even sees it coming, my hand is squeezing his throat and his body is being slammed against the wall.

"Things already got ugly the second you laid your hands on Wynter." I squeeze his throat tighter, cutting off his air supply. "Now you're about to feel what she felt; that crippling fear that kept her in your grip for days as you beat her bloody. You're going to feel that and so much more. And I don't share."

I loosen my hold on his throat, giving him a little space to breathe. I don't want this ending too soon. Not before I get a chance to fucking play.

There's some noise behind me so I turn around to see Ace swing out and punch some dude in the face.

"This fucker wasn't here last time," Ace says, while slamming him against the wall. "Says his name is Riley. He's a bit of a fucking smartass. Can I just kill him now?"

"Not yet, brother." My lips tilt up into a twisted smile as I release Kevin's throat and headbutt him down to the ground. "He's not going anywhere either. Anyone else still here?"

"Nope."

"Good. Let's take these fuckers for a little walk in the woods and see what kind of fun we can get into."

My words have Kevin scrambling to his feet in fear and rushing toward the stairs again. I quickly catch his leg and pull him toward me before tossing him down onto the ground and stomping on his hand. He cries out in pain. I twist my foot, digging my boot in until I hear the snapping of bones and Kevin screaming even louder in pain.

My rage has me grabbing onto his shirt with one hand and his neck with the other as I drag him up the stairs and out the back door.

He's too busy crouching over and cradling his broken hand to attempt to run this time.

A few seconds later Ace appears beside me with his hammer across Riley's throat. "Let's have some fun, little brother. You know I've always loved playing in the woods."

"You and me both." I grab the back of Kevin's shirt and pull him to his feet.

There are woods just on the other side of the street from this fucker's house, so we head there. I want the privacy, need it for the damage I'm going to do to this asshole.

We stop so Ace can go to the vehicle and grab a bag that has all the "toys" we'll need for tonight. I don't know if I'll kill Kevin tonight, but I do know that he'll be begging for mercy by the time I'm done.

Once we make it into the woods I push Kevin to the ground. I hear him grunt as the impact knocks the wind out of him, and I can't help but grin at that.

Ace is busy tying the other fucker to a tree, no doubt saving him for later, and preventing him from being a pussy and running off. Ace then comes over to me.

"Get up, asshole," I say and reach for a cigarette. I light it, knowing I should quit them, but for what I am about to do I need that nicotine kick.

When Kevin stands I gesture for him to put his back toward the tree. Like a good little asshole he does what I say. I can see he's scared shitless, and he should be, rightfully so.

I'll fuck him up.

Kevin cradles his busted-up hand, and I gesture for Ace to secure him to the tree as well. Once Kevin is where I want him, I grin.

He's all but strung up like a pig about to get its belly cut open.

"Come on, we can work this out." Kevin tries to barter with me, but I am not all about that. He fucked up, and his pleas for me to be merciful aren't going to fly.

I grab a dirty rag out of the duffle and walk over to him, shoving the cloth in his mouth.

He struggles against his bonds. He knows he isn't getting out of this, not unless he's dead or barely able to move.

I want to get this the fuck over with so I can go be with Wynter.

"So, what's your plan for the fucker?" Ace asks, coming to stand right beside me.

"I want to make this quick since I got shit to do, but he also needs to suffer."

I roll up my shirtsleeves to my elbows, my heart racing, the blood pumping through my veins.

This is going to be some back alley dirty and raw bloodshed. Now that I think about it there is no doubt that in the end this motherfucker will be dead. If he's lucky.

I take one more hit off the cigarette, but instead of putting it out on the ground, I walk up to Kevin and stub the butt out in the center of the prick's head.

He screams out, and I grin wider.

Ace chuckles behind me. "Here, you want these," Ace says, not phrasing it like a question.

I turn and grab the brass knuckles, slip them through my fingers, and curl my hand into a fist. It feels incredible to have them on.

I face Kevin again. "Get ready to feel some major pain, fucker," I say right before I step closer and start beating the fucking shit out of him.

I deliver an undercut to his jaw, and then a punch to his temple so his head cocks to the side. I start to punch his gut over and over again, loving the sounds of pain coming from him.

"Let me have a few goes at him," Ace says, and I step aside, despite not wanting to stop.

Blood drips from Kevin's mouth, his lip is busted, and his eyes are swollen. I watch as Ace gives the fucker blow after blow and after a moment steps back, looking at his handiwork.

I don't waste any time going back to town on the prick's body, busting up his ribs now. The grunts, cries, and pleas for me to stop fall on deaf ears.

I love every fucking minute of it.

I do have to give the asshole credit; he isn't begging for his life.

"How's it feel to be the one getting the beatdown?" I say with a grin. I slam the brass into the side of Kevin's head again. His skull cracks to the side. Blood is everywhere, even covering my knuckles and shirt.

Kevin grumbles and spits out a mouthful of blood. Rearing my arm back, I slam the metal so hard into the side of the bastard's jaw I hear bone crunch under the onslaught.

I finally step back and look at my handiwork. Kevin looks like he is a piece of meat that has just gone through the grinder.

I almost laugh at that.

Blood is soaked into his shirt, as well as mine, and pieces of flesh have torn off from Kevin's face, skin and meat barely attached anymore.

"Not that I give a fuck, but he's about to check out from

blood loss. You better finish it so you get the satisfaction of delivering that final blow," Ace says from behind me and I can barely hear him from my heavy breathing.

I desperately want to get back to Wynter, to make sure she is okay and let her know that she's safe now and Kevin has been taken care of.

I grab Kevin's chin in a brutal hold, and bare my teeth. I need to give that final blow while the fucker is still conscious.

Ace hands me a knife and I take hold of the ten-inch blade.

"She's mine, and you'll never put fear in her again." Without anything else being said, I start to go to work on Kevin's face, opening it up, giving him a nice Joker-esque smile. Then I take the blade and slowly slash it across his chest, watching as blood drips down his body and onto the dirty ground.

He'll never be able to look in the mirror without seeing the fucking horror I inflicted on him.

I take a step back and stare at Kevin's body. We'll untie him and leave him here, let him crawl his ass back to his place and lick his wounds. "Surely this fucker gets the message now," I say before turning to face Riley, who is now quivering in fear. "Do I need to send you the same message?"

He quickly shakes his head and begins pulling at the ropes. "No. Please," he begs. "I have no desire to ever look in her direction again. I promise. It was a mistake to try to have her as mine, but Kevin never showed her the attention she deserved. I never meant any harm, I swear. I fucking swear."

I glance at Ace, who's eyeing Riley as if he *needs* this too. "Have at him, brother."

Ace grins and starts beating the shit out of Riley, letting him know as well that messing with Wynter, or anyone associated with the Locke brothers, means they get fucked up.

My grin widens as he reaches for his hammer and swings it around before slamming it at Riley, connecting it with his leg.

Riley screams out in pain and begins crying like a little bitch as the bone snaps.

I take Ace's place and get in Riley's face, so close that our noses are touching. He's snotting all over me like a fucking baby. "Don't make us come look for you. This isn't even half the shit we're willing to do to you. We're some savage motherfuckers."

Needing to release my anger with one more blow, I swing out and plunge my brass knuckles into the side of his skull.

Satisfaction swarms me as I watch him go limp in the ropes. Hope both these fuckers have a nice little nap.

Now it's time for me to go back to Wynter, to make her see she's mine and no one fucks with her.

14

Wynter

I've been pacing around the living room for the last hour, my heart racing and my chest and neck covered in sweat as I wait to hear anything about Sterling.

They've been gone for hours now and Aston hasn't gotten any word that they're okay. Sterling's phone also keeps going to voicemail.

I can't handle the idea that something bad could've happened to Sterling. I feel sick to my stomach and somewhat wish I would've insisted he just stay with me and forget Kevin, but I knew that wasn't an option.

There would've been no stopping Sterling from going.

"The boys are fine." Kadence steps into the living room with a glass of water. She smiles and hands it to me. "Sterling wouldn't like you worrying so much about him. He wants you resting and taking care of yourself. The Lockes can handle their shit. Trust me."

I grab the glass and take a small drink before setting it down on the coffee table. "I can't rest. I've tried. I haven't been able to sleep since I woke up late last night. I just keep thinking about Sterling and all the bad things that could possibly happen to him. I can't stand the thought of him getting hurt."

Aston takes the knife that he's playing with and tosses it across the room and into the wall with a grin. King jumps to his feet as if he hears something. "Looks like the boys are back."

I find myself rushing through the door and out to the porch, watching as the SUV comes to a stop at the end of the driveway.

My gaze stays trained on the passenger side door, waiting for it to open. I can't stop my heart from beating out of my chest the moment the door opens and Sterling steps out, covered in blood.

"Sterling!" A surge of panic shoots through me as I run down the steps and through the grass to meet up with the man that's had me on edge with worry for the last ten hours. "Are you hurt?"

I reach out and grab his face, running my hands over it, looking for any cuts, before I move down to his chest and arms. Instant relief takes over once I realize that the blood isn't his.

But then something else moves through me at the fact this *isn't* his blood.

"I'm fine." He reaches out and grabs my waist with a small growl, yanking me against his hard body. He moves his hips slightly, showing me that he's hard. "But I need to shower and get this prick's blood off me."

I let out a surprised gasp as Sterling picks me up and begins walking past his brothers and Kadence and into the house.

Even when we reach the bathroom, he keeps a hold on me as he pushes open the shower curtain to turn on the water.

"Is Kevin..." I can't even finish saying the words.

"He's still breathing..." He places his blood-covered forehead to mine and sets me down on my feet. "I didn't want him to be when I left, but I let him as a reminder of how badly he fucked up. I wanted him to suffer a pain far worse than a quick death and trust me, he's suffering right now with half his face missing."

The vision of what Kevin must look like now, after Sterling having his violent way with him oddly makes me smile. Maybe I'm just as savage and twisted as the Lockes.

"He didn't hurt you at all?" I run my finger over his cheek, wiping some of Kevin's blood off and watch as he clenches his jaw and moans. "He didn't touch you?"

He shakes his head, looking me over with his amber-colored eyes as if he wants to ravish me. “No, baby. He didn’t lay a finger on me and he’ll never lay another finger on you. Not for as long as I fucking live.”

With that he kicks his boots off and lifts me up. His lips crash hard against mine, claiming every part of my fucking soul and owning me irrevocably. He steps into the shower and presses me against the wall with force.

His hands work at my shirt, lifting it up and over my head before he tosses it aside and begins running his lips up my neck.

There’s blood washing down our bodies and down the drain and even that isn’t enough to make this moment any less perfect. I’m with Sterling Locke and that’s all that matters right now.

His strong body against mine. His teeth digging into my flesh as he continues to undress me. That’s all I’m focused on, but I’m pretty sure the way Sterling takes care of a woman’s needs is enough to distract someone even from death.

Before I know it, Sterling is crouched down in front of me, ripping my pants and thong from my body before he begins to make his way back up, running his tongue along my flesh.

I tug at his wet hair, pulling him up to let him know that I need him inside me. I need him filling every part of my body and soul.

I want him to make love to me before my entire body explodes with need…

Sterling

I LOSE it when she tugs on my hair and I want nothing more than to be inside her, claiming every inch of her tight little body.

Grabbing the back of my soaked shirt, I lift it up over my head and toss it outside the shower. I quickly strip myself of my jeans and boxer briefs until I'm standing nude before Wynter.

It's the first time she's seen me fully naked and from her wide-eyed stare, I'd say she's more than impressed with what I have to offer her. Maybe even a little scared of me hurting her.

But I'll never hurt her. All I want to do is make her feel good. And I will. Fucking hell, I'll make her feel so damn good she's screaming my name and begging me for more.

I pull her body close to mine again, cup the back of her head, and slam my mouth on hers. I force my tongue between her lips, stroking her, making her moan.

I mouth-fuck her like I'll be doing between her thighs soon enough.

Moving around to bite her neck, I turn around and press

her back to the wall. I move my hand down her hip and curve it around her ass. I give the mound a squeeze, her skin wet, soft. I'm so hard, stiff like an iron rod between us.

I lift her leg up and wrap it around my hip, grinding myself against her, needing her to see what she does to me. The little sound she makes has me groaning like an animal.

"You see what you do to me?" I say against her mouth, kissing her between the words, making her see exactly the kind of arousal I have for her. "You see how hard you make me? You're the only one who can make me like this, who can make me feel this way."

"God, Sterling."

She's panting against my mouth, all but rubbing herself on me. I don't want to wait. I can't.

"Ask me for it. Beg me for the dirty things you want." I pull away from her and cup the side of her throat, my thumb right below her ear, feeling her pulse beating rapidly. I stare into her eyes, seeing her pupils dilate, and feeling the rapid rise and fall of her chest as it presses against mine.

Yeah, she's primed for me, ready for me to thrust into her and fuck her good and hard.

"Go on, baby. Tell me what you want me to do. Show me where you want me."

And then she takes my hand in hers and places it right between her thighs, right over her hot, soaking pussy. I clench my jaw, gritting my teeth at the feel of her. And then I slip two fingers into her cunt, stretching her for me.

"Right here, Sterling. I want you right here." She breathes those words out, her warm breath tickling my neck.

I start pumping my fingers in and out of her and move my thumb to her clit, rubbing it back and forth, over and over again. The sexy little sound she makes goes straight to my fucking cock.

Before I can come right here, just get off all over her and the bathroom tile, I pull my fingers out and hold them up. I show her the glistening digits and bring them to my mouth, sucking them clean.

"Ask me for it," I demand, needing her to say the words. "Ask me to fuck you, to fill your tight little pussy and come inside you."

"Give it to me, Sterling. I want you inside me. All of you and only you."

"Fuck yes, baby."

And just like that I grab my cock and stroke it a few times before placing the tip at her entrance. I stare right in her eyes, and without waiting another minute, without torturing us further, I thrust all of my inches into her.

She throws her head back, her mouth opening, her eyes closing. Wynter cries out, maybe from the sudden movement, or maybe because I'm splitting her in two.

This way right here, me inside her, our bodies molded together, is the only pain I'll ever give her.

But as her hands go to my shoulders, her nails digging into my flesh, I know she likes it. She finally looks at me, this flush stealing over her face.

"God. Yes."

I start pumping in and out of her, unable to stop myself from the frenzied motions, unable to be gentle. I have my hands on her hips, digging them into her sensitive skin, most likely leaving marks.

But I want to leave bruises on her flesh to replace the memories of the bad ones. I want her to look in the mirror and see what I have done to her, how I've claimed her.

And I won't stop, not until she is fully mine. I'll make Wynter see that to me she is everything.

I growl out and quickly flip her around so that her front is against the shower wall, her ass facing me, ready for me to take her in ways that no other man ever has.

I've already made it fully known to her that I plan to claim every part of her body and I won't be completely satisfied until I do just that.

The way her tight little round ass is spread for me, her asshole waiting for me to take it, has me close to losing my shit and coming all over her.

But I'm not done with her sweet little cunt yet, so I place my hand to the back of her neck and thrust back inside of her. She screams out and curls her fingers against the shower wall, the sound of her pleasure echoing throughout the small bathroom.

I have no doubt that my brothers and Kadence can hear every last noise we make in here, but I couldn't care less. I'll let them listen to me claim my girl so it's just as clear to them as it is to her that she's mine.

I want the whole fucking world to know.

Wynter releases a moan against my arm as I continue to fill her with my cock, making her take every inch of me.

"I want all of you," she says, out of breath. "I want you to take all of me as well. Every last bit of me."

My lips turn into a savage smile as I slowly pull out of her tight little pussy and move the head of my cock up to meet her asshole.

I feel her tense up, so I place my lips against her neck and gently kiss it as a way to distract her from me slowly entering her from behind.

I smooth my fingers along her pussy, coating them with her wetness, and moving it back up to her ass. I lube her hole up good, make her primed for me, ready for me to stretch her ass.

But I know that's not enough. I move away from her only long enough to grab some lube from the bathroom drawer, one I've used to jerk off to while I thought about her.

I pop the cap and spread the liquid over my dick before

putting a hefty amount on my fingers and smoothing it along her asshole.

She leans her head back, letting out a small painful noise. I quickly bite her neck, drawing the pain somewhere else, until I can push my cock halfway in.

I move slowly at first, giving her time to adjust to the mixture of pain and pleasure, before I finally push all my inches in and stop.

I'm buried balls deep in her tight little ass. "Am I the first to be back here, baby?" She nods for me and I growl out low. The fact that I'm the first and only one to ever claim her this way has me almost coming, but I stop myself.

"Fuck, baby." I press my lips against her ear and slowly begin moving in and out as I scrape her flesh with my teeth. "This ass is mine..." I reach around to rub my thumb over her clit. "This pussy is mine. And this cock..." I thrust hard inside of her, causing her to groan out and dig her nails into my arm. "Is yours. I'm yours..."

"Say it again," she whispers against my arm.

"I'm yours." I smile against her neck before kissing it. "I'm Sterling Locke and I fucking belong to you. Every last bit of me."

"Yes..." she moans. "I love the sound of that."

"Me, too," I admit. "Now hold on tight, baby. I've been about as gentle as I can be."

I pull out of her ass and let the water wash over me as I quickly swipe my hand over the bar of soap on the wall and wipe it over my dick. My jaw clenches hard as I slam back into her tight pussy, fucking her so hard that I'm pushing her up the shower wall with each thrust.

This has her biting my arm so hard that I won't be surprised if she's drawn blood. But I want that, need it. I need her to leave her mark on me just as badly as I need to leave mine on her.

I keep moving my hips, taking her hard and deep until I feel her pussy clenching around my cock, causing me to come deep inside of her.

"Fuck, baby..." I reach around to grab the front of her neck before I trail kisses up and down her back, while fighting to catch my breath.

I can hear her struggling to slow her breathing as she goes limp in my arms, my body holding her up against the wall.

"I've imagined this moment for a really long time. What it would feel like for you to take me. How rough you'd be."

I pull out of her gently and turn her around, placing my wet body against hers. "And?" I grab her hand and gently kiss her fingers as the water runs down them. "Was I too rough for you?"

She smiles and shakes her head. "I think I'd like you to be rougher next time. I want to feel you inside me weeks later and not just days because that's what you do to me. You make me want to feel your pain... want to feel *you*. All of you."

"Fuck, baby. You're so fucking perfect for me." I lift her up and she wraps her legs around my waist. I slam my lips against hers, needing to feel her breath against my mouth. Needing to feel her *want* for me.

"Let's go get some rest. I have somewhere I want to take you later. Just the two of us."

I reach over and turn the shower water off before stepping out of the tub with her still in my arms.

There's nothing I love more than taking care of my woman and she's going to feel that with every fucking breath I take.

And that's exactly why I need to take her to where my love for her first started. A place I visit often late at night just to clear my head.

She's part of the reason I kept fighting when all I felt like doing was giving up.

15

Wynter

I slept so good last night that I feel like energy is running through me at a high rate. But then a good fucking, and sleeping next to the man I love can do that to a person, I suppose.

I'm surprised when Sterling walks over to his motorcycle and straddles it with a cocky grin, while looking me over. "Get on."

I move over to him and he grabs my hand, helping me onto the back before he hands me his helmet to put on.

I can't contain my excitement as I quickly strap it on and loosely wrap my arms around Sterling's body, placing my hands on his firm chest.

He lets out this animalistic growl and grabs my hands,

pulling them farther around him so that I have a better grip. "Hold on, baby." His body vibrates as a deep laugh moves through him, before he lowers my hands down his ripped abs and down to his hard dick. "Even if it's onto my cock. Just hold on tight."

Electricity shoots through my body and down to my pussy, remembering how it felt for him to take me just hours ago in the shower.

I love the way he's so bold with me and just says and does what he wants with no fucks given.

Turns me on so damn much.

I squeeze his dick and gently bite his ear before moving my hands back up his body and gripping tightly onto his chest, to let him know there's no way I'm letting go. Then I rest my head against his back, moving in as closely as I can. "I'm ready."

"Good, because I think we both need fast right now. A little escape from this fucked-up reality."

As if he was waiting to make sure I'm secure, he revs the engine a few times before taking off fast.

I have to admit that I'm a little nervous since it's my first time on a motorcycle, but the idea of Sterling being the one in control is keeping me cool and calm.

I trust him with my life more than anyone.

And why shouldn't I? He's already proven the lengths he'll go to make sure anyone who hurt me will pay with blood. Lots of blood.

Oddly, that makes me feel safer than I have my entire life.

It's not long before we're pulling up at our old high school. He gets off only long enough to jimmy the lock on the fence that keeps people off of school property. Once he's back on the bike he's driving through the grass, toward the football field.

Old memories of Sterling walking through the halls with bruises covering his body, his dark gaze trained on me as we passed each other take over and I find myself wanting to be closer to him.

I find myself wanting to comfort the quiet, dark soul that I spent my days and nights thinking about and wondering what his life must've been like.

Not once did I ever think I'd be pulling up back at this place in the middle of the night and on the back of a Locke brother's motorcycle, no less.

"Do you come here often?" I find myself asking once we stop. "It feels so... I don't know. I haven't been here in years."

He's quiet as he cuts the engine and helps me off his bike. He looks around at the field as he pulls my helmet off and sets it on the seat. "I like to come here at night and think. It helps get my head off all the fucked-up shit my brothers and I deal with on the daily. When we came here... it was the one place I could go and not have to worry about what my parents would do next. How they would hurt my brothers and me. I knew that as soon as I walked through those doors that I had at least seven hours where I could breathe easy and not have to watch our backs."

His words break my heart.

"Unless it was me asking for the trouble, but I was always prepared for that."

It's like this thick silence descends upon us after he speaks. I know he's reliving that time in his life and I hate it. I want to take it away from him, want to make him only feel happiness and love.

He takes my hand and leads me toward the center of the football field. There are a few security lights on, but the only other illumination comes from the full moon above us.

I remember coming to some of the games when I was younger, not really caring about it, but just wanting to get away from the control of my father. Even though I had moved away after graduating, he was still an unpleasant and demanding presence in my life.

He had always tried to control me, and even breaking away hadn't stopped that. It had helped, given me a little bit of my own life back. But still he saw me as this child that needed to be molded and controlled.

He ruined my mother that way and I refused to let him do the same to me. That's why I left, but it seemed I put myself in the same fucked-up situation anyway with Kevin.

Sterling stops in the center of the field and we both sit down. He pulls me in close so I'm resting right up against his body. For long moments we don't say anything, but I don't need us talking to feel comfortable around him.

We both lay back and I rest my head on his chest, hearing the steady beat of his heart. It's strong, just like him.

I take his hand in mine and intertwine our fingers. It's nice spending time with him, just enjoying nothing but each other. The silence is comforting even.

I don't want this night to end. I don't want to have to go back to reality, to the fact I still have to deal with my father, or what happened with Kevin.

"Do you ever think about the future?" I ask but stare at the stars above, continuing to listen to his heart beating, wondering if he sees a future for himself.

I know the Locke brothers are hardcore and violent, that they live on the edge and take one day at a time. But do they think about what they want in the long run?

Do they think about what they *want* in their life?

Because the truth is I do think about the future. I think about it all the time and Sterling's in it.

When he doesn't answer right away, I brace myself up on one elbow and look down at him. His eyes are closed, but I can tell he's thinking, concentrating. And then when he opens them and stares at me, his pupils so dilated the black almost eats up all the color, I wonder what is on his mind.

Is my question too deep for him? Is he afraid to tell me

that he really doesn't see a future for us despite what he has said this whole time?

He lifts his hand up and cups my cheek, and the feel of his thumb stroking along my skin sends shivers down my body.

"Yeah, I see a future." He continues to stare at me in the eyes. "I see a future with you, Wynter. I've always wanted that."

And if my heart weren't already his, he would've taken it right then. His words would have made me fall in love with him, just given myself over as if nothing else existed.

I lift my hand, cup his face, lean down and place my lips on his. For long seconds, all I do is kiss him, nothing sexual, nothing heated. It is me sealing my love for him, showing him that I am here and not going anywhere.

His lips against mine feel too good to stop, so I don't. Not until my lips go numb and my arm gets tired. But I finally pull away.

It surprises me when Sterling places one hand on my face and the other one on my hip as he flips us around so that I'm lying on my back in the grass with his body resting between my legs.

The feel of his hard body against me, his arms, his thighs, everything that is Sterling, has me sucking in a breath and breathing in his air.

"I love you," he says against my lips. My entire body ignites with heat from his confession and the feel of his fingertip brushing over my lip as he continues to look me in the eyes has me fighting to catch my breath. I know without a doubt that he means what he just said. "I've loved you for a long fucking time, Wynter."

"I'm yours, Sterling. I love you, too." And I say those words so he knows. Even if I only have this one moment, it's already ingrained, memorized in my entire being.

And I'm lucky to have that.

"Good. That's real fucking good, baby." As soon as the words leave his lips, they're pressed against mine again. The intensity of his kiss sucks the air straight from my lungs and I find myself grabbing at his strong back, digging my nails in as I fight for air around his lips.

He must notice me shivering beneath him from the cool night air, 'cause he stops kissing me long enough to rip his long-sleeved shirt off over his head and help me put it on.

I look up at his hard body, my lips tugging into a smile as I watch his muscles flex as he continues to hold himself above me. "Relax and lay with me, Sterling. I like the way it feels with my head on your chest."

Without hesitation, he lays back down on his back and pulls me into the same position we were in before we started kissing.

With my head on his chest and his hands wrapped into my hair, I know without a doubt that there's nowhere else I'd rather be.

I could lay like this for hours and we do.

16

Sterling

It's been a few days now since my brother and I left Kevin and his douchebag friend bleeding in the woods behind his house.

Wynter hasn't heard a peep from that motherfucker and I'm hoping that either means he's scared shitless to ever contact her again or that his ass is suffering in the hospital, unable to move without screaming out in pain.

My lips curve up into a sickening smile as I imagine him lying there in the hospital with his beat-to-hell face wrapped up in a cloth.

It only makes me want to mess up the motherfucker in front of me even more and shake him up until he's pissing in his pants.

"...under the sink. It's under the sink!" He's shaking below me, while holding onto my boot as if that's going to stop me from stomping on his face.

This asshole fucked over the mother of his child and emptied out their joint bank account, leaving her and their two-year-old son with no money.

"Oh yeah." I kick his hand out of the way and rest my boot against his throat. "Under the fucking sink, huh?" I nod to Aston. "Check it out. See if I need to crush little old Bobby's throat with my favorite boot until he's no longer breathing."

Aston pulls the cigarette from between his lips and flicks it at the wall with a grunt. "This is the third place he's told us it's hiding. I say if it's not here that I take that knife over there..." He nods toward the knife on the counter that Bobby attempted to attack us with when we broke down the door. "And carve his motherfucking eyeballs out and feed them to him."

"No! It's under there. It's there, just look! She can have it all. Every last dollar. Fuck!" He swallows, watching Aston open the cabinet under the sink and pull out a little lock box. "Yes, that's it. Take it. Let that bitch have it."

"Watch your fucking mouth before I cut it off." I press my boot down harder, crushing his throat until he begins turning red.

"It's locked. Damn, this would be a good time for our other fucking brother to be here." Aston turns behind him and begins looking through the drawers for something. It takes him a few minutes but finally pulls out a small hammer. "Not as big as Ace's, but this should do the trick."

I keep my foot on Bobby's neck, but relieve some of the pressure as I reach into my pocket for one of my joints. I light it with a smirk and watch as Aston takes his anger out in the little box.

He beats it to hell, even after it's already open and money's flying out of it. Thousands of dollars that this asshole believed was his for the taking.

A real man cares for his family first and himself second, but apparently this asshole is nothing but a lowlife animal.

Aston finally puts the hammer down and reaches for the money. "Here." He tosses me a rolled-up five-dollar bill. "At least his ex was nice enough to leave him a little something for dinner."

I lean in close to Bobby's sweaty face. "This is more than you left for your family to eat on, you piece of shit. Hope this shit tastes good." With an angry growl, I shove the bill in his mouth to the point where he's choking on it and then I reach for the glass of water next to me and pour it in his mouth, causing him to panic and begin gripping at my arm.

"See if that lasts you for two weeks, you piece of shit." Aston steps up beside me, lights a cigarette and pulls the bill out of his mouth before shoving the lit cigarette inside and holding his mouth closed. "Here's a little dessert to go with it, bitch."

It's getting late at this point and all I can think about is getting back to Wynter and having a chill night with just my woman and my family. "Let's get the fuck out of here."

"I'm ready, brother."

THE CRACKLING of the fire has us all staring at the pile of wood before us, watching as it slowly burns into ashes.

This is our time to relax and forget about everything for just a few hours as a family. It feels good as shit having Wynter here for this one and not just her showing up at the end with bruises all over her body.

The memory of that night has me squeezing her tighter, pulling her into my lap as close to me as I possibly can. Her body against mine instantly calms me and takes me to a place where my head doesn't seem so fucked up and my thoughts don't seem so dark and twisted.

I need Wynter more than she'll ever know. She's maybe only been mine for a week now, but it feels like a fucking lifetime.

Maybe that's because even when she wasn't mine all those years ago, in my head I always wanted her to be. I spent my nights getting lost in thoughts of her, wondering how it'd feel if she were mine. It helped me escape my hell.

I owe her all of me. Every last bit of me belongs to her for as long as she'll have me.

We all look over when we hear the crunching of footsteps coming down the long driveway.

Ace is the first to stand, but Kadence laughs and grabs Ace's arm to let him know it's okay. "It's only Melissa. She's bored at home."

I see the slightest hint of a smile on my big brother's lips, before he quickly tilts back his beer bottle, keeping his gaze on the dark shadow coming toward us. "I could've picked her up."

"It's a five-minute walk," Kadence says with a huge smile. "You boys are crazy protective."

"Damn straight we are, babe." Aston stands and moves over to where Kadence is sitting. He crouches down in front of her and cups her face. "Because we protect what we love. And even though Melissa is still unsure about us, she's your family and that makes her ours too."

"That's right," Ace agrees. But it's becoming clearer with time that Ace wants to get his hands on Melissa and work his way under her skin. He wants to change her mind about us. Or at least about him.

"Right here, darlin'." Ace smirks and gives his chair to Melissa, before he leans down into her neck.

"Ouch!" Melissa yelps. "You just bit me."

A twisted smile tugs at Ace's lips. "And you liked it too, babe."

Ignoring my asshole brothers, I press my lips against

Wynter's neck before I push her up to her feet and stand. "I'll get you another beer."

I get ready to walk away, but she grabs my arm, stopping me. She smiles and stands up on her tippy toes to wrap her arms around my neck. "I love everything about you, Sterling. I love everything you do for me, but I want you to know that being with me is all I expect from you."

I run my thumb over her plump bottom lip before I lean in and suck it into my mouth, and then I bite it. "You're my woman and this is my way of taking care of you. Get used to me doing a lot of shit for you, 'cause I won't be stopping anytime soon." I run my tongue over her lips before moving up to whisper in her ear. "Taking care of you gets me hard. So fucking hard."

I hear a small rush of air leave her lips before I walk away to grab some more beers from inside.

Just as I go to open the fridge, I hear the crunching of tires in the driveway, causing me to close the fridge and rush toward the door.

An instant smile forms on my lips when I notice Killian's black, lifted truck come to a stop.

I step out onto the porch and watch my brothers stand around with huge smiles as Killian jumps out of his truck and tosses his cigarette at the gravel.

"What are all you fuckers staring at?" He gives us a crooked smile before walking over to Aston and grabbing his beer from him. “You act as if you haven’t seen me in years, when it’s only been eleven months.”

His dark hair has gotten longer, to the point that it’s falling over his left eye and he’s now grown out a beard.

“Good to see you, uncle.” I walk over and grab his shoulder, looking him over before I give him a one-armed hug, squeezing him harder than usual. “But fuck you for taking off for so long.”

He laughs and moves around to give my brothers hugs. Just as he pulls away from Ace, his eyes go wide once he notices three girls sitting around the fire. “Whoa. This is some new shit for you boys.”

“Yeah, well I guess we needed a little change.” I lift a brow and look over to see Wynter talking and laughing with the other two girls. She turns my way for a quick second and smiles at me. It has my heart jumping like crazy in my chest.

“She’s yours, I’m taking it.” He wraps his arm around my neck and squeezes. “Good for you. I’m proud of you. I know shit hasn’t always been easy in your life. For any of you boys, but every fucking one of you deserves to be happy. Don’t ever question that. Got it?”

Aston nods his head. “I’ve realized that over the last seven months.” He grabs his beer back from Killian and tilts it back, emptying it. “It took me a while, but thanks to Kadence, I believe it now.”

“And the third one over there?”

"She'll be mine... soon enough."

We all look over at Ace, not expecting those words to come from his mouth.

Ace keeps shit inside more than the rest of us.

"It's going to take some work, brother." I laugh and slap his back. "Good fucking luck. You're the most twisted of us all."

"Deep down inside she's craving for me to twist her up. Trust me, brother."

"Well, assholes. It was a long fucking drive. Got some more beers before I thank you guys for taking care of that fucker Paul?" He grinds his teeth, no doubt still wanting to kill that asshole for messing with Camille's son, even though we took care of him already.

Ace nods. "Yeah. I'll bring some more out." With that he takes off inside, while the three of us make our way back over to the fire.

Kadence smiles the moment her eyes land on Killian walking beside Aston. "Uncle Killian, I'm guessing."

This has Killian grinning, showing off his perfect teeth. "You've heard about their badass uncle. I knew I loved these boys."

Wynter laughs and joins in. "I've heard a lot about you from my father. I have to admit that I'm sort of excited to meet you."

"Oh yeah?" Killian grabs a beer from Ace as he holds one out for him. "Who's your father?"

"Officer Lowe."

"Oh fuck." He tilts his beer back, taking a huge swig. "That's your father, huh? And you're here with a Locke?"

Wynter nods and takes a seat in my lap as I pull her down to me. "My father doesn't control me anymore. I do what I want and what I want is Sterling."

"Good shit. I like that."

We spend the next few hours drinking and sitting around the fire, everyone enjoying having Killian back.

Even Melissa seems to somewhat like Killian.

Having Wynter here and Killian back is truly beginning to feel like our family is whole.

I could really get used to these kinds of nights.

This feels too good to ever let Wynter not be a part of.

Wynter is distracted, talking with Ace and Aston, but I can tell she's tired and needs to rest. So I grab the beer from her hand and toss it down beside us before I straddle her lap and capture her mouth with mine.

Everyone around us begins whistling and throwing things at me as I grind myself against her and move around to whisper in her ear. "Let's go inside, baby. We can do whatever you want. Even fucking sleep, but don't let these nut sacks keep you up."

"Oh fuck you!" Ace says with a laugh. "I'll keep her up all night." He grabs his dick and smirks just to piss me off.

I stand up and kick his chair over. "Good night, fuck face." Then I grab Wynter's hand and pull her up to her feet.

"My brother's dick will never get close to you. I'll cut that shit off and then smash it with his precious hammer."

Wynter smiles and wraps her arms around my neck. "That sort of amuses me. Is that bad?"

"Not at all, babe." Killian leans forward and tosses his empty beer into the fire with a grin. "Only means you're a part of the family now."

"I like the sound of that."

"Me, too, baby. Me fucking too. Now let's go upstairs."

If it wasn't for Wynter needing to rest, I'd fuck her nice and loud with every damn window open so my asshole brothers could hear her screaming my name from all the way out there.

A little reminder of how she's mine.

17

Wynter

Spending the other night with Sterling and his family around the bonfire felt really amazing, and the way he wasn't afraid to show everyone that I was his girl felt even better.

Their uncle Killian seemed pretty shocked at first to see two of his nephews settled down, but you could see in his eyes just how happy he was for them.

I know he took them all in every chance he got even though he's probably not more than ten years older than Ace.

I like their uncle, but I can definitely see why my father has hated him for as long as I can remember. He seems like the type of guy that doesn't take shit from anyone and doesn't allow anyone to tell him what to do. Not even the law.

Sterling decided he wanted to go for a ride after dinner so, after riding around for a couple of hours, he asks what I want to do before we go back to the Locke house.

It's been a long time since I've been to Benny's ice cream so I suggest we stop for some.

Even with everyone's gazes following us around as if we don't belong here, being here with Sterling feels good. Feels normal. Like something a normal couple would do.

It makes me happy because truthfully, I want everyone to know we're together. All my old friends, old teachers and anyone I've ever met in this shitty little town.

I want them to see that Sterling is loved. I want them to see that he's just like the rest of us when it really comes down to it.

He eats, sleeps and breathes just like everyone else.

They may fear him, may think he's a savage beast, but he's capable of love too.

"Come here, baby."

He's straddling his motorcycle, but grabs my arm and scoots back, pulling me in front of him so that I'm straddling his bike, facing him.

He smiles at me and then leans in and runs his tongue along my chocolate/vanilla swirl cone. "Mmm... it's been such a long time since I've tasted their homemade ice cream. Probably since I was ten and my uncle brought me here."

I take my free hand and wipe the chocolate from his mouth with a smile. "Sure you don't want me to walk over and grab you a cone?"

He shakes his head and leans forward to run his tongue around my ice cream again. "This is the last lick. I promise."

"You sure about that?" A twisted smile takes over my face as I shove the cone against his lips, leaving a huge smudge of chocolate and vanilla. "You have a little..."

Before I can finish what I'm saying, he grabs the back of my head and crushes his lips against mine. I moan out and run my tongue over his lips, realizing that my dessert tastes so much better served on him.

He squeezes my thigh and then bites my lip right as I'm pulling away. "We can get messy if that's what you want. I'll lay you right over there on that picnic table, cover your body with ice cream and lick it off with my tongue. Every fucking last inch of you."

His words have me getting excited, feeling needy for him to take me. It doesn't even matter that we're still getting dirty looks from people.

I let out a small moan when he pulls me farther onto his lap and grinds below me, letting me feel how hard he is.

"Sterling..." I lean in and run my cold lips over his ear. "I think I'm ready to leave now."

"Fuck, me too, baby." He grips my hips, squeezing them

hard as he pulls me in and kisses me again. He sucks and tugs on my lips, giving me a small taste of what's to come.

It's not until his phone begins yelling at us that we pull away from each other so that Sterling can see who's calling him.

"Those fucking assholes." He squeezes his phone. "Ace and Killian need my help with moving my uncle's ex and her son into their new place. I swear I could kill them right now."

"I would help you too right now." I move my hips above him, giving him a small tease before I climb off the bike and kiss his cheek. "Let's go so you can get this over with and hurry back to me."

"Fucking shit." I hear a frustrated growl leave his lips as he grabs my ice cream and tosses it before helping me onto the back of his motorcycle and taking off.

My whole body is aching for Sterling to take me at this point and waiting for him to get back is going to be torture.

STERLING and the boys have been gone for over three hours now, helping Camille move. Us women offered to help, but the men refused to let us to a "man's job."

So I've been sitting here with Kadence and Melissa playing games and talking about the Locke brothers.

Melissa cracks me up every time someone mentions

Ace's name. She's trying really damn hard to fool us into believing she isn't attracted to him, even just physically, but we call bullshit.

She's into him, even if it's only for a good fuck from the oldest Locke.

"I'm not into him for the last time, so please stop." Her face is red because Kadence has been talking about Ace slamming her against a wall and having his way with her.

"Mm-hmm... we all know you've wondered if he fucks just as rough and twisted as he is."

"Is that right?"

Us women look over toward the door at the sound of Ace's husky voice.

Apparently, we've been too wrapped up in messing with Melissa to hear the guys pull back up.

Killian walks in after Ace, wiping his shirt over his sweaty forehead, followed by Aston and then Sterling.

My heart instantly reacts to seeing him, along with my body that is still aching for him to take me.

The guys are barely inside for two minutes when everyone's ears perk up at the sound of another vehicle coming down the driveway.

"Wonder who the fuck that could be," Aston grunts from the couch.

Red and blue flashing lights have me walking toward the window and looking outside. My stomach drops and my throat instantly goes dry when I see my father's squad car pull up at the end of the driveway.

I watch with my heart racing as my father and his partner, Officer Newberg, step out of the car and look up at the old house in disgust.

Apparently, now that Kevin's had almost a week to recover from what Sterling and Ace did to him, he's regained enough energy to contact the one person he knows will attempt to control me since he can't.

"Shit... my father's here." I close the curtain and turn around to see Sterling already making his way outside. "Sterling! Wait..."

I hurry to the door, but Aston blocks my way, not allowing me to step outside. "Stay inside," he growls at me. "My brother knows how to get rid of these assholes and if not, then my brother and I will help."

"Aston, move." I push his arm, but it stays firm. "I'm not going to make Sterling deal with him alone. He's my father and he's been controlling me for as long as I can remember. It ends today. Now. Move."

When Aston doesn't move, I bite his arm, surprising him and causing him to move just enough for me to slip past him and out the front door.

My eyes go wide when I look over to see Sterling right as he headbutts my father, causing him to stumble backward into his car.

I cover my mouth as Officer Newberg rushes over to Sterling and tackles him facedown onto the ground. He falls hard, but it doesn't stop him from swinging his head back in just the right amount of time to hit my father's partner in the forehead.

Apparently, getting himself arrested is his way of getting rid of them.

After a few seconds, Sterling stands with his hands in the air with a cocky little smirk on his face as my father curses and pulls out his handcuffs, ready to detain him.

"Don't you fucking dare!" I yell, getting my father's attention. "This has nothing to do with him and everything to do with your need to control your family. I'm not going anywhere and neither is he."

I take quick steps, stopping right in front of my father.

His eyes go wide with anger at the realization that I'm putting my foot down for the first time. Well, I'm tired of being controlled. First him and then Kevin. I will never allow anyone to control me again.

"Get in the front seat," he demands. "There's no way in hell I'm allowing you to stay here with these fucking savages. Especially after what Kevin told me this morning. This family..." He points at the house with his jaw clenched. "Is no good. Do you know how many times I've had to come here because of their drunken, drugged-up parents in the past? Do you know how many times I've had to arrest their uncle for stealing and fighting? It's in their blood to be bad. These boys aren't any different."

"No. It's in their blood to protect their own. It's in their blood to love hard and fierce, and take out anyone who stands in their way or threatens to harm them." I step up to Sterling and wrap my arms around his neck. "This savage... this man that you claim is no good is the only one who has ever made me feel safe and protected."

My father looks shocked as he lowers the cuffs. "How could you say that when I've done everything in my power to protect you from harm since the day you were born?"

I stand in between Sterling and my father and place my hand on my father's chest, pushing him away from us. I don't want him laying even one finger on my man. "No." I shake my head, feeling the pain and anger in my chest grow as I think back to just over seventeen years ago. "Do you really think I was too young to remember you coming home drunk and beating my mother until you had to rush her to the hospital? Or the fact that she never came home after that?" My whole body shakes as anger and rage takes over. "You lied to me my whole life. You told me she was in a car accident and didn't make it, but I always knew the truth. Why do you think I stayed away as much as I could and moved away the first chance I got?"

I feel Sterling's hand grab my waist, then he pushes me behind him as if to protect me from my father, but there's no mistaking the shock in my father's eyes at hearing the truth. The one he thought he'd kept hidden from me all this time.

"Back the fuck up," Sterling barks. "If you ever come

near her again, I'll rip your fucking throat out and throw you in the river. Let them lock me up for good, but at least you'll get what you truly deserve."

I look around me to see that Aston and Ace have now joined us outside, looking fierce and ready to strike if it comes down to it.

Then two seconds later Killian steps outside, shirtless. The fierce look on his face as he stares my father down has him in complete silence.

"Wynter..." My father looks defeated as he runs his hands over his face and takes a few steps back. "You're mistaken. Of course your mother died in an accident. Stop with that nonsense. You're all I have left and I'm not leaving you here with these animals."

"No," I cry out. "You lost me the day you took my mother from me. Now. Leave. I don't want you in my life."

Sterling stands tall, intimidating my father as he slowly walks around to the other side of his squad car and opens the door. "You're really going choose to stay here with these *people* over your own father?"

"You better fucking believe it," I say stiffly. "These *people* have done more for me and have made me feel safer and more welcome in the last week than you've ever made me feel in twenty-four years. I'm done being controlled. This is where I belong. If I *want* to see you, then I'll make that decision and *I'll* come to you. Now. Go."

My father nods his head, but looks disappointed as he

slips into his car and shuts the door. His partner immediately follows his actions and jumps into the passenger seat.

We all stand outside and watch as he pulls away, none of us bothering to speak until we can no longer see the taillights of his squad car.

"You didn't have to do that." Sterling places his hands on my face and leans in close to me. "I was going to get rid of him on my own."

I run my finger over his bottom lip and smile. "Oh yeah. How's that?"

"I was going to threaten to spend all my time watching his every fucking move until he learned that I'm not going anywhere and you're *mine*. I'm not easy to get rid of and my family is even harder to get rid of. Especially my uncle. Trust me. It wouldn't have been worth it to him to try to keep you from me or control you."

"I don't want you to have to take care of my father, Sterling. As much as I appreciate it, he's my responsibility to take care of. You have enough to deal with."

Sterling grabs my waist and pulls me against him. "And you're my responsibility. See how that fucking works, baby?" He smirks. "Now let's go upstairs. I'm ready to be alone with my woman."

18

Wynter

Sterling led me up to his room and we made our way to his bed. We've been lying on his bed for the last twenty minutes, just talking about random things that make my heart full. After the situation with my father and Kevin, and everything coming around full-circle, this finally feels like the closing to a nightmare.

Sterling runs his hand through my hair and tingles race up my spine. "What are you thinking about right now?" I ask and smile at him, staring into his eyes. Despite the solemn atmosphere in the air, the heavy, comfortable sensation of being with him, I want to know how he truly feels.

"I feel pretty fucking incredible, if I'm being honest." He leans in and kisses me, his lips firm, strong.

I feel the heat of my body rising, my erogenous zones tingling. In this moment I want him. I don't want soft and gentle. I don't want sweet and slow. I want Sterling the way he wants to give it to me. I want him to show me what it's like to really be with a Locke brother.

"Be with me, Sterling. Fuck me." Before I know it's happening he has his hand on my waist and is hauling me on top of him. I'm breathing heavy now, beads of perspiration dotting the valley between my breasts. My heart is racing and my palms are sweating. It's as if I'm finally feeling alive, free from this weakness that's been holding me down my entire life. It's all because of Sterling, what he did for me, how he opened my eyes and made me see I don't have to be afraid anymore.

And then in the next instant I'm under him and my pants and panties are being pulled from my body. My ass shakes from the force, and I moan at the roughness he shows me.

He spanks my ass especially hard, and I curl my hands in the sheets, my eyes widening, my breath stalling.

"You want me to fuck you?"

I nod, his voice deep, serrated.

"I'm the one in control."

I hear the zipper of his jeans go down, and glance over my shoulder to see him getting undressed.

"Take the shirt and bra off." I can see he's frenzied, ready for this, ready for me. And just like that I feel just as frenzied as he is.

I rise up just enough to take off my shirt and bra, and when I'm naked, the same as he is, I rest back on the bed.

He spanks my ass again and again, and the pain and pleasure morph into one.

"Ask me for it rough and raw, just the way I want to give it to you."

I'm gasping for air, nodding at his question. "Give it to me rough. Give it to me the way you want to, Sterling."

He pushes my legs apart and I feel the hard, thick head of his cock right at my entrance. I know this will be a fast fucking, so damn intense that I won't even be able to walk straight tomorrow. I look forward to it. God, I am looking forward to it all.

"I hope you're ready, because this is going to be fucking intense, baby girl. I'm still pumped up from earlier." He pushes just the head inside. "When you're with me, I'm the one that does the fucking." He slams into me fast and hard and I slip up the bed from the force.

He starts really fucking me then, pulling out and shoving all his thick inches back into me. My inner muscles clench around his length, and he grunts, picking up his speed.

"Fuck, you feel so good, Wynter." He flips me over, my face smashing into the mattress as he slams back into me.

All I can do is hold on as he fucks the hell out of me.

He grabs my ass and spreads the cheeks so wide I know he's watching his cock move in and out of me. He picks up speed and slams harder into me.

"Your cunt is so fucking tight and wet. And it's all mine." Sterling leans forward and runs his tongue up the length of my spine. He works his dick inside of me in deep, long strokes.

I force myself to hold off on coming because I want this to last, but God, I just want to let go. He pumps three more times into me before stilling, his balls pressed against my pussy, his cock lodged deep inside of me.

"You want me to let you come?"

"God, yes."

He pulls out so the tip is at my entrance again. "Come all over my dick. Soak me in your cream." Sterling thrusts back in so powerfully I do come for him.

The world swallows me whole, and the pleasure is like nothing I've ever felt before.

He keeps fucking me, drawing out my pleasure, making me beg for more. Right before the climax ends, Sterling pulls out and turns me around so I'm on my back now.

He has his cock back in my pussy and is fucking me hard and fast. I cry out and close my eyes. I have my legs around his waist, and he's so deep in me I can't see straight. He grabs my thighs and pushes them toward the bed, keeping me spread for him, open for his penetration.

I'm so filled, so stretched. My pussy is tender, but it's the kind of discomfort that turns me on even more.

"Tomorrow you'll still feel my big dick in your pussy." His voice is so rough.

My body slides up the bed even more when he starts moving again, my skull hitting the headboard.

"Watch as I tear this pussy up, baby."

I lift up and brace myself on my elbows, my focus down the length of my body. He slowly pulls out of me, and I watch his cock become visible, my cream coating the thickness. Then he fucks me like a madman, over and over, making me gasp and moan.

I can't hold off anymore. I have to come. I have to let go.

"Do it. Get off for me."

And then I'm crying out and coming for Sterling. He pumps into me once, twice, and on the third thrust, he buries his cock so far inside of me I know I'll feel him tomorrow.

He comes long and hard, filling me with his seed, making me take every last drop.

"Fuck. You're mine, baby." He collapses on top of me. My heart is thundering so hard in my chest.

He quickly rolls off of me but keeps me close, our bodies sweaty, sated. He places his hand between my thighs, pushing his finger into me, making his cum stay up in my pussy.

"Get some sleep, baby." He kisses the top of my head

and I feel myself start to drift off to sleep. "You're safe. You'll always be safe with me."

And I know he means that, know it's the truth down to my marrow.

Sterling is where I belong. He's where I've belonged since the first day our gazes locked in the classroom of our high school and finally I'm his and he is mine.

EPILOGUE

Sterling

Six weeks later

My woman and me can't seem to get any damn peace with my brothers always the fuck around, knocking on doors and asking for shit.

That's exactly why I made the decision to move out and get a place with the only person I want to be around twenty-four-seven.

I love my asshole brothers, don't get me wrong, but I can only take so much of them without wanting to choke them out.

Plus, my woman deserves to have her own space, especially now that she's been working at the local bank.

She's tired after long days of work and I want her to have the peace and quiet she deserves.

"Put that shit over there." I point at the corner, but Ace sets the table in the middle of the floor, anyway, ignoring my order. "Thanks, prick."

"Always welcome, dick." He stops to look around the large room. "I think there might be room for me to move here too. What do you think?"

"Nah, hell no. Time to leave, brother." I push him out the front door and lock it behind him.

When I look over to see Wynter and Kadence unpacking boxes and smiling and talking, this pride takes over me that I'm providing my woman with what she needs. As long as she's mine she'll never have to want for anything.

"You do realize the back door's unlocked, right?" Aston grins as Ace bursts through the back door with his hammer over his shoulder.

"I was about to break a door down..." He points his hammer at me. "So you're lucky."

"Really?" Wynter stands and gives Ace a stern look. "Give me the hammer."

Ace exhales and hands his hammer over to Wynter. "Really? It's like that?"

She nods. "Yup! I think I'll be holding onto this until we're done."

Ace looks to me. "You see this shit?"

I laugh and walk over to my brother to slap his shoulder. "I do, brother. Fuck, I love that woman."

I feel Wynter's soft arms wrap around my neck from behind, before she walks around to stand in front of me. "I'm so excited for our first night here. I love it. I really do. And it's close to your family home. I love that even more."

I lean down and brush my lips over hers. "I love it because you're in it with me." I reach out to grab her waist, not realizing that I'm digging my fingers in until she bites me. "Fuck, I'm sorry. I'm trying my hardest not to take you right here in front of everyone."

"You've had me every night for six weeks. I think you can handle a night without making me scream for you." She grins against my ear. "Besides, it's our very first bonfire at our new home. It might be a late night."

"Fuck me. Do we have to?" I growl and pull her bottom lip into my mouth, trying to persuade her. "We can always do it tomorrow night and just kick everyone out right now. They won't mind."

"We're not going anywhere, nut sack." Aston drops a box in the middle of the floor. "This is the last one. Now let's get this fire started. I need a fucking beer."

I watch my brother as he walks over to Kadence and scoops her up, throwing her over his shoulder before he heads out the back door.

Then I look over to see Ace lift a brow in Melissa's direction, but she places her hand on his chest and pushes him back.

"I don't think so, big guy. I can walk my damn self."

My brother throws his arms up and cusses to himself as he watches her walk past him and out the door. "See how much she wants me, brother?"

"You're a fucking idiot." I laugh as he walks outside after her, most likely to bug her some more and get under her skin. He's been doing that every chance he gets now.

It's as if the fucker is desperate to make her want him.

She's sassy as fuck with him, so I somehow see them working out if she ever gives up and lets his ass in.

My heart does this little jump when I feel Wynter's hand wrap around mine as she kisses my arm. "Let's make this house a home, baby." She tugs on my arm. "Come on."

When we walk outside, the fire is already started and Aston and Ace are pulling chairs up around the flames.

I have to admit that it feels good having my family all here in the place that Wynter and I will be calling a home.

It all just fucking feels so complete now.

It's late into the night now, but no one seems to want to leave, so I just sit back in my chair, with Wynter in my arms.

Killian showed up an hour ago and he's been telling stories about some fucked-up shit he's done over the years.

It's keeping everyone entertained, other than Ace, who seems to be focused on getting all up in Melissa's space.

She tries to hide it, but I see a small hint of a smile when

Ace presses his lips to her ear to most likely whisper something inappropriate.

"Think they'll end up together?" Wynter turns to face me, cupping my face in her hands.

"Maybe," I whisper. "Doesn't really matter to me."

"Oh yeah?" She smiles and leans in so that our lips are brushing. "Tell me what does?"

"You," I whisper against her lips. "Always you. Because I fucking love you more than life."

Her gaze locks on mine and just stays there for long moments before she speaks. "I love you, too. More and more with each day that passes." I move up so that our lips are touching. "You're mine and I'm never letting you go, Sterling Locke."

I let out a little moan before sucking her lip into my mouth. "Always. I fucking belong to you, Wynter Lowe. And one day I'll give you my name. That's a promise."

Wynter

HEARING STERLING SAY he's going to give me his name someday has an emotion I've never felt before taking over me and swallowing me whole.

I'm pretty sure that if it weren't for the chattering of the voices around us that Sterling would be able to hear my heart pounding in my chest.

I've managed to only fall more and more in love with Sterling Locke with each passing day. Just the thought of not being with him feels like my heart's being ripped from my damn chest.

He's changed my life. He's given me a happiness I never knew existed until the day I showed up at his house with my face beat to shit.

There's nothing I wouldn't do for this man and I know there's nothing he wouldn't do for me.

He's even managed to take care of my father the times he's called me, even though I told him he didn't have to. It's been over a month now that I've heard from my father and when I did talk to him, he only asked me how I was doing and said he just wanted to check in with me.

No more being controlled by anyone and being with Sterling, I know the only place he'll control me is in the bedroom, which I prefer anyway when it comes to him.

"I'd want that too," I say. "To have your name someday."

"Good. That's what I was hoping to hear." He kisses my forehead and then pulls me back against his chest so we're both facing the fire.

Everything about this moment feels perfect. Sitting out here with family, just enjoying each other's company with the man I love. No worries. Just happiness.

The End

TWISTED LOCKE

LOCKE BROTHERS, 3

Cover model: Andrew Biernat

Photographer: Wander Aguiar

Cover Designer: Dana Leah, Designs by Dana

Editor: Kasi Alexander

Ace Locke

Damaged.

Savage.

Twisted.

Those three words describe us Locke brothers to the motherfucking T.

We were wronged by the ones who were supposed to protect us. The ones who were supposed to love us ... to show us how to love.

It doesn't matter though. 'Cause we taught ourselves how to love in the best way we know how. When it comes to giving our heart away, we do it with everything in us. We may be dangerous sons of bitches, but we love hard as shit.

Melissa doesn't quite get that yet. But she will.

She got dragged into our fucked-up world, afraid and unsure of us.

Well, I'm about to change that.

I'm going to twist her up and shake the fucking innocence in her.

And by the time I'm through with her, she's going to be my beautiful, twisted angel.

She'll be mine and I'll be hers.

I'll make damned sure of that.

Melissa Anderson

I was pulled into the Locke life when my roommate got involved with one of the dangerous brothers.

I should have left, should have minded my own business, but the attraction I feel for Ace is stronger than I can ignore.

I can feel the way he watches me. The ownership I feel from him, the possessiveness and obsession, lets me know he wants me too.

But common sense tells me I don't want this in my life, don't want to let a Locke brother mark me as his.

But that reality isn't what my heart wants, isn't what my body craves. Truth is I want to have Ace claim me, want his hands on me, his dominance showing me that all I want is to submit.

We may not lead the same lives, and he may have darkness in him, the likes of which I've never seen before, but for once in my life I want to skirt with that danger.

I want to forget everything else and just let Ace own every single part of me.

And I have a feeling he won't stop until he does.

WARNING: Twisted Locke is a short co-written, kind of twisted love story from NYT Bestselling Author Victoria Ashley and USA Today Bestselling Author Jenika Snow. If you like it hot and a little rough... this is the book for you. 18+

1

Ace

I place the joint between my lips and look down to see red covering my knuckles. It gets my adrenaline pumping once again, making me very aware of what happened less than five minutes ago.

My hands are busted up, covered in blood, but I don't feel shit.

Nada.

No pain and definitely no motherfucking remorse for almost taking a man's last breath.

This motherfucker should've known better than to cross an angry, homicidal Locke.

It's obvious he was very unaware of who was sitting across the bar from him when he decided to punch his woman in the face and then proceed to grab her by the hair and drag her across the bar as if she was a fucking ragdoll.

The fact that he felt the need, had the fucking balls to do that in a roomful of people, told me he did even worse things to her when no one was around.

He barely made it out the door before I was on his ass, pulling him from her and showing him what it's like to be the fucking ragdoll.

I wanted to make sure he knew what it felt like to be the *helpless* one and I have no doubt he's still feeling it this very moment.

It feels so fucking good to know that some son of a bitch is suffering right this very second, because they chose to make someone weaker than them suffer first.

I'll never get over that feeling... the high it brings me to crush a motherfucker even harder than they crushed someone's world.

To leave that permanent scar they deserve.

I'm barely halfway through smoking my joint before I pass it to the woman beside me with the busted-up, swollen face.

"Here. Finish that while I take care of this prick." I slap the trunk and a twisted ass grin crosses my face when I hear a few desperate pounds come from the inside.

He should've thought about his actions. If he had he wouldn't be shoved in some stranger's trunk like a little bitch right now.

Good thing I decided to take the old Dynasty out of the garage tonight.

"Are you going to kill him?" she says, the pain on her face clear as she places the joint between her busted-up lips. She takes a long hit, holding the smoke in.

"Probably not. It depends on him."

My response has the noise coming from the trunk getting louder and more desperate.

"Shut up in there you, fucking asshole!" Her whole body is shaking in anger as she slaps the trunk repeatedly. "Fuck you! I hate you! I fucking *hate* you so much! You're done hurting me. Done! Do you hear me?"

Next thing I know she falls to her knees and bursts into tears.

There's nothing I hate more than seeing a woman hurting and her tears are just enough to set me off again.

"Fucking piece of shit!" I growl out, reaching into the backseat for my hammer.

Before I can even think about what I'm doing, I'm popping the trunk and dragging the sorry motherfucker out by his neck.

"Get up on your hands and knees." I give him a shove in her direction. I help the woman up so she's not kneeling any longer. "In front of her, bastard!" I yell, losing my damn patience. "Now!"

"I'm sorry." He looks up at me, snot covering his pathetic, beat-up face as he does what he's told. "I'm so sorry. I promise I'll never lay a finger on Amanda again. I swear. I fucking swear."

Stepping up behind him, I grab his hair and force him to look straight across so he can get a good view of the damage he did to her. "Look what the fuck you did!" I bend down beside him to make sure he's actually looking. "Do you see the fucking damage you caused?" I slap the back of his head before grabbing his hair again and tilting his head up. "Do you?"

"Yes," he whines. "Yes. I see it."

His woman is backing up and crying so hard now that her whole body is convulsing as she attempts to catch her breath.

"You were damn right when you said you'd never lay a finger on her again. You wanna know why, Frankie?"

He shakes his head back and forth. "No. No. Please!"

"Too motherfucking bad. Place your hands flat on the ground."

Now he's the one shaking.

Good. He should be.

"Now!" I scream and kick him over when he doesn't listen. "Be a man and get this over with, Frankie. Do this for her!" I point my hammer at Amanda, who still looks scared shitless at him being near her.

From the old bruises on her face and arms, it looks as though he's been hurting her for a while now. This shit ends here and now.

"It's either going to be your hands or..." I place my hammer to the back of his skull, which has him immediately splaying his hands out on the ground in front of him.

"Fuck, fuck, fuck..." he cries to himself, while squeezing his eyes shut. "I'm sorry. I'm sorry..."

"Well, I'm not."

Gripping my hammer, I take one hard swing at his right hand, hearing the bones crack as he screams out in pain.

I barely give him a moment to really feel the pain before I take a swing at his left hand, causing him to scream out again before he falls over and begins crying.

Keeping my eyes on him, I reach for a smoke and place it between my lips before bending down beside him. "Just be lucky you're not fucking dead. You'll heal."

He doesn't say anything and from the excruciating pain he's clearly in, I don't expect him to be able to.

I take a few seconds to enjoy my handiwork before I pat his back and walk over to check on Amanda.

She almost looks relieved as she watches him suffer on the ground, as I'm sure she's done plenty of times since she's met this piece of shit.

"I should take him to the emergency room." Her voice is void of any emotion. "He may be hurting for a while."

I honestly don't give a fuck if he writhes in pain on the ground, but Amanda seems worried, and I feel for her. If this will make her feel better, getting this piece of shit to a doctor, then so be it.

"Yeah," I say between drags. "Pull your car up and I'll shove him into the backseat."

She backs up, keeping her eyes on Frankie the whole time. "Yeah... okay. I'll be right back."

A black '95 Corvette pulls up a few moments later and I can't help but to laugh to myself. He's going to be real comfortable shoved into the backseat of that thing.

Not my problem and not my damn concern.

"Come on, asshole." I flick my cigarette across the mostly empty parking lot and reach underneath Frankie's arms to lift him to his feet.

Amanda already has the car door open and the seat pushed forward, so I give him a shove toward the car and stuff him into the backseat.

It may seem a little fucking twisted, but I get pleasure from hearing him whine and cry like a little bitch.

I guess that's why I'm the twisted one.

Hurting others brings me pleasure and I'm the first one to admit that I enjoy doing what we do.

It's because of me that my brothers are the way they are. All it took was years of abuse from our sorry ass excuse for parents and seeing the secret lifestyle that our uncle Killian lived.

I did this. I brought my brothers into this lifestyle and twisted is what I do best.

2

Melissa

A text comes through from Kadence asking me to bring her the leftover scones and muffins when the coffee shop closes for the night.

If we don't take them home, then they just end up getting thrown away, so I send her a quick text to let her know that I'll bring the leftovers home with me.

I'm just about to shove my phone back into my pocket when it vibrates in my hand with another message from my *sometimes* roommate.

Kadence: Bring them to Aston's. I'm already over there.

Kadence: Pleeeeease...

I huff and put my phone away without bothering to respond to her message. She's knows I'm still not very comfortable with going to the Locke house, yet it seems she always finds a *reason* for me to show up there.

What she doesn't know, though, is that I'm attracted to the oldest Locke. The most twisted one of them all, the more I see him, the more I'm drawn to him physically.

I've been doing *everything* in my power to make sure I don't fall for a Locke when I've spent the last four years fearing them.

When Kadence fell for the youngest Locke I was against it and wanted nothing more than to keep her away from Aston.

I'll admit I've softened up toward them over time, but I still don't quite understand their violence and that part scares me.

Especially Ace.

He's vicious and mysterious in ways that his brothers aren't, yet when I look at him I feel as if I'll melt into a puddle at his feet.

Ace has this *power* to make me want to fall at my knees with just one glance into his amber eyes.

I've never met a man so dangerously sexy in my entire life and a part of me is unsure if I can stop myself from falling for him if I keep getting sucked into being around him.

Releasing a deep breath, I lean over to clean off a table,

but freeze when I glance out the window to see Ace standing across the street, leaning against his truck.

He's got a cigarette between his lips and I can't help but stare at his mouth as he takes a drag from it.

His gaze is trained on the building but I can't tell whether or not he can see me watching him. It has my heart beating at an alarming rate, but I can't seem to pull my gaze from him.

He's dressed in a snug white T-shirt and a pair of black jeans that fit his body to perfection. I hate that he's impossible to turn away from and I hate that he's so physically flawless.

"Too bad a man so incredibly sexy has to have such a bad reputation."

I pull out of my haze at the sound of Gia's voice. I hadn't even noticed she was standing beside me until now.

"It's weird that he's just standing there, staring at the building, right?" I glance beside me to see her staring out the window as she speaks. "He's the oldest one? What's his name..."

"Ace," I say on a whisper before she's able to finish thinking. "And yes; he's the oldest one."

A small smile tugs at the edges of Ace's lips before he flicks his cigarette across the street and jumps into his truck.

"I heard that he once cut a guy's finger off and force fed it to him," Gia says, watching as he drives away. "That's some crazy stuff. I can't believe that Kadence dates one of those guys. I'd be terrified."

"They're not that bad," I say on a swallow. "It's not like they go out and just hurt random innocents. They have reasoning behind everything they do."

I'm not sure who I'm trying to convince that the Lockes aren't what they seem, Gia or myself.

The only reason I choose to still be cautious is because I know I *have* to in order to keep Ace at a safe distance.

"Then maybe it's not so bad that the oldest one is hanging around." She smiles and turns away from the window. "Maybe he'll come in next time. I'd love to see that one up close. He's absolutely gorgeous and terrifying at the same time."

The idea that Gia is attracted to Ace for some reason bothers me. It's stupid for me to feel this way.

"Maybe," I say, wiping off the table. "I have a few things to take care of in the back and then I'm going to take off. Do you need help with anything first?"

Gia is the owners' daughter and she's been coming in almost daily for the last few months. I have a feeling it's because she'll be taking over the coffee shop soon so that Cheryl and Bryon can retire.

"No, I don't think so. We'll be lucky to get one, maybe two more customers stopping by so I should be good to handle things."

"Sounds good."

After cleaning up in the back and organizing things for tomorrow, I pack up some leftover pastries and jump into my car, hoping that maybe Ace won't be around when I drop these off to Kadence.

After seeing him already once today, I'm not sure I can handle seeing him for a second time and not end up spending the rest of the night thinking about him.

It's something I've been doing a lot lately and the last thing I need is to keep the habit going.

I need to be strong when it comes to the oldest Locke.

I'm just not sure for how much longer I can manage that.

3

Ace

I place a joint between my lips and watch as the asshole before me struggles to get out of the ropes.

His attempts are only making the rope tighter, digging into his already bloodied wrists even more. I know how to tie a fucking knot, and his struggles only have me grinning. He won't be able to get out of it unless I fucking want him to.

"Take it easy," I finally say and glance down at his wallet, "Troy Foster. You keep pulling at those ropes and you're going to lose your hands."

Hell, keep pulling at those ropes. Give me more entertainment tonight.

He struggles to scream at me, but with the tape wrapped

around his mouth, nothing but muffled sounds come out. Tears are coming out of the corner of his eyes, his face is red as a fucking beet, and I can see snot starting to slip out of his nose. The fucker isn't used to this. He wants out, no doubt. He probably wants at me with all that rage. I should just let him go, should just let him get a punch or two in so that I can feel that pain then really go fucking psycho on his ass.

He mumbles something again, his eyes narrowed, the anger coming from him clear.

"What was that?" I kick away from the garage door and walk over to yank his head back. "I couldn't understand you." I push his head down and take a long hit off the joint before yanking his head back again and blowing the smoke in his eyes.

He squints and struggles harder.

"You know..." I pull the knife from my boot and run it along his skin as I walk around him. "I'm not sure what to do with you yet. You see... I don't like the idea of some stranger coming to my motherfucking house in the middle of the night with a gun."

I stop in front of him and tug on his wrists, which are tied above him. His scream is muffled behind the tape as the ropes dig further into his skin, causing blood to drip down his arms.

"I could *kill* you to make sure that you're never a threat to my family again."

My threat has him struggling against the ropes again, clearly desperate to get away—or maybe to get to me—no matter how much pain he's currently in.

I tilt my head and watch as he shakes his head and attempts to scream.

"Or... or I could just chop both your hands off so you can never hold a gun again, never pick a lock, hell," I chuckle, "open a fucking door handle again." I stare at him in the eyes. "I haven't quite decided yet which route I should go, though."

I scowl deeper, letting him know how serious I am. This asshole really has no clue who he's fucked with.

King caught him on the side of the house last night and dragged him down by his foot from the window he was attempting to climb into.

He tore into his leg pretty good before I was able to run outside and see what was going on.

The piece of shit pulled a pistol on me. Aimed that shit right at my head, but King attacked his arm before he could manage to get a shot off.

This asshole fucking almost shot at me. Could've shot at my family and now he's going to pay the price.

Just thinking about it has me wanting to rip his throat out with my bare hands.

With an angry growl, I take my blade and run it down his cheek, watching as the blood drips from the wound.

I'm already covered in his blood as it is, due to the

beating I gave him thirty minutes ago after returning from the coffee shop.

I needed something to hold me back from killing this motherfucker tonight, and seeing Melissa always seems to calm the demons inside my head just long enough to get me thinking clearly.

If it weren't for her, he'd already be dead.

Something in me snaps and I find myself taking the blade and running it down his chest, watching as the knife moves easily through his skin, opening up the flesh just superficially, blood welling up immediately.

I'm a sadistic fucker so I make a few more cuts on his chest, the asshole struggling, mumbling behind the tape. His eyes are wild, and sweat is dotting his forehead, mixing with the blood as it runs down his cheek and cut. No doubt that shit stings.

I laugh at that.

I take a step back and stare at my handiwork. He has his fingers clenched tightly, and I see blood on his palms. He relaxes his hands and sags against the bonds, crescent shaped cuts from his nails littering the insides of his hands.

But I'm pissed about him breaking in, about thinking he could threaten me. I'm seeing red, picturing if I'd had Melissa here, how she'd be scared, in danger. I grab one of his hands and start breaking his fingers, snapping the digits back until I hear him screaming, hear the bone splintering in two. Only then do I exhale roughly and move away.

"We're done for tonight, Troy." I take one last hit from the joint and toss it at his face, embers bouncing against his skin. "Expect me when the sun rises. I have a few games I want to play with you tomorrow."

Tears run down his face and I grin, but other than the pleasure I feel at exacting pain in him, I don't feel shit for this sorry fucker. He didn't give a fuck when we came here with the intent to hurt whoever was inside, to take what wasn't his.

He wasn't sorry when he aimed that pistol at my head and tried to take my God damn life.

But he sure as hell is sorry now.

Rolling my head around on my neck, I hear it crack. I step out of the garage and grab a cigarette from my pocket, closing my eyes for a second and just inhaling and exhaling. I open my eyes again and place the cigarette between my lips and look up as headlights come from the driveway.

I stand here and take a drag, needing some kind of release before I lose it on whoever has decided to show up invited.

It's not until the vehicle gets closer that I realize that it's Melissa's car.

Fuck.

This isn't how I wanted her to find me.

She steps out of the vehicle, her gaze immediately landing on me.

From the way her eyes grow wide as she checks out my

bare chest, I know without a doubt that she notices the splatters of blood across my skin.

She's heard of the things we do, no doubt. Hell, I know Kadence had probably told her shit that Aston has done with us all in the name of fucking over a Locke. She's even been around after a few jobs, but she's never actually seen me covered in another man's blood before.

I keep my gaze on her, watching intently as she swallows and fights to pull her gaze off me.

I can see the struggle on her face, until she finally manages to turn away and walk to the front door.

Fuck me, she's so damn beautiful that all I want to do is slam her against the side of the house and fuck her right here and now.

I don't even care that I'm covered in another man's blood.

I want to be buried inside her pussy, making her scream for me.

The problem with that... Melissa hasn't quite come around to our lifestyle yet.

That's something I plan to change real soon. I've already given her enough time and I'm tired of waiting.

I want her as mine and when I get to her, she's going to want to belong to me just as much as I want her to.

4

Melissa

I don't know what to think right now. All I can picture is Ace, the blood covering him, his expression feral, his body tense. I picture his cut muscles just under his skin as he stood there, staring at me, maybe wondering what I would do, if I'd run. The light from the garage had silhouetted him, making him seem even more dangerous than he already was.

I haven't been able to get the picture of him covered in blood out of my head. He was standing there looking lethal, as if he could rip a man's heart out with his bare hands and there I was, unable to turn away from him.

What the hell is wrong with me?

I'm so confused with the fact that even knowing he was

just hurting someone, I still found him to be sexy as he stood there staring at me.

I almost hate myself for how aroused I was, how much I wanted him in that moment, even covered by the gore and violence of what he'd just done.

I knew I needed to get away from the Locke house as quickly as possible, before he was able to walk through that door and catch me staring for a third time in one damn day.

After I'd left, Kadence had explained to me what happened with someone trying to break into the house the night before.

It is all so crazy. It seems like an eternity ago that I first met the Locke brothers. I can still remember rooming with Kadence, knowing about them and what they did to anyone who crossed them. They are bad news but I saw the curiosity on Kadence's face and I hated it.

And now here I am just as curious about one of them.

The most lethal and twisted one of them all.

Ace.

Anyone who doesn't know him, anyone who doesn't know of his reputation, his clean-cut appearance would make him seem like the boy next door. But he's far from that. His skin might not be inked like his brothers, but he's even more dangerous than they are.

His hammer is his weapon of choice, and he has no empathy for people who cross him or people who hurt others who are weaker than them. Maybe that's why I'm captivated by him even though I try my hardest not to be.

Maybe that's why I want him so much.

Yes, I'm drawn to a Locke, but I will never admit that to anyone, least of all him. Hell, I try to not even admit it to myself.

But then I see the way he looks at me, the way he touches me, even around his family. He makes me feel owned already and I haven't even done anything sexual with him. But God, I want to. I want his hands on my body, rough, demanding. I want him to hold me down and take me the way I know he can, with a savage brutality that will make me know there is no one else for me.

I've been feeling this way more and more with each day that passes and I don't know what to do with that. I don't know what the hell is wrong with me.

"Miss?" I snap out of my haze and look at the customer in front of me. She lifts an arched eyebrow and gives me this stiff glare. "I ordered a latte. But you're just standing there."

"Sorry," I mumble and turn away to make her drink. I need to get Ace out of my head, need to worry about working and myself. He might've told me in more ways than one that I was his but a part of me wants to not get involved with a Locke because I know he can be dangerous.

But he's like a drug to me, my addiction that I can't walk away from, can't ignore. I felt that again last night stronger than before and it's been eating at me.

The rest of the day flies by as I try and focus on work. Once I clock out and grab my purse and car keys, my intention is just to go straight home. But as soon as I step out the back door and head to my car, I feel someone watching me. I stop and lift my head to see Ace standing there leaning against his truck, which is parked right beside my car.

The sight of him causes my heart to about leap from my chest. This is the last place I expected to see Ace.

He's got a baseball cap on, a white T-shirt stretched across his muscular chest and arms, and a pair of faded jeans that fit his long, lean body to perfection. His boots are black, slightly scuffed, his legs crossed at the ankles. Shit kickers are what I aptly call them.

He pushes away from his truck and walks over to me. The grin on his face can't be called anything but shit eating. I don't know what to say, or how to act. This is the first time he's ever shown up at my work other than when he was parked out front yesterday.

"Hey," I say and look up at him. He might be lean and muscular like a swimmer, but he's tall and I have to crane my head back just to look at his face. "What are you doing here?" He takes my bag from me and we walk over to my car together. He hasn't said anything yet, but he doesn't have to for me to feel like I'm walking on a tight rope.

"I haven't seen you in a few days and you took off so quickly last night..." He looks me right in the eyes and I take my bag from him and toss it in the back of my car.

“I've just been busy with work.” I lie easily, my voice tense, stiff. I am trying to not let him see how much he affects me, but I feel I’m failing miserably. I glance at him out of the corner of my eye, see his brows lowered, this look of confusion on his face, or maybe he’s pissed. I can’t tell half the time with him. He’s so hard to read.

The truth is I've been avoiding him. It's not that I don't want to see him, because that's actually the opposite. I want to see him all the time, and that scares me.

What scares me even more is the fact that I still feel this way even after what I witnessed last night.

“You've been busy at work?” He leans against his truck again and crosses his arms. It's obvious that he knows I'm lying.

“I have been.” I clear my throat and look away for a second before staring at his face again.

“Let me take you somewhere. Just you and me, a place where we can talk.”

I look at his hands, his knuckles, which are scabbed over, and it makes me wonder just what he did to that guy last night. But I know better than to ask what happened. Because the truth is I don't want to know the answer.

The violent side of Ace, the dangerous part, scares me, even though I know he will never hurt me.

“You want to take me somewhere?”

He nods. “Just you and me.”

The thought of being alone with him has my nerves kicking in.

I don't want to fall for him. I *can't* fall for him.

When I don't give him an answer, he backs me against my car and closes in on me. His toned arms surround me, and his scent, which I can only describe as intoxicating, fills my head and makes me drunk.

I find myself breathing hard and fast as he presses his body against mine and leans down so that his face is in my hair. I may even be trembling a bit, both out of fear and desire for Ace. "I'm not leaving until you say yes." I feel his lips move against the strands before he lowers his mouth to my ear and lets out something between a growl and a moan. "Fuck, Melissa. You have no idea how hard your scent gets me. But I'm not here to push myself on you and make you realize how much you truly want me inside of you. No... I'm here to take you somewhere alone so we can think in some peace and quiet. Now say yes."

His words have my entire being feeling as if it's igniting into flames and the closeness of his hard body has my brain in a mush. I can't think straight when he's so damn close.

"Okay," I say on a tremble. "We can go somewhere alone. But just to relax, to talk." I somehow find the strength to push him away so he's no longer practically glued to me. "And you have to leave your hammer at home. No violence."

He flashes his usual twisted grin that always seems to spark something in me I can't seem to understand. "Done. I left it in the SUV." He reaches out with his scabbed-up knuckled hand and closes my car door. "We'll take my truck."

Oh shit, is the only thing that runs through my mind as I allow him to lead me to the other side of his truck.

What am I getting myself into by allowing the scariest Locke of them all to get me alone?

5

Ace

It may be twisted to admit, but feeling the way Melissa's body trembled when I pressed mine against hers fucking turned me on and had my cock jumping with excitement.

I know a part of that is because she somewhat fears me still, but the other part is because she wants me just as much as I want her.

She knows how dangerous I am. She knows I'll kill any motherfucker who threatens my family. But what she doesn't know is that I love just as hard as I intimidate, maybe even more.

I hear a small breath escape her as I grip her waist and hoist her into my truck.

I'm not sure I can ever get used to how damn good it feels whenever I touch her. That's why I need to do everything in my power to make sure she wants me to keep touching her.

Things may get a little ugly, but I'm going to twist her up and shake the fucking innocence in her.

And by the time I'm through with her, she's going to be my beautiful, twisted angel.

When I climb into the vehicle and take off, I can feel her gaze on me as if she's taking this moment to take me all in, most likely thinking that I won't notice since I'm driving.

But fuck me… it's hard not to notice.

"Do you like what you see?"

From the corner of my eye, I catch her quickly turn away from me so she's now looking out the passenger side window. "Just checking for any fresh blood or any warning signs that I should jump out of this moving truck and run for my life. Don't get too cocky."

"Is that a deal breaker for you? Because I'm pretty sure you saw me covered in blood last night…" I glance over at her and raise a brow. "Yet you're still here in my truck with me."

She's silent after that.

That is, until she notices me pulling onto a side road and into the woods.

"Is this one of your kill spots?"

I laugh. "You're supposed to relax, remember?"

"How am I supposed to be able to relax when the woods are where axe murderers bring their victims before they cut them into tiny pieces and hide their body parts? Or in your case…" She turns behind her and begins looking into the backseat. "Smash your victims' body parts until they come off."

"That's not a bad idea. I've never tried that before. It could be a good workout." I park and look over to see her staring at me all wide-eyed and somewhat shocked. "Do you really think I'd do that?"

She watches me as I reach for my cap and take it off before running a hand through my messy hair. "God, I hope not. I'm not that twisted." I offer her a half smirk and reach over her to open her door. "Come on."

I'm the first one to hop out and I can't help but be a bit amused that she hesitates before getting out herself.

I really have my work cut out with Melissa.

"What are we supposed to do out here in the middle of nowhere?"

"Lay back and relax. Talk, shit like that." I flash her a grin. I grab a blanket out of the back of the truck and make my way to the tailgate. I pop the back and lay the blanket down. I jump up before reaching out for her hand. "This is the most peaceful place to think. I've been coming here for years but this will be the first time I've *not* come alone."

"Really?" She finally gives me her hand, allowing me to

pull her up beside me. "What do you like to come here and think about?"

I lay back and rest my hands behind my head. "I don't know. Just whatever's going on in my life at the time, I suppose. It's kind of hard to relax and have some *me time* when my brothers are always around and there's always some fucked-up shit for us to handle. This is the one place that is *mine* alone."

She's sitting on the edge, hanging her legs off as she looks up at the sky. "I have to admit that this is a pretty nice spot. I can see why it's so relaxing."

"Come here," I say softly, wanting her to see that I'm not all that bad. I hold my hand out for her to grab. "Lay with me."

It takes her a few seconds, but she eventually takes my hand and allows me to pull her down beside me.

Her gaze locks with mine. I should try to be a gentleman or some shit, but being so close to her has me all in knots, has the possessive side rising up. I crawl above her, spread her thighs with my knees and place my hard body between her legs. I can see her eyes go wide, feel her chest start to rise and fall faster. She breathes harder, and I know that she wants this just as much as I do. "Does this make you nervous?"

I see her throat work as she swallows. After a second she nods. "A little."

I press my body farther between her legs as I lean in to

brush my lips against her ear. I know she can feel how hard I am for her. "How about this? Does it make you nervous to *feel* how badly I want you, Angel?"

She nods again. "Yes," she whispers.

"That's all I needed to know."

With that, I roll over and lie back in my spot, allowing her to breathe easily again.

The next hour goes by in silence.

I've got Melissa alone for the first time and although I'd love nothing more than to fuck the fear out of her, to make her see that she is meant to be mine, I hold back because I can tell it's too soon.

I'll take things easy this time, but I can't say the same for the next. My willpower only goes so far.

After a while, she finally sits up and turns to face me. "It's getting kind of late. I should probably get home. Mind taking me back to my car?"

Without saying a word, I sit up and get off the tailgate, grab her hips and pull her closer to me so her legs are hanging off the side, and stare at her. I look into her eyes for a second, wanting to kiss her, to possess her. But I hold back and instead help her down as well.

"Let's go."

Once we get back to her car, I lean across the seat and unbuckle her seatbelt.

I can feel her heavy breaths hitting my neck and I know without a doubt that I've got her walls slowly crumbling.

"Goodnight," she says quickly. "Appreciate the relaxing night. I actually needed it."

I turn my head so that my lips are right above hers as I speak. "Good" is all I say before I lean back to my seat and listen to her uneven breathing.

She'll go to bed thinking about me and that's enough for tonight at least.

It definitely won't be enough for next time.

6

Melissa

I spent the entire night tossing and turning, thinking about Ace and how good it felt to be alone with him.

When he first asked me to go somewhere with him I was nervous. I was scared, not sure of what to expect from a guy like him. I never would've imagined that I'd be able to have a *normal* moment with him and enjoy the night as if nothing else mattered.

I'm so damn confused right now, because even though I know he's twisted and dangerous, I also know that there's more to him. There's a side to him that I could easily fall for and get hurt.

Kadence is sure to get a kick out of this and that's why I

need to keep my feelings from her until I know exactly what they mean.

"Why did you leave in such a hurry the other night?" Kadence questions from across the diner booth.

"I told you," I say over my glass. "I had a headache and I was tired. Why do you keep questioning my motives?"

She smiles and takes a bite of her cheesecake. It's the whole reason we're here. "It had nothing to do with a shirtless Ace that came inside a few minutes after you left?"

"Why would it? We didn't even talk. I don't know what you're talking about."

She laughs and stands up. "So it had nothing to do with the fact that he looks pretty damn good in red."

"That's messed up." I shake my head and try to fight back the smile. "It was someone else's blood, Kadence. Of course not. I wasn't attracted to him no matter how good he looked."

"So… you admit that he looked good?"

"Don't you have to get to work or something? I knew I shouldn't have met you here. I should've known it would lead to me watching you scarf down your cake while you try to get something out of me that will never happen. Ace is…"

"The guy you can't stop thinking about." She grins when I give her a dirty look. "Okay. Okay. I'm going. You should get some lunch or something while you're here."

I shake my head. "I'll just finish my drink and eat at

home. The cheesecake is on me so leave before I change my mind."

"Thanks, babe." She smiles that annoying smile at me again before finally turning away and walking outside.

I take a moment to finish my drink and pull myself together before I walk out of the diner and to my car.

It's not until I reach for the door handle that I notice Ace's truck parked behind me in the lot.

My stupid heart betrays me at the sight of him and about flies from my chest again. It only gets more intense the more I see him.

I swallow and walk over to his truck at the same time that he hops out and shuts the door behind him.

The way his amber gaze roams over my body makes me hot, and when his gaze stops on my lips, I find myself wondering what it would feel like for Ace to kiss me.

Surely, he'd be rough and demanding.

"What are you doing here, Ace?" I lift a brow and watch as he tosses his keys up and catches them. "Is a Locke brother stalking me?"

His lips pull up into a half smirk that causes my breath to catch in my throat. "You haven't eaten yet. I'm here to buy you lunch."

My heart stops mid-beat as Ace grabs my hand and begins walking us back toward the door of the diner.

A few glances land on us as he opens the door and

guides me right back to the table that Kadence and I were just sitting at.

I have to admit that being seen with Ace in public is sort of a rush. I know without a doubt by the surprised looks on everyone's faces that there's not one person in this place that doesn't know that I'm here with a *Locke*.

Ace pushes one of the menus in front of me but doesn't say a word as he grabs for the other menu and begins looking it over.

I find it to be crazy that he can make me feel excited and nervous just by sitting across from me in a diner. He doesn't even have to speak to evoke these emotions inside me.

We both place our order when the waitress comes by a few minutes later. I can tell by the slight shakiness in her voice that Ace makes her nervous, yet she can't stop checking him out and it's driving me crazy.

Just the thought of Ace touching her or kissing her has jealousy rushing through me.

I look across the table to see Ace's attention on me, instead of the waitress who has barely finished taking our order. It's as if he's trying to figure me out.

"Have you ever been in love, Melissa?"

I nod and thank the waitress as she drops off two glasses of water. "Once. What about you, Ace?" He watches me as I take a drink of my water. "Have you ever been in a long-term relationship?"

"No," he says, his gaze locked on mine. "I've been

waiting for the right girl to claim as mine. Once I find her..." He runs a hand through his messy brown hair before licking his bottom lip to wet it. "She'll be mine for good. That's how us Lockes work."

My heart hammers around in my chest at the idea of belonging to Ace. He wants a girl to possess.

Why do I find that to be so hot?

The food comes a few minutes later and we eat in silence, both of us glancing up to look at the other every few minutes and every time that he does, excitement courses through me.

I can't help but to feel this way and it's driving me insane.

I'm not sure if I'll ever be ready for Ace Locke, yet I can't help but want him...

Ace

CALL ME TWISTED. Call me a fucking stalker and I won't deny that shit. I'll do anything when it comes to getting Melissa.

Melissa looks up when the waitress sets the bill down in front of us, but I decide to keep my attention on her, wanting to show her that I could care less about the hot girl that is checking me out for the tenth damn time since we've walked through the door together.

I'm here for her and her only.

"What are you doing when you leave here?" I ask, tossing down a fifty-dollar bill.

She stands up and reaches into her pocket to pull out some cash. I grab it from her hand and shove it back into her pocket, getting up in her personal space.

Just like before, my closeness has her breathing picking up. This has me lifting her chin up and leaning in close as if to kiss her, but I stop right before our lips can meet. "Are you going to answer me, Angel? Or make me guess."

"Work," she says on a breath. "I have to be at work soon."

I can hear her swallow as I raise my thumb up to brush over her lips. "What about after work?"

"I don't know." She backs away from my touch, but I take a step further, backing her up against the side of the booth. "Probably going home. To bed."

"What if I don't want you to?" I run my hand up the side of her neck, before reaching around to cup the back of it as I lean in close to her mouth again. This has her fighting to catch her breath. "Come for a ride with me tonight. What time do you get off?"

"Ten. Or a little after. It depends."

I release her neck and smile as her gaze lowers to my lips. "I'll be out in the parking lot then."

She nods as I back away, giving her room to walk around me.

I know I'm not exactly *easy* to fall for, but I can promise that after she does, she's not going to want to go a day without me *inside* her.

I've just got to move slow with Melissa and let her see how much her body craves me first. That's exactly why I haven't kissed her yet.

I have to prepare her for me first.

7

Ace

It's half past ten and Melissa is just walking out of the coffee shop. She looks around for a few seconds as if she thinks that I've left her, but smiles once she finds me parked toward the back of the lot.

I shift my truck into drive and pull up beside her. I lean over and push her door open before reaching out my hand for her to grab. She's hesitant at first, but grabs it and allows me to pull her up.

There's a part of her that's still not sure if she should be alone with me yet. That's exactly why I need to take her where I have planned tonight... to soften her up toward me.

She's quiet as she shuts the door and fastens her seatbelt.

"How was work?"

I can feel her watching me as I pull out of the parking lot. "Boring as usual, but it pays the bills."

"How long have you worked there?" I pull my eyes away from the road just long enough to catch her checking out my thighs in these ripped up jeans I threw on before leaving the house. They're snug and easily show the imprint of my dick, which her gaze now seems to be focused on.

I laugh and look back up at the road. "Glad my body can be entertaining for you after a boring day at work."

"I was just thinking." She quickly turns away as if that'll make up for being caught staring at my package. "For four years now. I've had other jobs on the side, but this has been my main job for a while now. Do you have a job other than... you know..."

I let out a little chuckle and head toward the garage. "Yeah, we're actually headed there now. A mechanic. I have a little project I need to finish and thought maybe we could talk while I work."

I want Melissa to see the side of me that many don't get to see. The *me* outside of what I do with my brothers.

"You're a mechanic?" she asks, her smile widening.

"Why are you smiling so big?" I glance over at her again to see her watching the muscles in my arms flex as I grip the steering wheel.

"I don't know..." Her face reddens. "I guess I can just picture you all greased up, working on vehicles. "It's–"

"*Hot.*" The word leaving my mouth has her swallowing and fidgeting with her hair, as if she's turned on by what she's picturing now.

"I work on motorcycles mostly." I pull up in front of the garage and park. "I have a hard time sleeping some nights so I like to come here and work myself into exhaustion. That is, of course, when I'm not working with my brothers."

She follows me into the garage, looking around as I flip a few of the lights on. "So if my vehicle ever breaks down?"

I lean in close to her ear, causing her to slightly jump when I speak. "I'll fix it. Naked if you want."

She sucks in a breath and I walk past her, making my way to my old Harley. I reach for the stool, pulling it up for her to take a seat.

I can feel her heated gaze on me as I yank my shirt over my head and stuff into the top of my back pocket and I can tell that I have her picturing me naked now.

She sits there quietly for a long while, just watching me work, and I love just knowing that she's here with me. It has this weird warmth spreading throughout my body, making me feel at peace.

An hour passes, maybe longer, before she finally speaks.

"How long have you been a mechanic?"

I look up from my bike and wipe my hands on a towel. "Since I was fifteen. My uncle taught me to work on vehicles back when we used to stay with him off and on. It helps to clear my head sometimes and keep the demons at bay."

"It's nice having a distraction, something that you enjoy doing."

"It does." I stand up and walk over to stand in between Melissa's legs. She lets out a small moan as I cup the back of her neck and press my body against hers. "You're a distraction for me, Melissa. In a good fucking way. Feel that?"

She sucks in a small breath when I grind my erection between her legs and growl.

"Yes. Oh God, yes." Her gaze roams over my shirtless body before moving up to land on my lips. "It's kind of hard not to *feel* you, Ace. Or not to notice you. You're a distraction for me too, no matter how much I try and fight it."

"Good," I whisper.

I grip her thighs and pick her up, carrying her over to the closest car. She lets out a little surprised gasp as I set her down onto the hood and roughly pull her toward me so that her legs are wrapped around my waist.

I watch her watching me with curious eyes and I can tell by her heavy breathing that she desperately wants me to make the next move. So I lean in and pull her bottom lip between my teeth.

She moans and wraps her arm around my neck, pulling me in closer as I give it a soft nibble before running my tongue over it.

She wants me to kiss her, but I hold back, wanting her to wait a little longer.

I want her to fucking want me as much as I want her.

I want her to fucking crave me.

But I know, and my body sure as hell knows, that I can't hold back for much longer.

Fuck, I need to get her home.

"I should get you home." I back away and run my hands through my hair in frustration.

The twisted side of me wants to fuck her on top of every vehicle in this garage and make her scream my name until her voice goes out. I want her nails in my back, making me bleed as I fill her with my long, thick cock.

I want to fucking possess every part of her body and soul until she can't even breathe without thinking about me.

My fucked-up, twisted side won't even be a concern for her once she really *feels* me.

I'm going to make sure of that.

8

Melissa

I feel Kadence staring at me and finally glance at her. I am on my break with a latte in front of me, a half-eaten scone beside that, and my mind consumed with Ace.

"What?" I know she has something on her mind, and I know she'll voice it.

I lean back in the chair and cross my arms over my chest, waiting for it to come.

She stares at me for a prolonged second, maybe trying to guess what I'm thinking about, or what's really going on. Kadence is pretty perceptive, and I know that she'll figure it out without me having to say a word.

"Are you going to tell me what's going on or do you really want me to start naming off things?"

I really don't want to talk about this on my break, but I do want to discuss it with her. With Kadence now being with Aston, she spends a lot of her time with him. And with me working more, our time together is limited.

I hate that, hate that the majority of when we see each other is at the Lockes' house. We used to do so much together, and I want that back.

"This is about Ace, isn't it?" She phrases it like a question but I can hear in her voice that she already knows the answer.

I exhale and glance around me. Even though we are semi-secluded, it still feels like a million people can hear me. Not that I care if anyone knows I have strong feelings for Ace, but I've never been one to open up about how I feel.

"You know you can trust me, right? You can tell me whatever you want."

I look into Kadence's eyes and nod. Of course I know I can trust her, but it isn't about that. It is about me finally admitting out loud how I feel and what I want, when I'm not even sure what it all means yet.

I've never done that, never been the person to open up like this. But I know I need to talk about it.

"I trust you, Kadence. It's myself I don't trust, especially where it concerns Ace." There, I said it, all but admitted that I have no self-control when it comes to a Locke brother.

This sympathetic look crosses her face and she leans forward. When she smiles I can see that she understands what I mean, how I feel. Hell, she went through the same thing.

"I'm here. I'm listening."

"I have some pretty strong feelings for Ace, and they scare me because of the type of man he is, the violence that I know he houses." I glance away, the words spilling from my mouth for the first time ever. I've thought them plenty of times, but actually saying them out loud is another thing.

"I know." Kadence says and gives me a genuine smile. "The violence and danger that the Locke brothers have within them is not something that just anyone can accept. It was hard for me at first too." She gives me another sympathetic look. "It takes a really strong woman to be with one of those boys, and we are those women, Melissa."

I nod, knowing she speaks the truth. "I guess I'm just afraid to fully give myself over. I don't know what to do."

"Is that what you want, though? I mean, do you want to give yourself over to Ace completely? Because once you do there's no going back. He won't let you go. You'll be his irrevocably."

"Maybe." This is not something I haven't thought about before and now, after I've gotten to spend some one on one time with him, the feeling has only grown stronger. The need is becoming overwhelming, even though I'm trying to fight it. "I don't know, Kadence. I think at the end of the day that's what scares me the most when I think about it. I'm afraid that if I give myself to Ace in every way imaginable, I will be his and I'm not sure I'm ready for that." I can already see the possessiveness in his eyes when he looks at me, when he touches me. It ignites something deep in my body, makes me yearn for more than I've ever wanted before. I'm confused by it, not sure if I should accept it or run the other direction. A part of me is afraid, terrified of what it means to want him, what it will mean if I give myself over.

A part of me fears that, but another part, a bigger one, anticipates and wants it so damn badly. It's that part that's dominating me, controlling me ... consuming me.

"Look. I'm going to be honest with you about something, Melissa. And listen carefully."

I sit up straight, nervous to hear what she's going say. Especially since it will undoubtedly involve Ace. "Okay," I say a little hesitantly. Kadence can be a little abrasive when she wants her point made. But I love her because of it. Hell, right now maybe that's what I need. "Give it to me."

"All right..." She sits up straight too now. "Ace is twisted in ways that his brothers aren't. It's simply because he went through hell the longest and had to stand up and become the Locke that his younger brothers could look up to for protection. But I know without a doubt that Ace or any of the other brothers would never hurt someone they care about, especially a woman. They protect those who need it. It may be scary giving your heart and body over to a Locke, but I can tell you with everything in me that it's the best feeling in the world once the initial fear wears off. It's even exciting in ways that you've never experienced before. At least it was with Aston for me. I can't even imagine what it'd be like with Ace."

I feel my stomach sink because I hate to hear how Ace and his brothers were forced into becoming who they are today by parents who physically hurt them and put them in danger. I've heard some of the stories and they're ugly and unimaginable. It's one of the reasons I've softened toward Ace a bit. Because no one should have to go through what they went through. "I know Ace would never physically hurt me, Kadence. It's not the physical part that I'm worried about. Everything about him is so damn intense."

"Well, you shouldn't be worried about him hurting you in any way. When the Locke brothers find someone they care about, they never stop loving them." She smiles as if just remembering something. "Oh, and I almost forgot that Sterling and Wynter are having a fire at their house tonight. You're coming. Ace is coming. The whole crew is coming. It's going to be great."

I feel my heart speed up at the thought of seeing Ace again so soon. Truthfully, I haven't stopped thinking about him since he dropped me back off at my car last night.

The moment he set me down onto the car and pressed his hard body between my legs, I almost forgot how to breathe. Especially when he pulled my bottom lip between his teeth. That scared me even more.

If he could make me feel that way simply by touching me… I can't even begin to imagine how he'd make me feel if he kissed me.

I've dreamt about those sexy lips on my body more times than I can even count and I know for a fact that I'd be done for the moment I feel them owning me. Because I know that's what he'd do.

He'd own me with just a single kiss and I need to make sure I can handle being his before I allow that to happen.

"Do I have a choice?"

She shakes her head and stands up. "Nope. You're family. If you even think about not showing up, you'll have one of the Lockes at your door, breaking it down."

"I don't doubt it," I huff.

And I'm sure Ace would look sexy as hell doing it too.

9

Ace

I lean against Bobby's door and pull out the rest of the joint that's stuffed inside my jacket pocket and light it up. "Don't make me bust this door down, Bobster..." Placing it between my lips, I light it and take a few quick hits, keeping the smoke in my lungs for a second before blowing it out. I glance down at my watch. "I've got somewhere to be. That means you have about twenty fucking seconds to unlock this door before I break it down, come inside, and drag you out by your fucking balls."

"Ten seconds now..."

I hear the clicking of the handle unlock, and then a second later the sound of footsteps running through the house comes through.

"Really?" I flick the rest of the joint across the porch before I speed walk around the house and to the back door. This idiot tried this shit last time. You'd think he'd know it's pointless for him to run from me.

As soon as I round the corner, I get a clear view of Bobby jumping off the back porch and racing for some shitty little bicycle that's laying in the yard.

"This is pretty fucking comical, Bobster." I watch as his overweight ass struggles with the little bike but gets nowhere.

"Shit!" He screams as it falls over.

"Chasing you is like chasing a toddler." I make my way over and stand above him as he struggles with getting back up. "Why do you insist on running every damn time? Is it simply for my entertainment or is it because you really believe you'll get away?"

"I don't have the money," he spits out, kicking the bike away. "I told Jim I'd have it next week. Can't you just give me a break, buddy? Come on... I promise I'll have it by next Friday."

For a second I just stare at Bobby, and although I'm pissed at this little fucker because he owes me money, I can't help but start to chuckle at the comical routine he always delivers.

This isn't the first time I've had to chase his ass around, but in the grand scheme of things he's harmless.

He's a dirty bastard, and I mean that in a literal sense.

Overweight from only eating fast food, and reeking of cheap-ass beer, Bobby's always getting himself in shit.

And I'm the stupid motherfucker who lets him get away with it.

I should just put a stop to it, but because of all the dark shit I've gone through—and still go through—this is almost like a little reprieve from all of that.

"Get up, Bobby." I take a step back as he tries to stand upright. His white shirt is stained with grease, and the hem hits him right above his bulging stomach. He's even got some fucking lint in his belly button.

I just shake my head at the state he's in. He's a sorry sack of shit, that's for sure.

"I'm sorry, Ace. I swear I'll have your money next week. I swear it." He starts crying over and over again, sweat starting to cover his forehead and dripping down his temples. He needs to calm the fuck down or he'll have a heart attack. "I'm really, really sorry—"

I reach out and slap him across the face. His fat cheek jiggles and he stumbles back a little bit. His face instantly becomes red and I know that he's going to start crying any second. I don't have time for him to be apologizing continuously.

He's panting, breathing like he just ran a fucking marathon. "Calm the hell down, Bobby." I cross my arms over my chest and eye him up and down. The asshole is out of shape. If he wants to fuck over people then he should at least work out so he can get away. "Because I'm in a good fucking mood, I'll give you three days to get me my money." He opens his mouth as if he wants to argue, or maybe tell me again how he needs a week, but I hold my hand up and give him a hard fucking look. "No, you have three motherfucking days to get me my money. If you don't I'm gonna come back here and I'm going to open you up like a goddamn fish. Do you understand me?"

He starts nodding furiously, and then starts repeating over and over how thankful he is. I turn, leaving him standing there, wondering why the fuck I let him off the hook.

On any other day I wouldn't have given him a second chance. But the truth is I *am* in a good mood, the thought of Melissa still running through my head. Although I will never change who I am, or how I do things, even knowing that Melissa can soon be mine has me feeling ... different. I don't know if I like it, but I sure as hell don't want it to disappear.

I head back to the truck and climb in, and for a second I just sit there, staring out in the distance and thinking about Melissa. She's all I've been thinking about lately, but hell, I like that. I want her on my mind always. I want her by my fucking side. It is hard as hell not to just make her see that she's mine. But I don't want to rush this, don't want her to see me as some arrogant fucking bastard who can't keep his dick in his pants.

But the truth is I want her so damn badly. I want her under me, naked. I want her arms above her head, her breasts thrust out as she parts her thighs. I want her begging me for more. And I want to bury my face between her legs and lick her pussy until she comes in my mouth.

I reach down and adjust my massive erection, groaning at the very image of me thrusting in and out of Melissa. Fuck, I'm so damn aroused, so ready to claim her and make her mine. And I know that time will come, sooner rather than later. I'm a patient man, but when it comes to Melissa I want her like a fucking fiend jonesing for his next fix.

Shit, I need to get control of myself. I can't be going off the handle. This isn't like me, isn't how I operate.

I want Melissa like I want to fucking breathe. I want her as mine, forever, with nothing stopping me, no one telling me that she isn't mine. I want her to see we belong together, that we've always belonged together. She's afraid, I see that, but I'll show her that if she were mine she'd be treated like a fucking queen.

I am coming to realize that when it comes to Melissa, all bets are off on how things play out. I am so not in my element with her, but I like it.

I fucking love it.

10

Melissa

I got off work hours ago, but took the time to decide if I should make an appearance at Sterling and Wynter's or not, knowing that I'd be seeing Ace there.

Yet, when I arrived thirty minutes ago, and everyone was here but him, I couldn't help but to be filled with disappointment.

I've been sitting beside Kadence and Aston, and although Kadence has been making attempts to talk to me every few minutes, my mind has been too distracted to pay attention to anything she's been saying. The way Kadence is with Aston makes me long for that with Ace, and a part of me hates myself for wanting that, knowing the type of man he is. He's dangerous, but not to me. Never to me. He helps people, even if that is violent, destructive. But that's the way he is, who he is. I wouldn't want to change him ever.

I keep finding myself staring out into the darkened street waiting for Ace to show up. Hoping he'll show up.

"Why is your leg bouncing?"

"Huh?" I pull my gaze away from the road and take a sip of the beer in my hand. "It's not. What are you talking about?"

She just laughs and places her hand on my knee, stopping it from moving. "Why are you acting all weird?"

"I'm not. What do you mean?"

"Okay... if you're not acting weird then why have you ignored everything everyone has said to you since you got here?" She looks out toward the street at the same time I find myself doing it again. "Ah... I see."

I shake my head and let out a small laugh. "What is that supposed to mean?"

"Oh, never mind." She's silent for a moment. "But Ace isn't coming."

My heart sinks in unwanted disappointment. "I thought you said he was?"

She shakes her head and reaches for her beer. "He got held up with a job and said not to expect him tonight." I feel like this weight settles on me, holding me down. He's not coming tonight, and that makes me feel like shit. I realize, even if I want to hide it, try to pretend to myself that it's not true, that I am well and deeply into Ace and there's no going back.

She smiles as she takes in my disappointment. "You wanted to see him, didn't you?" Her voice rises and I have to shush her before everyone else hears.

"I don't know what would make you think that. I never once said that."

"Really?" She pauses for a second before speaking again. "Look up."

"What for..." I look up and my breath gets sucked right from my lungs at the sight of Ace walking through the yard right toward us with King at his side.

He's here. I feel like that weight is gone, that I can breathe easier now. I don't know if that feeling should scare the fuck out of me or not.

He's wearing that damn baseball cap again, and the way his intense gaze is trained on me as if he wants to devour me right where I sit, has me squeezing the beer bottle tighter.

I find myself looking away.

Ace keeps walking straight toward me, and before I know it, he's kneeling in front of me and grabbing the beer from my hand.

He doesn't say anything as his gaze meets mine and he tilts the beer back, drinking half of it in one go. When he pulls the bottle away, a little bit spills on his lips and I can't help but notice how sexy it is when he wipes it away with his tongue.

"Vanilla," he whispers with a twisted little grin, leaning in close to smell my lips. "You probably shouldn't wear that on your lips unless you want me to lick it off."

He stands and winks before walking into the house and leaving me sitting here with my damn heart practically beating out of my chest with excitement at the idea of his tongue on my lips again.

Ace Locke is so sexy that I can hardly handle it.

I'm so caught up in what he just said that it takes me a few seconds to realize that he never gave me my beer back.

He's good at getting what he wants, so I don't doubt that he did it on purpose to lure me away from everyone, but still I find myself doing what I do next, feeling like I *need* to.

"I need another beer." I stand up and wipe my sweaty palms down the front of my jeans, my nervousness claiming me, taking hold, refusing to get control. "I'll be right back."

I swallow down my nerves and make my way into the house, fully aware that Ace could be hiding somewhere in the darkness, waiting for the moment I step into his trap.

With my heart racing, I walk through the kitchen and, just as I'm about to turn down the hallway, Ace backs me against the wall, closing me in with his strong body.

My breathing picks up when his rough hands grab my wrists and pin them against the wall above me.

Silently, he watches me, as if he's trying to figure me out.

He slowly moves in closer, teasing me with his lips close to mine, but stops before there's any contact. His mouth twists into a satisfied grin when he notices my chest quickly rising and falling. The anticipation of what he's going to do next moves through my veins.

Closing his eyes, he squeezes my wrists tighter and gently runs the tip of his tongue over my lips, tasting me.

"You didn't take it off..."

I find myself breathless as I attempt to speak. "Didn't have any reason to..."

"Fucking good, Angel."

Slowly, he lowers one of his hands down my arm until he moves it around to grip my throat and lightly squeeze.

It's then that I feel his massive erection pressing against my belly.

I should attempt to get away, leave before I no longer have that option, but I don't.

Instead, I close my eyes and moan out as he thrusts his hips further against me, completely unashamed that my taste has aroused him.

"That's all I needed to hear..."

He releases my throat long enough to yank his cap off and toss it aside. Then he squeezes my throat a little harder than before. His actions have me breathing so heavily that he lets out a small laugh before he speaks against my lips. "Don't go passing out on me, Angel. We haven't even gotten to the good stuff yet."

As soon as he speaks the last word, he sucks my bottom

lip into his sexy mouth, causing me to moan out and grip at his muscled arm, digging my nails in.

His teasing has my body on edge, about ready to explode just from the anticipation alone.

But I have a feeling he already knows this, because he seems to be enjoying it a hell of a lot. This is even more torturous than last night.

With his mouth still on mine, he moves down to grip my thighs, pulling me up so that my legs are wrapped around his waist.

The feel of his erection has me so turned on that I accidently moan out his name.

This has his lips twisting into a smirk. "My name sounds damn good coming from your mouth, Angel. I can't wait to make you scream it."

My heart thunders, beating hard, like a war drum in my chest. I need to get myself under control.

"Are you two coming back... whoa... whoa... am I interrupting something here?"

I push my way out of Ace's arms at the sound of my best friend's voice. Once I have my thoughts clear, I look over to see Kadence smiling at me over the top of her beer bottle. I purse my lips. I know I won't live this down. "No," I say pathetically. "We were just grabbing some beers. You need another one? I'll grab it." I can hear myself rambling and I know my face is probably so damn red.

Clearing my throat, I squeeze by Ace's hard body, which

hasn't moved an inch since I wiggled my way out of his arms, and move over to the fridge, opening it. My heart is pounding relentlessly as I reach for two beers, grab Kadence's arm and quickly pull her outside, away from Ace.

"Looks like you two have been having a little more fun than you mentioned to me earlier."

"Shut it," I whisper. "We haven't done anything."

"Yet," she says with a small laugh as we take our seats by the fire again. "Ace is going to erase the worries from your mind completely and soon you won't even care about his dangerous side. You'll crave it. Just wait."

I know she's not wrong about that and it terrifies me that he has the power to do that.

Ace Locke has the power to own me completely and he's barely even touched me yet...

11

Ace

I can't help but grin as I watch Melissa leave the house. She's embarrassed that Kadence saw what we were doing. Hell, I don't care if anybody watches, if anybody sees what I was doing with the woman I care about, with the woman I want as mine.

I'll show every fucking asshole on this planet who has doubts that Melissa is mine. And she is, all of her.

She's mine. There's no doubt about that, no going around it.

Never in my life have I gone slowly, refrained from going after what I want. But with Melissa I'm taking my time. I want her to be right there with me, primed and ready for what I have to give her.

I walk over to the door and lean against the frame, staring out the screen and watching Melissa. She sits down in front of the fire, her body tense, the taste of her still on my lips. I reach out and adjust my cock, the bastard thick and long, painful.

My body knows she's mine, and it reacts accordingly. My heart races, my muscles tense, and my cock gets harder than fucking steel. Just one look at her and I'm ready to go.

Damn, I want her so fucking badly. I want her on my bed, want to spread her thighs and devour her pussy. I know she'll taste so sweet.

As slow as I am going, it is damn torture. But I can tell she is right here with me, wanting the same things I do. But I want her to know that she has control. I want her to see that I will never push her.

I feel myself smile as I watch her tip her head back and laugh. This isn't just about sex where Melissa is concerned. I want her by my side. I want to defend her because she is mine, want to tell everyone that if they mess with her they'll deal with me.

She looks back and our gazes clash. I smile and she returns the gesture. I want to go out there, pick her up, throw her over my shoulder and take her upstairs to a spare room.

Hell, I have no idea why I am refraining from doing just that. Maybe she sees my expression and knows what I am thinking, or maybe she wants the same thing, but a second later she stands and starts walking back toward the house, while Kadence is distracted by my brother.

I open the front door and move to the side so she can come in. And then I take her hand and lead her upstairs; neither of us saying anything, both of us knowing exactly what is going to happen.

Maybe we'll have sex. Maybe I'll be able to claim her for the first time, something I've wanted to do since the moment I met her. Or maybe I'll just hold her and listen to the sound of her breathing, knowing that she is here with me, bringing me pleasure with her company alone ... bringing me peace.

I don't really give a shit one way or the other what we do, because she is here with me and that's all that I care about.

Once we reach the top of the stairs, I guide her down to the end of the hall, where I know there's a spare bedroom.

For what I have planned I don't want anyone to interrupt us.

But before I open the door, I pin her up against it with my body, as I lean in close and brush my lips up her neck, stopping below her ear. "Are you sure you want to be alone with me right now, Angel?" I whisper, my voice this husky growl of need. "Once we step inside this room, I can't promise that I won't taste you where I really want to. Where I was holding back from last night."

I feel her shiver in response as I run my tongue along

her neck, giving her a feel of how badly I want it on her body.

"I'll twist you up with my tongue alone," I whisper. "I'll make you come undone before you even have time to hit the mattress."

Without saying a word, she nods, giving me permission to go forward.

Fuck, how I love that.

Keeping her against the door, I lower my way down her body and grip the top of her jeans, yanking them down until they hit the floor.

Her standing there, the wet spot I can see between her legs, her arousal soaking her panties, has me practically ripping them down her legs before I lift her up to straddle my face.

I can hear her heavy breathing as she grips my hair, the anticipation of me tasting her working her up.

"Hold onto me tighter. You're not gonna want to let go."

Her hold on my hair tightens and a long moan leaves her lips the moment I flick my tongue out and run it along her wet pussy, tasting her.

Fuck, I want to own her flavor. I want to make it mine and mine alone.

It will be. She'll always be mine. Only mine.

I won't hesitate to kill any motherfucker who thinks he has a right to her taste ever again.

She moans again as I bury my face further between her legs, shoving my tongue inside her to memorize her flavor.

"That's right, Angel. Moan for me. It makes me so fucking hard."

The combination of my words and tongue has her crying out and gripping my hair as if her life depends on it.

"Ace..." I feel her legs squeeze my head as I continue to lick and flick at her pretty cunt, hitting her right where I know she needs it. "Keep going... keep... yes... yes..."

I growl out against her pussy, the vibration of my mouth causing her to squeeze my head so tightly that I can barely breathe. Even that doesn't stop me from licking until she's coming undone around my face, her release tasting on my tongue.

Needing a moment to breathe, I press her back against the wall and hold her there until her grip on my hair loosens and her breathing evens out.

Then I slowly lower her down the wall, setting her on her feet.

"Holy fuck... what just happened?"

"The beginning of me showing you that you're mine." I grip her face and lean it back before sucking her bottom lip into my mouth and growling. "I'm not sure you're ready for what's to come next."

She's still fighting to catch her breath when Kadence calls her name from the kitchen.

This has her cussing under her breath and moving away from me. “My clothes. I need my clothes.”

Keeping my gaze on her, I reach for her panties and help her slide them up her legs, before doing the same with her jeans. “I want to spend time with you soon. I’m busy tomorrow night, but I’m free on Friday. I’ll pick you up after work.”

She just looks at me as if she doesn’t know what to say before nodding. “Okay. Yeah, I get off at seven.”

I smile and stand back and watch as she takes shaky steps down the stairs, being careful that her legs don’t give out on her.

Pride fucking fills me that it’s because of me that she’s having a hard time walking right.

If she thinks it’s hard to move now, she hasn’t felt anything yet. Once I’m inside of her all bets are off.

I have a feeling she won’t be leaving my bed for days.

12

Melissa

It felt strange, Kadence being the one to grill me last night about a Locke brother. She kept trying to get me to confess to doing something *naughty* with Ace, but I kept denying it, not ready to confess yet.

I finally managed to call it a night, before I could manage to spend the rest of it drooling over Ace from across the yard.

Every single time he looked at me, I felt my insides burst into flames at the reminder of him tasting me.

I've never had such an intense orgasm in my entire life and I feel as if I'm still recovering from it.

Just the thought of his lips and tongue sends my body over the edge with this powerful need.

That's exactly why I need to reconsider allowing Ace to pick me up tomorrow night. I said yes without even thinking and now I can't *stop* thinking of excuses I should've come up with.

"...some pretty hot guys here. What do you think about that one?"

I focus my attention on Gia long enough to catch the end of what she's saying. She's pointing at some pretty boy from across the bar and although he's cute, I can't help but to compare him to Ace.

I compare all guys to Ace, it seems. Maybe that makes me crazy, but it's inevitable anymore.

"He's okay." I shrug and take a sip of my drink.

"What do you mean okay?" Gia gives me a strange look. "Do you need glasses or something? That man is *fine* and so is his friend."

I turn away from Gia and give the guy a second glance before turning my attention to his friend. "I guess. I don't know." I spin the stool back around to face the bar. "Let's just focus on our drink. I'm not here to check out guys. I just want to unwind a little."

"That might be a problem now," she says in a voice mixed with excitement and nervousness. "They're coming this way and his friend's attention is on you."

Just great.

I exhale, squeeze my eyes shut, and pray I can make them leave without them giving me a hard time.

A few months ago, I would've been excited at the opportunity to meet an attractive guy and possibly get to know him. I haven't dated anyone since Jordan and I broke up two years ago and I've missed having a companion in my life. But no one has ever piqued my interest long enough for me to give them a chance, to allow them in my life.

That is, until Ace came along.

He is a bad boy, rough around the edges, and something in me feels alive around him. I want to feel that danger and violence that I know radiates from him, covers him like a second skin. I want to feel like, with him, I'm on the edge of this cliff and not even caring if I fall over and never reach the bottom.

And I do feel like that when I'm with him. He's the only one who has ever made me want more.

But now, the idea of meeting some random guy in a bar doesn't sound the least bit appealing. Especially when all I can think about is Ace and how it felt when he made me come; the way his mouth felt so amazing on me. There's no way I'll be able to focus on some other guy when physically he doesn't even compare to Ace.

"Ladies. Can we buy you two some new drinks?"

I keep my attention straight ahead, not speaking, not even acknowledging them. I know if I do they'll get the wrong idea. They usually do. I'm trying to think of the best way to get out of this situation without upsetting Gia. I know she's attracted to the dark-haired guy and there's no way I can leave her here alone with two strange men.

"Sure. I'd love one," she says happily.

My stomach twists into nervous knots, not knowing what to expect from this night now.

I force a smile and turn around to face the two of them. The friend is taller and thicker, with light hair and a clean-shaven face. He's cute, but does nothing for me. "I'm good, but thank you."

The dark-haired guy's friend nods and takes a seat next to me. I hear the scraping of the stool as he scoots it closer to me, but I keep my focus on something else so that he doesn't get the wrong idea.

I can feel him watching me and it's making me uncomfortable, but I do my best to ignore the feeling so that Gia can get a chance to at least get her guy's number.

"Where is your ring?"

"Excuse me?" I pull my glass away from my mouth and look beside me.

"Your ring?" The friend says with a cocky grin. "I don't see a ring on your finger, yet you're refusing a drink from me. That's not something that happens to me often."

Great, he's one of those guys. If he'd been decent he wouldn't have mentioned anything about me not accepting a drink from him. At least from my experience that's how it usually goes.

"I don't need a ring to refuse a drink from a stranger," I

say stiffly. "I'm good with the one I have. I appreciate the offer."

Feeling uncomfortable, I turn my attention to my left to see Gia laughing and talking with the other guy. Clearly, she's forgotten that I didn't even want them coming over here.

"Come on," he pushes. "Our friends seem to be hitting it off. Let me buy you a drink and we can talk. What you're sipping on is practically just juice. It's not going to get you drunk."

"I'm good," I say tightly, removing his hand as he places it on my leg. "Save your money and your time. Just because our friends are getting to know each other doesn't mean we need to."

"You know..." He grabs my arm and squeezes it when I go to reach for my drink again. "You're being a real bitch when all I'm trying to do is–"

Before he can finish what he's saying, his head is being slammed into the bar in front of him with so much force that my glass shakes and falls over.

I feel my eyes widen as I look up to see Ace standing there. He's the one who has a grip on the back of the asshole's hair and from the look on his face, he doesn't plan on letting him up anytime soon.

My heart drops to my stomach as his intense gaze turns to meet mine. There's this animalistic quality inside of his eyes, reminding me of just how dangerous and unpredictable he is.

It somewhat scares me, yet I can't turn away from him.

It also turns me on.

There's something incredibly sexy about Ace when he's angry.

With a growl, he pulls the guy's head back and whispers, "Touch her again and I'll cut your scalp off with the knife I have shoved inside my boot. It won't be the first time I've played that fucking game and enjoyed it." After he pulls his lips away he slams his head down again, not once, but two times, before he releases his hair and steps back.

The guy that Gia is talking to stands tall, as if to come to his friend's defense, but suddenly takes a step back and throws his hands up in defense once Ace steps up to him with a tilt of his head.

The look in his eyes screams that he'll kill anyone who challenges him, and that is enough to keep everyone at a distance, including the guy whose mouth is now covered in blood from his nose, which Ace just busted.

Everyone in the bar seems to be watching Ace as he steps in close to me and cups the back of my head with force. "This is not the place for you to be hanging out at. There's drunken assholes everywhere."

"How did you..." I shake my head and stand up when he grabs my waist. "How did you know I was here? I thought you were busy tonight."

"I was," he says on an angry growl. "I got done early

and asked Kadence where you were. It's a good thing too, because if this motherfucker would've gotten any further with you, I'd have to do much worse to him than I just did."

As if no one else is in the room, Ace presses his body flush against mine and leans in to speak against my lips. "I'm fighting with everything in me to not turn back around and kill that asshole for touching you the way he did. *Leave* with me before I lose my willpower."

I take a step back and swallow. His closeness has my heart racing so fast that I can hardly catch my breath. "I can't. I'm here with a friend."

"Looks like she's ready to leave too." He glances over my shoulder, his eyes narrowed as if to give a warning.

That's all it takes for the dark-haired guy to walk away from Gia and leave her standing there staring at me.

"What the..." I can't tell if she's mad or just in shock at the fact that I'm standing here with Ace right now. "I should get going anyway. It's late. I'll see you at work tomorrow."

"Gia!" I call out her name as she quickly walks away, but she doesn't stop to look back at me. I look around at all the attention on me and suddenly feel as if I need some air.

I barely make it outside before I feel Ace's hands on my waist, gripping me from behind as he moves his body in close.

He's hard all over, and as much as I crave to feel him against me, my head is screaming at me to run from him.

Tonight was just too much ... too real. I need to think, to breathe and collect myself.

I feel like this was a warning sign, reminding me before it's too late that falling for Ace could be disastrous.

"I'll walk." I take a deep breath and find the courage to walk away from him, but the moment he stops me again and his breath hits my neck, I feel weak again and I want nothing more than to give in and leave with him. "It's not that far, Ace. I'll be fine."

"It's too far for me to let you walk alone. I wouldn't give a shit if it was right behind this place. You're not going anywhere alone tonight." He brushes my hair away from my neck and runs his lips along it. "Come with me, Angel."

My breathing picks up and, just like usual, I can't control my thoughts when he's so damn close to me. I should be walking away from him, yet I can't seem to.

"I want to but..."

"But what?"

"Was that true?"

He lets out a deep, throaty laugh that vibrates my ear. "Is what true?"

"That you once scalped a guy?"

He's tense, but then I feel him nod before he speaks the words. "Yes. That wasn't just a threat. I'd do it to that asshole inside in a heartbeat if he ever touched you again. That's a fucking promise."

His confession makes it hard for me to breathe. Hard for me to move and before I know it, I'm allowing him to guide toward the motorcycle I watched him work on the other night.

I stand frozen, watching his biceps flex as he reaches for his helmet and slides it on my head. Ace is completely hypnotizing and in this moment, I feel as if I'll do *anything* he tells me to.

He takes a moment to look me over, maybe seeing how I look wearing his helmet, before he straddles the motorcycle and grabs my hand, pulling me on behind him.

"Hold on tight. I have somewhere I want to show you." He grabs my arms and places them around his body when I don't make a move. "Don't let go."

I finally snap out of it and lean into him, while holding onto his firm body as tightly as I can.

Once I've got a good grip on him, he takes off, heading toward an area I've never been in before.

We ride for a good fifteen minutes before pulling up to an old abandoned building that looks like it hasn't been used in ages.

My heart races with anticipation as he helps me off the bike and leads me into the old place.

"My brothers and I spent a lot of time here when we were kids. When my uncle wasn't around to save us..." He opens the door and turns to face me. "I had to. This was the only place I knew we'd be safe."

I feel my heart sink at his confession as I follow him inside.

He doesn't move at first. He just stands in place and looks around as if being here is bringing up old memories.

"There's a room I want to show you." His jaw flexes as he grabs my hand and gives it a light squeeze. "I feel like I need to put it to use right now."

I'm not sure what he means by *putting it to use,* but I allow him to pull me through the darkened house anyway.

"Your parents hurt you and your brothers a lot, didn't they?"

He stops and takes a deep breath before pushing one of the hallway doors open and stepping into the room. "Almost every fucking day."

"I hate that," I admit. "I hate that they hurt you guys. It's not fair."

"It's not," he says stiffly, turning on a few lanterns to give the room some light. "That's why I made this."

I turn to face the wall when he nods toward it. There's a huge target painted onto a piece of plywood that has huge chunks missing from it. You can tell it's gotten a lot of use over the years.

"Was this for you and your brothers to let off some steam?"

He shakes his head and kneels down to reach into his boot. "It was for me."

I jump when he quickly stands up and throws a knife into the target, hitting the bullseye.

His heated gaze lands on me and I can tell that he must notice how nervous I look now that he's got a knife.

I'm alone in an old abandoned building with a pissed-off Locke, a knife and a target.

I should probably be more nervous than I am, but the moment he pulls the knife from the target and hands it to me, I relax as I look down at it in my hand.

Ace is showing me a piece of *him* and I'm going to take every last bit of that I can get.

13

Ace

I saw the way Melissa stiffened when I pulled the knife from my boot and threw it at the target. There was a split second that I hated she was afraid I could harm her.

I'd never hurt her, never even dream of it. Hell, I'd kill, maim anyone who thought of putting fear in her.

It fucking kills me and I want to give her every reason to know that she'll *always* be safe with me.

"Throw it at the target, Melissa." She pulls her gaze away from the knife to look up at me. "If anyone has ever hurt you, they're that fucking target. Throw it."

"I've never been hurt enough by anyone to want them to be the target, Ace." She brushes past me to stand where I was just moments ago when I threw it. "But I'll be more than happy to pretend it's your parents."

Before I can say anything or react to the fact that she hates my parents so much for hurting us, she throws the knife at the target but misses it, hitting the wall beside it.

"Here." I walk over and pull the knife out of the wall before I make my way back over to her. "Don't think so much next time. Just relax and aim."

She takes the knife from me as I hand it to her.

I stand back and watch as she throws it again. A satisfied smile spreads across her face when it hits the target this time.

I fetch the knife and allow her to throw it a few more times. She seems to be enjoying it more with each throw and I can't help but to get turned on by watching her.

As much as I'm enjoying watching her let loose, I still can't get that look of fear that was in her eyes when I grabbed my knife out of my head.

She throws the knife one last time, but instead of handing it to her and stepping away, this time I hand it to her and back her against the wall.

"I'll never fucking hurt you, Melissa. I *need* you to know that."

Keeping her pressed against the wall with my body, I grab the back of my shirt and pull it over my head. I toss it aside and look down to see her breathing heavily, her gaze roaming over my body.

"I wasn't afraid of you hurting me, Ace. I'm just in an unfamiliar place and the knife caught me off guard..."

Her words trail off when I grab her hand and place the blade of the knife to my chest. "I'd let you cut me before I ever let any harm come your way. I'll always fucking protect you." I stare into her eyes, seeing them grow wider, her shock, maybe even a little bit of fear of the situation, claiming her. But I can also see she knows the truth, can see it in her expression. "Now. Cut me."

She shakes her head and attempts to pull the knife away from my chest, but I push it farther into my skin, drawing blood. "Ace – stop. I don't want to hurt..."

I move her hand along my body, digging the blade in, stopping at my collarbone. "I've never let anyone cut me before," I say, my voice a low growl. "That's how much I trust you and *need* you to trust me back."

Once I release her hand, she tosses the knife aside and runs the tips of her fingers over my wound. "I trust you, Ace. I know you won't physically hurt me. But I'm not sure I'm ready for the things you do. The violence you bring to others. I don't–"

"Touch me, Angel." I place my hand on hers and lower it down the top of my jeans. "Let loose and forget about everything else for once. Fucking touch me." I bow my head and run my tongue across her lips. "Take my cock out and stroke it until I come in your hands."

She releases a sharp breath when I lower her hand to

my erection. She looks surprised at how hard I am after what I just made her do to me.

"The pain doesn't bother me," I whisper against her lips. "You can hurt me all you want and I'll still be hard and ready for you. *Always.*"

I lean my head back and close my eyes as Melissa's hands work on undoing my jeans. Our heavy breathing is the only noise in the room and I love that she can't control hers, just as I can't mine.

The moment her hand touches my bare cock, I bite my bottom lip and growl out my need for her. "Stroke me like you want to... like you *own* me, because you do."

With a small moan, she begins stroking me, her breathing picking up as if she can hardly handle the fact that she's pleasuring me.

I place my hands against the wall on either side of her head and watch as she runs both her hands over my long, thick cock.

Each time her fingers move over my head, I moan, feeling like I could come any second. She moans too once she notices the drop of pre-cum wetting the tip of my cock.

"I'm so fucking close, Angel. Squeeze tighter."

She squeezes me tighter, using the moisture from the head of my cock to make her strokes slicker and faster.

I growl and grip the wall, feeling a tug at my balls. I'm so fucking close and she's barely touched me.

But it's not about the way it feels to have her stroking

me, although it feels fantastic. It's about the fact that she *is* stroking me that has me ready to fucking explode.

I've wanted Melissa's hands on me for as long as I can remember and knowing that she's enjoying it just as much as I am is enough to send me over the edge.

"Fuck, yes..." I thrust my hips forward and move my hands down to wrap into the back of her hair as her strokes become faster and harder.

"Holy shit, Ace," she breathes. "I want you to come for me. I want to see you get off."

"Fuck!" Her words send me over the edge and within seconds, I'm busting my nut all over her hands as she continues to move them over my length, making sure to get every last drop out.

I fight to catch my breath as I grab her chin and tilt it up so that she's looking me in the eye. "Next time I bust... it will be inside your tight little pussy, Angel."

Her body shivers from my words as if just the thought is too much for her to handle. It makes my dick jump with excitement. "Ace... this is not what I expected tonight. I don't usually–"

"Pleasure twisted, homicidal maniacs?" I cup her face and move in closer when she removes her hands from me. "There's a first time for everything," I breathe. "But I can promise that it won't be your last."

I move in and press my lips against hers, kissing her

gently at first before deepening the kiss, until she's fighting for air.

Then I move away and grab my shirt to clean her hands off with.

She watches me in silence, her gaze raking over me, as I take care of her. I may do a lot of damage with my hands, but I can be gentle with them when needed.

After she's all cleaned up, I toss my shirt aside again and move in so that our bodies are flush. I slowly move my hands up her body, stopping once I reach the back of her hair. "It's late. I should get you home. I just wanted to show you this place first."

She swallows and nods. "Okay, yeah..." Her words trail off as she moves around me and heads for the door.

I stand here for a few moments, taking deep breaths before I follow her outside and help her back onto my bike.

The last place I want to take her is home, because it's not *my* fucking home, where she belongs.

I can feel that she's so damn close to where I need her to be and that is enough for tonight. Soon, though, I know what I have to do to really get her to where I need her.

I just need a little more time to show her that I'm more than just the twisted Locke she's feared since the moment she's heard about us.

14

Melissa

I've been at the coffee shop for seven hours now and the *only* thing I have been able to think about is Ace Locke. Truthfully, I haven't been able to stop thinking about him since the moment he dropped me off at my house and drove off on his motorcycle last night.

I knew if I allowed Ace to touch me, to kiss me and taste me, that I'd be completely consumed by him. Yet I allowed him to do those things anyway, because a part of me wanted to know what it'd feel like to give myself over to him.

To give him a piece of me that I know I can never get back.

He hasn't even slept with me yet, but he doesn't have to

for me to *feel* the way that I do about him. My feelings for him have slowly been growing with each moment we spend together and the fact that he took me somewhere so personal to him last night has my walls slowly crumbling down.

But it doesn't change the fact that I'm not sure if I'm ready for Ace's lifestyle and everything that comes along with it.

The violence.

The blood.

The worry.

We're not even *together,* but I find myself worrying about him. I'm terrified he'll get hurt or even killed and the idea of that makes me sick to my stomach.

After having his perfect mouth on me... and his rough, dangerous hands, I feel as if I'll go crazy without him touching me. I want him to touch me all the time and now that I've touched *him*... made him come for me, I'm addicted to the rush he gives me.

The sound that came from his throat when I made him come undone has haunted me all day, making me imagine him making that noise above me, buried deep inside me. I'm so wet, ready for him, primed in ways I've never even dreamed of. Only Ace can make me feel unraveled. I want more, so much more, but I'm afraid to ask for it, frightened to even imagine how real that would be.

Once that transpires, once I allow that to happen, I'll be

his and there will be *no* going back. I know this without a doubt.

And a part of me wants that.

My shift is over soon and I haven't decided where I should go yet once I get off. I could go home and spend the entire night thinking about the one man I *shouldn't* be falling for, or I could show up at the Locke house to see him.

Every part of me wants to see him. Wants to *feel* him despite the worry I still possess.

"What's your plans for tonight?"

I look up from cleaning the counter at the sound of Gia's voice. She hasn't mentioned last night yet, but I can tell she's been wanting to since the moment I walked through the door.

"I'm not sure yet. I may just go home and watch TV."

She crosses her arms over her chest and leans against the counter as I continue to clean. "Are you just going to pretend that the scariest Locke didn't show up at the bar last night and break a guy's face over you?"

I swallow and look up to see her studying me. "Ace is overprotective and that *guy* wouldn't stop pushing me to accept a drink from him. He wanted to get me drunk, Gia. I'm not sure I feel sorry for him."

Her face softens. "I'm sorry. I had no idea he was pushing you. I was too wrapped up in Rye. I should've been paying more attention instead of putting you in an uncomfortable situation."

I shrug and toss the towel into the sink. "It's fine. I'm actually pretty happy that Ace showed up when he did. He's not as bad as you think... None of them are, Gia. They're just..."

"Misunderstood," she says with a small smile. "I guess I can see that. Plus, they're completely gorgeous. All three of them. Maybe I should've landed myself a Locke."

We both laugh, but stop and look over when the bell on the door chimes.

The moment my gaze sets on Ace, who steps inside dressed in a white Henley, dark jeans and a pair of black motorcycle boots, I almost forget how to breathe.

I don't think I'll ever get used to how beautifully dangerous this man looks.

He stops and his gaze locks with mine as the door closes behind him.

The intense look in his eyes is almost as if he's close to losing his shit on someone and is fighting with everything in him to keep his cool.

"Is everything okay?" I ask, my gaze slowly trailing down to see his knuckles freshly busted open. "Ace..."

My words trail off as he comes at me, grips the back of my head and lowers his mouth to mine.

He kisses me hard and deep, his tongue slipping between my lips with an urgency that makes my heart beat fast against my ribcage. It's almost as if he *needs* me in this moment and the idea of that has my walls crumbling even more.

"Are you off work yet?" he asks the moment our lips part.

I shake my head. "Almost. I have another twenty–"

"She's off," Gia interrupts. "Melissa can leave now if she wants."

Ace nods to Gia as he releases my head and backs away. "I'll wait outside for you."

I don't even get a chance to respond before Ace is out the door, hopping into his truck.

"Whoa," Gia whispers. "That kiss was pretty damn intense."

"Yeah." I nod and clock out, unsure of how to feel at the moment. This kiss felt *different*. So much more intense than the other ones and I know it's because my feelings for him have changed. "Thanks for letting me leave early."

"No worries. Kadence will be here soon." Her attention goes toward the window. "Enjoy your time off. I know I would if I got to stare at *him* from the passenger side of his truck." She shakes her head. "I promise I'm not thinking dirty things about your boyfriend."

"He's not my–"

"I'm pretty sure he is, Melissa. Just stay safe."

Butterflies flutter around inside my belly at the idea of Ace being my boyfriend. I like the sound of that a lot more than I ever thought I would've.

"Yeah," I whisper. "I'll see you later."

I grab my purse and head outside to Ace's truck. Just like always, he leans over and opens the door before grabbing my hand to help me up.

"Where do you want to go?" he questions, placing my hand on his firm thigh.

"I don't know." I can't think straight right now because all I can think about is why his knuckles have busted back open. "What happened to your hands?"

"Troy." He keeps his eyes on the road as he drives, his jaw steeling at the mention of this Troy guy.

"Who's Troy?"

"The fucker tied up in my garage who thought he could *hurt* my family. I'll let him go in a few days, but not until he's learned his lesson." He glances over at me and, instead of being afraid like I would've just weeks ago, I feel the urge to climb into his lap and kiss him hard on the lips.

Without giving it a second thought, I unbuckle my seatbelt and crawl into his lap, straddling him.

A deep growl comes from his throat as I kiss him hard on the lips, needing to feel his mouth on me. Needing to taste him.

I love the protective side of Ace.

"Fuck, Melissa." One of his hands moves up to wrap into the back of my hair and I feel him grow hard between my legs. "Where do you want to go? I'll take you anywhere just as long as I get to be with you."

I look up at him as he focuses on the road, his hips slightly thrusting into me as if he wants to fuck me right here in traffic. My entire body heats up at the thought.

"Take me to the garage. I want to talk and watch you work, Ace. I want to spend time with you."

He pulls up at a stoplight and moves his hands to grip my waist. "Just talking tonight," he groans. "I have somewhere I want to take you tomorrow. I *need* to because I can't control myself with you any longer." We are both breathing hard, heavy. "I want you to really see what you're getting into."

I don't know what he's talking about, but I trust him. "Okay," I whisper into his neck. "I'll go anywhere with you, Ace. But for tonight I want to just be *with* you. I missed you."

The moment the words *I missed you* leaves my lips, a small breath of relief leaves Ace's as if that's the confirmation he needed to know that I'm falling hard for him.

And I am.

I know without him saying it back that he's missed me too.

I'm not sure where he wants to take me tomorrow, but I need tonight with him. I need to get to know him before he takes me somewhere that can change *everything.*

I'm not ready to for my walls to come back up. I'm ready to fall for him completely.

15

Ace

Not killing the fucker in my garage has been proving to be harder than I expected. Every time I look at the son of a bitch's face, I'm reminded of the fact that he had the power to *hurt* my family. That all it would've taken was one squeeze of the trigger for him to end my life or one of theirs.

I spent the last hour torturing him, reminding him of what will happen if he ever steps foot on our property again. The need to see Melissa in order to catch my breath and think straight was too overpowering for me not to show up at her work unexpected.

The moment my lips touched hers and her taste covered my mouth, I felt as if I could fucking breathe again.

I *need* her, and the more time we spend together, the more I know that I can't *live* without her. I don't want to.

We pull up at the garage and as usual, it's empty. Gage never stays past five because he knows I like my alone time here. My time to work and think.

Melissa is still in my lap, straddling me when I put the truck into park and it's taking every last fucking bit of my strength not to fuck her right here, right now and show her just how *mine* she truly is.

"Fuck, baby." I brush her hair back and move my lips across her ear. "I missed you, too."

My confession has her wrapping her arms around my neck and moving to place her forehead against mine. "Tell me what happened, Ace. I want to know about the asshole who got caught trying to break in. Did he hurt you?"

I shake my head and steel my jaw. "No. He almost did." I pause and run my thumb over her cheek. "If it weren't for King, though, I'd most likely be dead. He was two seconds away from pulling the trigger."

Her heart pounds angrily against my chest as her grip on me tightens. "Is there a target here?"

A small smirk crosses my face as I lift her up and out of my lap. The idea that Melissa wants to let some anger out in the same way that I've been doing for as long as I can remember somehow makes me feel even closer to her. "No, but there can be."

I watch as she jumps out of the truck and slams the door

behind her. Once I make it out of the truck and over to her side, she's pacing nervously. "You could be dead right now, Ace."

She looks up, her angry gaze landing on mine as I bow my head to look down at her. "Not just me," I say on a growl. "Aston and Kadence too. Who knows what that asshole was capable of. Still is once I free him."

She swallows hard before pulling her hair back into a ponytail. "I hate the idea of that with every fucking part of me. I want to kill that piece of shit myself."

I bring my hands up to cup her face, wanting to reassure her that he's no longer a threat. "He won't be hurting anyone after I'm through with him, Melissa. I won't fucking let him. I'd die before I let him get to you or my family. That's a promise."

Keeping her gaze on me, she nods, before reaching out to grab my hand to look at my knuckles. "I believe you, Ace."

Once we get inside, I flip on a few lights and guide Melissa into the back room that never gets used. Gabe may get upset about us leaving holes in the wall, but I'll rebuild the whole fucking wall if I have to.

I grab out my knife and hand it to Melissa before stepping back and crossing my arms. "Let it out, Angel."

She gives me a confused look. "What? Right here. Won't you get fired or–"

"I'll handle Gage," I say, cutting her off. I don't want her to think about any of that. "Don't worry about me getting into trouble."

I push away from the wall and step in close behind her, turning her to face the wall. "Pretend that piece of shit is the wall. Don't hold back." I can't lie and say I don't find pleasure in the fact she is looking out for me, that she cares enough to worry about me. Hell, it makes me really fucking happy, if I'm being honest.

She leans her head back and lets out a tiny moan when I kiss her neck. "Okay," she whispers. "I can do that."

"Good." I back away and pull the joint from my pocket as I watch her growl out and throw the knife at the wall.

A half hour goes by, and she's still not ready to give the knife back and all I can do is sit back and watch my beautiful, twisted angel with a smirk.

Fuck, how she was meant for me.

"Feel better?" I push away from the wall and walk over to the wall that has the knife stuck in it.

She nods, watching me as I pull the knife from the wall and slip it back into my boot. "I feel much better, actually."

I barely get a chance to stand back up, before her arms are wrapped around my neck and she's pulling me in for a kiss.

Fuck, how I love that she's starting to kiss me and touch me on her own. It says that we've come a long way since she first came into my life because of Aston and Kadence.

"Can I sit and watch you work now?" she questions

against my lips. "It brings me peace and comfort and I need that right now."

"Yes," is all I say before guiding her back into the garage where my bike is.

I dropped it back off last night because there's still more work to get done on her.

She watches me in silence for a bit before speaking. "Were your parents ever good to you guys?" There's genuine curiosity and worry in her voice. It warms a part of my cold fucking heart.

"No," I say honestly. "Not that I can remember. I think I came out of the womb fearing them. They should've never been allowed to have kids." I look up from my bike to see her mouth curve down into a frown. "What about your parents? Are they around?"

She nods. "Yeah, they live about twenty minutes away. I see them when I can, but they both work a lot of long, crazy hours, so family time is usually few and far between." She shrugs. "We're also not real close, but we don't have any issues either. It's just sort of whatever. We make time when we can."

"They treat you well?"

"Yeah. I don't remember a time where they ever even spanked me. I guess I should be more grateful than I have been." She looks sad as her eyes move up to meet mine. "I never realized that I had it good growing up compared to some kids. I'm sorry."

"Don't be," I say stiffly. I hate thinking about my parents. "They made us who we are and I don't regret that. It also helped us get close to our uncle Killian. He's taught us a lot about life."

"I like your uncle. I can tell how much he loves you guys."

"Yeah." A grateful smile forms on my lips. "He loves us something fierce and trust me... Killian is the last Locke you want to cross. You think I'm twisted. Killian is brutal."

She lets out a small laugh. "I'll be sure not to get on his bad side then."

"Good. Because if you did... then I'd have to be on his bad side too."

She's silent as she watches me, almost as if she's unsure of what to say. I love my uncle to death, but I'd do anything for Melissa. I'm right there with her, no matter where that is.

We spend the next two hours talking, laughing and playing around and it feels incredible to be doing this with her.

I've never seen her so relaxed with me and it scares the shit out of me that after what I have to show her tomorrow, that this night, and everything that we've shared and learned about each other, might not be enough to make her want to stay.

After tomorrow, I may lose Melissa forever and, to be honest, I've never been so terrified of anything in my entire life.

That's exactly why I need to take every moment that I can get with her tonight and savor it.

After I clean off my hands, I guide Melissa out to the back of my truck and pull her into my lap, holding her as we both stare up at the night sky.

Here with her, I feel the happiest I've ever been. But for her to truly be happy with me, she needs to accept me for who I am.

Tomorrow, she'll get to see that with her own two eyes.

16

Melissa

To say I am curious about where Ace is taking me is an understatement. I glance over at him, the road we are on is rocky, as if it is foretelling me that what is about to happen, that what I am about to see would be just as uneven.

But I think this is what I need to know, whether or not falling for him completely is something I can handle.

I need to know where to go from here. Especially after the time we spent together last night. Being with him, him talking and holding me, felt so damn good to ignore.

"You don't want to tell me where we're going?" I see him smirk, but it is more of a sinister one than anything else.

Goosebumps pop out along my skin, and I know that

what I am about to witness will probably shape how I feel for Ace more than anything else that has happened since meeting him. But then again, I have a feeling that that is the reason he is taking me with him. I know that he wants me to see this other side of him, to know *truly* who he is before things get even more intense between us.

But I know about him, about his brothers and after getting to know him the way I have over the last week, I'm hoping that nothing that he can show me or tell me tonight will change how I feel for him.

Truth is, I'm already in too deep with it comes to Ace but am too afraid to actually say those words out loud. Hell, I think I'm even too afraid to admit it to myself the majority of the time.

About ten minutes later we come to a stop. There are a few houses around, all of them looking pretty rundown and deserted. Only one of them has lights coming from the inside. I glance over at Ace and see him clenching the steering wheel so tightly the leather creeks under his hold.

I want to say something, anything, but I know he's not in the mindset for anything aside from what he's about to do. And I know that's going to include violence.

He's out of the truck and reaching for his hammer before I can even comprehend it, and although I think he might say to stay in the vehicle, he walks around and opens the passenger side door.

My stomach drops, my nerves taking over.

For a second, I just sit there and stare at him, seeing the way the muscle under his jaw ticks, how he's holding the edge of the car door so tightly his knuckles are white. I can see the pulse beneath his ear beating rapidly.

He's pumped up for whatever he's about to do, or maybe he's afraid of showing me the real him. I may know what he and his brothers do, somewhat accept it now even, but witnessing it firsthand is something totally different.

I know this and it's clear he does, as well.

He helps me out of the vehicle and I stand there for a moment just staring at the house. Part of the front window is patched up with plywood, as if the owner of the house figured this was a good enough fix. The light coming from the window is dim, almost lifeless. I look over at Ace and see him watching me.

"Are you ready to see who I really am, Angel?" I open my mouth but no words come out. I want to tell him that I know who he is, but I have a feeling I really don't know who Ace Locke truly is.

"I guess I'm as ready as I'll ever be." The words fall out of my mouth, even though I'm far from ready. I spent a long time fearing the Locke brothers, not knowing who they really were, what they really stood for. I thought they were careless and dangerous. I never in my wildest dreams would've imagined I'd be where I am at this very moment.

He grins but it doesn't reach his eyes; he looks less than happy. And then together we walk up to the house. My heart is thundering and fear waves war in me. Although I know Ace would never let anything or anyone harm me, knowing I am about to see the violence that he dishes out has me on edge.

We stop right before we reach the uneven, partially broken porch steps. Headlights illuminate the house for a second, and the sound of tires on gravel ring through the air. I turn and see a dark SUV come to a stop beside Ace's vehicle. More Lockes have clearly shown up for this, and that worries me even more.

Sterling is the only one to get out, but he looks less than thrilled to see me standing there.

"What the fuck, man?" he says to Ace, but his focus is on me. "You brought your woman here? You fucking mad?"

I look at Ace and see he looks pissed off, his expression dark as he stares at Sterling. "She needs to see what we are about. She needs to know how far we go."

Sterling just shakes his head and exhales. "You're fucking insane, dude," he says under his breath. He glances at the house. "I guess if you were going to bring her with you this would be the right house to do it at. Shit that we can control."

I'm so confused at this point that I don't bother asking questions. I have to assume this is one of their "less violent" runs, because why else would Ace bring me with him if it were really dangerous?

Or maybe they are so sure of themselves that they know how this will go down before they even step foot in the house.

The latter seems more likely.

"Well," Sterling says, rolling his head around and cracking his neck. He's just as pumped up as Ace. "Let's get this fucking party started."

And just like that, my heart sinks to my stomach as the unknown presents itself.

I lift my gaze and stare at Ace's hammer, his weapon of choice. He swings it into the door, one, two, three times, before the whole thing practically comes down in front of him.

I would think seeing him with his hammer, heated and full of rage would frighten me somehow, make me think less of him, but it doesn't. In some strange way, it turns me on, knowing that he has the power to hurt some asshole who deserves it.

Ace is fearless with his hammer and I'd be lying if I said I'm not curious to see what he does with it next. I know now they don't hurt people unless it's justified and deserved. It just took me a while to realize that.

With his jaw flexed, he turns behind him and reaches for my hand. Without a word, he pulls me inside, with him leading the way.

Sterling enters behind us, and I glance at him, seeing him cross his arms over his chest and lean against the wall. He's wearing a pretty big grin. "The fucker is in the basement. I'll let you take care of the prick. I'll stay up here for backup, but I'm positive he's alone down there."

Ace grins at his brother while rolling his head around on his neck. "This piece of shit is mine and Melissa's. Just stay the fuck right there."

My heart hammers against my chest, adrenaline pumping through me as Ace grabs my hand again and begins leading me down to the basement.

Mine and Melissa's?

What does that even mean?

Why does this situation excite me, yet make me so damn nervous at the same time?

It's almost as if I want to see Ace hurt someone and I don't know how I *feel* about that.

Maybe being around Ace makes me want to be just as twisted as he is. Maybe inside, I'm just as corrupted as he is and he's been able to see it all along.

And maybe that's why I feel we are perfect for each other.

Whatever the reason, I'm about to see what Ace is all about. I'm about to see him. The *true* him.

17

Ace

I've been watching Melissa since the moment we arrived. Been testing her body language, her breathing, to see how being here makes her feel.

I'm not sure she's ready to admit it just yet, but being here, about to hurt some motherfucker who deserves it, the excitement of it, has her just as pumped as I am.

She's just confused by these feelings. I know this, because my emotions were just as twisted and confusing the first time too. Still... she's here with me and it doesn't look as if she plans on running anytime soon.

The knowledge of that has me wanting to slam her against a wall and bury myself between her thighs. Call me a sick fuck, but the thought of catching this motherfucker, beating him until he's bloody and tying him up while I fuck *my* woman in the next room has me hard as a fucking rock.

But I school myself and gather my self-control. I can't lose focus.

This motherfucker thinks he can put his hands on a woman without her permission. Thinks he can fuck someone without their consent. But once I break both his hands and legs, let him really feel pain, he won't know the feeling of being inside a woman for a long fucking time.

I want him tortured and in agony.

Once we reach the bottom of the stairs, I turn around and back Melissa up against the wall with my body. With my free hand, I grip her neck and lean in to whisper in her ear. "Stay here." Her body is tense against mine, the anxiety practically pouring from her in waves. I close my eyes and place my hand on the center of her chest, just breathing in and out slowly, telling her, showing her without words that she's safe.

I pull back and look into her eyes. She nods in response to my statement, my demand. She's breathing a little easier now, a little more even. She looks into my eyes, her pupils dilated, her desire clear.

I smirk down at her, pleased to know that she's still turned on by me, despite the fucked-up situation I have her in right now.

With a small growl, I pull her bottom lip into my mouth,

tugging it between my teeth, before I release it. "Don't move. I mean it."

"Wait," she says on a heavy breath. "I need to know what he did first. I don't know if I can stay otherwise."

I stiffen, hating the idea of saying what this sick fuck did out loud, but for her to fully understand what we do, she needs to know.

"He's a fucking rapist. A sick son of bitch who takes what he wants, when he wants. He drugs women so he can control them. The last one just happened to stay awake long enough to know it was happening."

"A rapist," she says on an angry whisper. "How many women?"

I shake my head. "Five, maybe more." I grit my teeth and grip the wood of the hammer tighter. "One was enough to punish the sick fuck and that's what I'm about to do."

She nods again, her eyes filled with anger at the knowledge of what this fucker has done. "Give him what he deserves." She looks down at my hammer as if imagining what she could do with it. "Break both of that sick asshole's legs."

I back away and swing my hammer around, my gaze still locked on hers, until I finally turn around and head for the first closed door.

The room is empty, so I move on to the only other option left down here in this creepy-ass basement.

Her words have me even more worked up, my adrenaline pumping like fucking crazy to get to this son of a bitch and hurt him.

It's almost like I'm hurting him for her now.

Bringing my boot up, I kick the door open and step inside to see a single bed and dresser set up inside the tiny room.

There's no closet and the room is fairly clean, causing me to laugh at the fact that this fucker thought he could hide from me down here.

"Trenton." I stop in front of the bed. "Are you really going to make me drag you out from under there?"

It takes a moment before I hear shuffling from under the bed. Then I see Trenton haul his ass out.

I take several steps back, curling my fingers tightly around the handle of the hammer. I can feel the smirk covering my face as the asshole stands and faces me.

He won't look me in the eye, and I can feel the fear coming from him.

Good, he needs to be afraid, because what I'm about to do to him is what nightmares are made of.

Finally, he clears his throat and shifts on his feet. He looks at me, his eyes going wide as they take in the hammer I'm holding.

He knows why I am here, and what I'm about to do.

He's heard of me. Of us Locke brothers.

Trenton holds his hands up in surrender, but that just makes me laugh. "I don't know why you're acting like this isn't going to happen." I take a step closer and he retreats one back.

"Ace-I-I swear. It was a misunderstanding."

That just pisses me off even more.

I tighten my hand even harder around the handle of the hammer and take another step closer.

The rage boils up inside of me, causing my blood to pump hard and fast through my veins. "You're actually going to stand there and tell me it was a misunderstanding?" I cock my head to the side as I appraise him. "You held her down, took from her what she wasn't willingly offering." The words come out of me like an animalistic growl. "Tell me again how innocent you are."

He is shaking his head as he retreats even farther, but the wall stops him, cornering him. I'm only a couple of feet from him now, the anger inside of me so intense I can feel it tightening my muscles, preparing me for what is about to happen.

"A misunderstanding." He says the words on a whisper, now knowing that this is going to happen no matter what.

Hell, he should have known that from the moment he knew I was here.

I am not about to prolong this. I'm going to fuck him up and then I'm going to take my woman and make her forget about tonight, about all the shitty things that she's seen, felt. I'm going to make her only feel pleasure as she stares into my eyes, knowing she's in my arms, safe and protected.

I bring my arm back, swinging my hammer forward.

I'll never let anything happen to Melissa and I'll do anything for her. She's mine, and I'm going to prove that to fucking everyone.

I connect the steel on the side of Trenton's leg, going all Misery on his ass. He screams out in pain and falls to the floor. I kick him so he moves over, and then I swing the hammer down on his other leg.

The sound of his kneecaps crushing under the onslaught of my hammer has my heart racing faster. I feel the rush of adrenaline at knowing this fucker is going to be in pain for a long time.

This fucker deserves a lot more than I'm giving him.

I swing out and knock the hammer against his knee again, then do the same to the other one. Blood is pooling through his jeans where I broke his legs, and the sight of that crimson stain spreading brings me a hell of a lot of pleasure.

I turn and stare at the door, knowing Melissa is right on the other side, no doubt hearing the screams of this piece of shit.

I wanted her here, but I didn't want her to *see* this violence, didn't want her to have that image ingrained in her memory. She needed to know exactly who I was, despite the rumors she's no doubt heard, despite the shit she knows my brothers and I do.

And tonight I gave that to her, tenfold.

18

Melissa

I stare at Ace from the passenger seat, watching as his broad chest quickly rises and falls.

He's focused on the road, but I catch him glancing my way every few moments as if he can't keep his eyes off me. Or maybe he's wondering how I'll react after what I heard? But I want to imagine it's the former.

I want to think that he's so drawn to me he can barely manage the simple task of driving wherever he's taking me without wanting to pull over and fuck me right here on the side of the road.

At one point I would've been nervous not knowing where he's taking me, but right now, all I feel is this overwhelming need to be alone with Ace. For him to do with me as he pleases.

As twisted as it sounds, I've been wanting him to touch me, ever since the moment he stepped out of that room and his gaze landed on mine.

There was something about the twisted smirk on his face that turned me on like nothing else.

It didn't matter to me that he'd just hurt someone and that I'd just listened to his victim screaming out in pain and begging for him to stop.

I wanted him to suffer just as badly as Ace did, and the fact that Ace was the cause of his pain only made me want him more in that moment.

Maybe I am just as fucked-up as Ace. Hell, maybe I'm more so, but as soon as I heard what that animal did, *I* wanted to hurt him my damn self. I was no longer scared of Ace's lifestyle, or what was about to go down. All I wanted was to get justice for his victims, for all the women he'd hurt in the past and was going to hurt in the future.

Ace did that. Ace did what the law wouldn't have, which was take a dangerous piece of shit off the streets for good.

The truck is filled with silence as Ace takes a quick turn onto the side road that leads to his spot in the woods.

Excitement fills me at the idea of us being here again. The memory of his hard body between my legs makes me hot and breathless.

"Does being here alone with me after what I just did

make you nervous?" he asks the moment the truck comes to a stop. "Does it make you want to run now?"

I shake my head as he leans across me to undo my seatbelt.

His amber colored gaze locks with mine as he reaches his hand out and lightly squeezes my neck. It excites me more. "How about now?" His uneven breath hitting my lips has me swallowing, anticipating his next move. "Are you nervous now, Angel? Are you afraid of me?"

"No," I whisper, speaking the truth. "I wanted him to hurt. I wanted that sick son of a bitch to get what he deserved. I *wanted* you to hurt him." I lean in closer, bringing my lips close enough to brush against his. "I'm not afraid of you, Ace. I'm not going anywhere."

"Good," he growls against my lips. "I've been fucking dying to do this." He releases my neck to push the truck door open. "Don't move."

I watch as Ace jumps out of the truck. The moment he comes around to open my door and pull me down into his arms, heat fills me from the feel of his erection pressed against me.

Holding me up with one arm, he slams the truck door closed, before pressing me against it with his hard body.

"*Fuck*, Melissa. I can't control myself right now. I don't want to hurt you, but I can't be gentle. Not with how badly I *fucking* want you." The feel of his teeth scraping against my neck causes me to jump in his arms. "Tell me you can handle me or I won't touch you."

"I can more than handle you," I say honestly. I stare into his eyes when he pulls back and looks down at me. "I wouldn't want you any other way." I reach up and cup his jaw. His gaze is dark, deep, as he takes me in. "I know what I got myself into, and I'm ready for it all." I'm breathing harder, faster, unable to keep myself under control either. "I've been waiting for this for a long time, Ace."

He makes this deep growl, this animalistic sound that has chills racing along my body.

"I want you here, Ace. I want you now." I don't want a bed, don't want romantic or sweet and gentle.

I knew what I was getting into when I fell hard for Ace. There's no going back, but I wouldn't have wanted to anyway.

Before I know what is happening, or can prepare myself, Ace is leading me toward the back of the truck, pulling the blanket he has on the bed flush, and helps me up so I'm sitting in the tailgate. He sits beside me and pulls me onto his lap, my legs spread on either side of him, my chest pressed to his.

His hands are on my lower back, his fingers digging into the skin that is exposed because my shirt rode up. We are staring at each other, neither speaking, but nothing needs to be said. The magnetism I feel is tangible, like fingers skating over my body.

Then he slides one hand up my back, tangles his fingers around my hair, and tugs on the strands until my head cocks back and I gasp from the pain. But on the heels of that, this pleasure washes through me, making me wet, needy.

"You sure you want to go here with me?" he asks in a deep, guttural voice, one that is like a serrated knife moving over my body.

I get wetter.

I nod. "I want this." I am so ready for him. "I've wanted this for a while, Ace, but was too afraid to say anything, to act on it."

"And you're not afraid now?"

I shake my head slowly. I don't need to think about what he said, but I stay silent for a few seconds. "I'm not afraid of you, but of how I feel."

He seems to dig his fingers into me harder, as if he doesn't want to let me go. "And how do you feel, baby?"

My throat is tight, my mouth dry. I don't know if admitting this to him is the best course, but I also know I can't hide how I feel. I can't pretend anymore. I won't. "I want you so bad that it hurts."

And then he has his mouth on mine, his tongue speared between my lips. Ace kisses me brutally, violently almost, but I love it. I want more of it, so much more that I'm drowning in it. We are both panting, gasping for breath when he pulls away a moment later.

"I won't fuck you in the back of my truck, not when I need you on my bed, surrounded by my things, smelling like me."

I'm about to tell him I don't care where we do this, because I need him too desperately. But before I can get a word out he's helping me off the truck, back into the passenger side seat, and is driving, presumably to his house. It all happens so fast I am dizzy from it all, can't even take enough air into my lungs.

This is really going to happen, and I'm not going to stop it.

I feel like we are back at the Locke house faster than normal, but then again, I think Ace was driving well above the speed limit. It seems he's just as frantic to start this as I am. I glance down and see the massive erection straining against his pants. He is ready for me, just as much as I am, my panties soaked, my nipples hard. Every part of me is screaming to finally be with Ace, to let him claim me, own every inch of me.

We stare at each other for long seconds, the heat and air in the truck getting thicker, hotter. I want to just have him take me right here, right now. I don't care if anyone sees us.

In fact, this part of me wants it to be known that I'm claimed by Ace, that I am with a Locke. I want anyone who looks at me to know that if they fuck with me they'll get wrath tenfold in return.

"I hope you're really ready for this, Melissa."

I swallow, the lump in my throat thick. "I've been ready," I say again, meaning it more than I ever have.

I don't wait for him to help me out of the truck this time. I get out and meet him at the hood of the vehicle. He growls low, and I know it's because he wants to be in charge, to call the shots. I am more than okay with that.

I can feel my heart pounding in my chest, and I wonder if he can hear it, see it beating at the pulse point below my ear. He takes my hand and leads me inside, up the stairs, and finally into his room. Once the door is shut, we stand there in silence, this thickness coating both of us, drawing us together.

"Take off your clothes for me," he demands in a low, deep voice, one that lets me know this isn't going to be slow and gentle. I already knew that, but it's another affirmation of who I am with.

And then I'm removing my clothes, feeling like Ace is the predator and I'm his prey.

That analogy can't be further from the truth.

I know that after tonight there really is no going back. But then again, I am already Ace's.

I have been since the moment I saw him. I just didn't know it yet.

19

Ace

My cock hardens even more as I stand back and watch Melissa undress herself. Fuck, how it hurts to not be inside her right now, taking her hard and rough against every surface in this room.

She moves slow, almost as if to tease me, and it's driving me fucking mad, twisting me up until I feel as if I'm about to explode.

I can't handle the wait any longer.

Closing the distance between us, I press my body against hers as I back her to the wall and brush my lips against her smooth neck. "I need it all off," I growl. "I need you naked, Angel."

She lets out a small gasp as I move my mouth around to the front of her neck and gently dig my teeth in before licking her skin where I just bit her. "You're *mine*, Melissa. After tonight, no other man will get to kiss you..." I move my lips up to brush over hers. "To taste you. And honestly, after knowing you've been with *me*, no other man will want to come near you for fear of me breaking their fucking legs and arms. This is it."

I hear her swallow before she lets out a soft "I'm ready," across my lips, confirming what I already knew from the first moment we kissed. She's already mine.

As soon as the words leave her mouth, my hands are gripping her waist and flipping her around to press her front against the wall. The feel of her round ass against my hard cock has me moaning and biting my bottom lip with need.

She's about to be *fucked* by the most dangerous Locke brother of us all, when in the beginning, she feared us and wanted *nothing* to do with us.

Fuck, how that turns me on.

I move my hands down her body, slow at first, but the moment I reach the top of her thong, I rip the thin material down her legs and slam my body against hers, unable to be gentle with her.

"Take your jeans off, Ace." She sounds needy as she grips at the wall, taking heavy breaths. "I need you inside me. *Now*."

Pressing her harder into the wall with my hips, I undo her bra, pulling the straps down her arms before grazing my teeth over her neck, right over the pulse that throbs beneath her ear. My cock jerks.

With a deep growl, I reach between our bodies and undo my jeans, sliding them down enough to pull my hard cock out and slide it against her ass.

I take my hand and slap her ass a few times, causing her to throw her head back and moan out, my cock now so fucking close to her needy pussy. The sound of her moans has me close to coming all over her ass, before I can even get inside of her.

I position myself at her pussy, feeling how hot and wet she is, how tight and mine she is. I lean in and growl into her ear, "Hold on tight, Angel."

With that, I slam into her.

I do it so fucking hard that she turns her head and bites into my arm, cussing from the intrusion of me stretching her pretty little pussy.

Groaning against the back of her neck, I wrap my fingers into her long hair and pull as I use my other hand and reach around to grip her throat, pulling her back so I can graze my teeth along the side of her neck.

My thick cock fills her, taking her deep and hard, her wetness coating me as I claim her as mine.

Something in me snaps and I start thrusting back and forth, shoving my big, thick cock deep in her wet, hot pussy.

She's wet, so damn wet that the juicy sounds of me fucking her fill my head, echoing off the walls. I'm grunting like a damn animal, but I can't help it. I'm finally claiming Melissa as mine, and there's no going back.

I have my hands on her hips, my fingers digging into her sides. I know there will be bruises in the morning, but I like that. I want my mark on her, want anyone who sees her to know who she belongs to. And she belongs to me, the same way I belong to her.

I push into her and pull out several more times, both of us moaning, sweat covering our bodies. I could fuck her against the wall all night long, but I want her on my bed, covered in my scent.

I force myself to pull out of her, both of us groaning in disappointment. I have her turned around and on my bed in seconds flat. She's breathing hard, fast, her breasts shaking slightly, her nipples pink and hard, the tips making my mouth water. I reach down and grab my cock, stroking myself from root to tip, about to come just from the look of her.

Her legs are slightly spread, her pussy bare of any hair. I love that she shaves, love that I can see how pink and glossy she is, how primed I've made her. I start jerking off faster and harder, wishing my cock was in her pussy again, but I'm too aroused to even move. My dick is slightly slick from being buried deep inside of her, and I need that hot wetness coating me again.

I'm on her before I can even think, this primal instinct taking over. I force her legs apart with my hands on her inner thighs, this small gasp leaving her. I align myself at her pussy again, staring right into her eyes as I thrust in deep and hard.

The force of my action has her moving up the bed. She closes her eyes, tips her head back, and opens her mouth on this silent cry. I move my hands up to her waist, digging my fingertips into her again. And then I really fuck her.

In and out.

Faster and harder.

I'm growling like a madman, unable to stop myself. I'm holding off from coming because I want this to last, because I want to feel her cunt squeezing me as she climaxes.

"Come for me, squeeze me, Melissa. Get the cum out of me." Fuck, I'm a dirty bastard. And then she cries out and obeys so damn nicely. I feel her pussy clenching around my dick, drawing my seed from my balls. I can't hold off, not when she feels so damn good.

She cries out and I groan, my cock feeling like it's getting strangled. I'm not going to be able to hold out. I don't want to. I pull out and push back in. Pull out and push back in. On the third thrust I bury myself completely in her, my balls slapping her ass, my orgasm rushing up.

I fill her with my seed, make her take it all. The pleasure is intense, consuming. Only when I feel the ecstasy start to wane do I pull back, slipping from her tight pussy for a moment. I keep her legs spread open with my hands as I stare at where I was just buried. And then I see my cum start to slip from her body.

I slip back inside of her, keeping my seed where it belongs. I look at her face, seeing her drowsy, post-euphoric expression and feel possessive and territorial.

"You are mine."

20

Melissa

I can barely catch my breath from the way Ace fucked me just now. I thought I was ready. That I'd be able to handle his rough possessiveness in the bedroom, but truthfully, I'll be surprised if I can walk out of here after the way he just claimed me.

How will I be able to do that when I can barely even move because my legs are shaking so damn hard below his body?

"Are you okay, Angel?" His muscles flex above me as he lowers his soft mouth to hover over my mine. "This... the way I just *fucked* you was me holding back. It's too soon for me to give it to you like I fucking crave to. You're not ready for *me* yet."

"What if I am?" I ask on a whisper, closing my eyes as his tongue flicks out to run across my lips. "I'm ready for all of you, Ace."

He lets out this deep, throaty laugh and grips my chin, pulling it up so our eyes meet. With his gaze locked on mine, he pulls my bottom lip between his teeth, causing me to let out a small cry as he bites me. Hard. So hard that it draws blood.

Then he takes his tongue and moves it across the wound as if to ease the pain he just caused. "Not yet."

I lay back and stare at him as he watches me for a moment. He's yet to pull out of me and the thought of his cum inside of me, filling me, has me remembering a really important fact.

"You never asked me if I was on birth control," I point out, feeling a bit anxious over just having unprotected sex. I should be freaking out more, but something in me is holding that down, telling me everything will be fine.

"Because I don't care if you are or not. I was going to fill you with my cum either way." His breath hits my lips as he speaks and for some strange reason, the fact that he came in me without asking has me completely turned on. "You're mine," he whispers against my lips, while moving his fingers down in between our bodies, possessively. "It's been a very long time since I was with a woman and I've always used protection ... up until now. You're different, special. I want your pussy filled with my seed every fucking night, Angel."

With a growl, he pulls out of me and spreads my legs apart, bringing his hands up to grip my thighs. His lips curve into a satisfied grin as he looks down, no doubt seeing his cum slipping out of my pussy. "So fucking perfect."

After a second of just staring at me, he stands up and reaches for his shirt to wipe me off with. My heart races in my chest as I watch him clean me off and toss the shirt aside.

His naked body is pure perfection as he stands before me and it's hard for me to pull my gaze away, but I manage to long enough for me to crawl out of bed and get dressed, too.

When I turn back around, he's standing there, naked, with a cigarette hanging between his lips as he watches me.

"I should get going now."

He doesn't say anything. He just lights up his smoke and opens the window, before walking over to lock his bedroom door.

He doesn't have to say anything. I know he's telling me to stay, and to be honest I want the same thing.

Ace

I DON'T WANT Melissa to go. Ever. Although I'm not a dumb fuck, and I know she can't be by my side at all times, the possessive fucker in me wants her locked in my room.

I sit in a chair in the corner and watch Melissa sleep. The soft rise and fall of her stomach underneath a thin sheet. The sheet has fallen just below her breasts, and my focus is trained on the perfect mounds, the fact her nipples are hard, the cool air kissing them. She is perfect.

She is mine.

She might have been afraid of the person I am, the things I do. But she is strong. She came with me, saw me in action, well, as much as I'd allow her to see. I didn't want her witnessing the gruesome and violent things I did even if it was the life the Lockes led.

I also don't want to hide who I am from her. And the fact she hasn't run screaming tells me she is perfect for me. I was right about that from the beginning.

I stand up and leave my room, shutting the door softly behind me. I know she's going to be hungry when she wakes up, so I head down to the kitchen to make us some food.

I see Sterling at the table, a half-eaten plate pushed aside, his foot kicked up on the edge of a chair. He's shirtless, with his jeans unbuttoned and unzipped, and his hair a wild fucking mess. The asshole doesn't even live here anymore, but him and Wynter still stay here some nights.

Looks like I'm not the only one who claimed my woman last night. He gives me a funny look and I grin, shaking my head, telling him without words to not even ask. What I share with Melissa is pretty fucking private. Even though I love my brothers and would die for them, kill for them, talking about being with Melissa is not something I want to do.

Which to be honest is pretty damn strange, given the fact I don't hide anything from Aston or Sterling.

"Looks like you had a long night," Sterling says, amusement in his voice.

I look over at my brother and scowl. "I could say the same thing to you." I laugh. "Looks like you've been ridden hard and put away wet." Sterling snorts and runs a hand over his face.

"Dude," he shakes his head. "I'm not even going go into my relationship with Wynter, but I can see you're right there with me where Melissa is concerned." Sterling grins. "And it's about damn time you fell hard."

And then Aston comes in, the third Locke looking worse than either of us. Sterling and I both start laughing, knowing that all of us are good and fucked where our women are concerned.

Aston stops and stares at us, his brows furrowed. "You guys look like shit, like you got no fucking sleep last night."

I look at Sterling and we both start laughing harder.

Hell, all of us are sure as fuck something to look at now. Yeah, I did fall pretty fucking hard. But hell, I'd bring down the whole damn world if it meant Melissa was happy.

I grab some food and go back upstairs, head into my room and shut the door softly. I set the food aside, get undressed, and slip under the covers beside Melissa. She smells so damn good, and her body is so soft, so warm. I feel her stirring beside me, and she shifts, turning over so she's looking at me now, this sleepy expression on her face.

I don't say anything, just cup her face and lean in, kissing her softly. After long seconds we're both breathing hard. My cock is stiff as fuck, pressing against her belly, needing to be inside of her. I roll her over so she's now on her back. I am on top of her, using my knee to spread her thighs, fitting my body between them, my cock running between her folds.

I kiss her again, reach between our bodies, and align myself at her pussy. And then I thrust in nice and slow. I'm not fucking her right now, even though I want to go fast and hard, be raw and rough. I take my time, pushing in and pulling out, driving her higher, making things hotter.

She's so fucking wet for me, and the soft mewls she makes has me becoming frenzied. But I go slow, make this sweet and gentle. This might be the only time I am like this, but right now this is how it has to be.

Right now this is what I want with Melissa. She's mine,

every part of her, and I want to take my time, savor every moment I have with her.

Because after this moment there won't be any more making love. There will just be hardcore claiming my woman.

21

Melissa

I got off work an hour ago, but came home first to change for the bonfire that's at Ace's house tonight. The fact I'll get to see him, maybe even make what we have official in some capacity, makes my heart speed up. I'm done hiding, pretending like I am too afraid of my own feelings to let them be known. I want the whole damn world to know that Ace is mine and I'm his.

I've slept the last two nights at his place and have only been home for twenty minutes at a time, just long enough to grab clean clothes to change into before I head back to see him. He makes me feel whole, like the person I truly am has been dormant this whole time, just waiting for him to spark it to life.

This is the first time that I've been here for longer and it feels weird all of a sudden, like I'm in someone else's place, as if this is no longer mine and Kadence's home. A part of me feels a bit sad about that, simply because this has been my "safe place" for a while now, where I felt sheltered and safe.

But I feel that way with Ace, and no matter where I am, as long as he's there I'm golden.

I grab the rest of my stuff and head out to my car. After tossing the bag in the backseat I climb behind the wheel, crank the engine, and turn on the radio. I drive around for a bit, wanting to take a moment to drive by mine and Kadence's old place. Once I arrive outside I can't help but look at the house across the street. It all started there, seemingly ages ago.

That's when I first came in contact with the Locke brothers, when they weren't just rumors to me. It's then that I should have known I was in deep, that I couldn't just ignore this ... that I'd be swept under in the best of ways. When I saw Kadence with Aston I felt like she was living for the first time. I never told her, but I'd been jealous of her, envious of the kind of fire I saw between the two of them.

I have that now, though. I have it for myself.

I finally arrive at the Locke property and already see a blazing bonfire lit up. There are chairs around the fire pit, and I immediately notice Sterling and Wynter, Aston and

Kadence sitting around. I even see the Locke brothers' Uncle Killian standing off to the side, a beer in his hand.

I park the car and cut the engine. As soon as I'm out I see Ace striding over, a grin on his face. My heart jumps to my throat. It seems whenever he's around I get this instant reaction, like I haven't seen him in years. Part of me knows that this won't ever change, that it will always be like this between us.

He wraps his arms around me and pulls me close to his chest. He has his hand on my nape, tips my head to the side, and slams his mouth on mine. I can't help but moan at the flavor of him as he strokes the seam of my lips with his tongue.

When he pulls away I'm left breathless, wanting more, craving it. I look over at the bonfire and can see the brothers and their women looking at us, each one wearing a smile. I feel my face heat. Although this is what I wanted. I want them to know I'm with Ace. Hell, I need everyone to know that he's mine in the same way he wants them to know I'm his.

We're not that different.

We walk over to the fire and he sits down, immediately pulling me onto his lap and holding me close. It feels good being on his lap, his arms around me, everyone staring at us. I don't feel weird that we have all this attention. It's what I want, what I need.

I turn and look at Ace, and feeling my emotions rise up,

I'm the one who kisses him this time. I press my tongue to his lips, stroking so he opens for me, and then I delve inside. I'm normally not so wanton or brazen. I like when Ace takes control, has the power. But I want him to see, to feel that I'm right here with him, that I want him as much as he wants me.

I hear Sterling whistle under his breath, can hear Aston saying something to Kadence about the PDA between Ace and I, but I don't care. I'm focused on the man I love.

I love him.

He groans but pulls away, and I'm left there panting, wanting more. Needing it.

"If we don't stop I'll have you in my room in my bed."

I smile. "Maybe that's what I want."

He groans again and rests his forehead on mine.

"You're just as fucking insatiable as I am."

I chuckle.

But I face the fire, knowing that being here with Ace, without us being naked, is just as good as when we are alone in his room. It might be better, if I am being honest.

For long moments he just holds me, and I listen to the brothers bullshit, even hear Killian telling a story or two about all the shit he used to get into when he was their ages. There are laughs, a lot of touching from the guys and their women, and for the first time in a long damn time I feel like I belong someplace.

Like I really belong here.

These guys are family, and I am now part of that circle. But this has me thinking about what and who Ace is, and more specifically, whom he has in the garage. I twist slightly and look at said building, knowing who is behind those double doors, who has crossed a Locke.

"Ace?" I ask softly and face him again, looking into his eyes.

"Yeah, baby." He lifts his hand and smooths his thumb over my bottom lip.

"Show me him." I know I don't have to elaborate on who I'm talking about. I see the way Ace's expression changes, how he becomes tense beneath me.

"You want to see him?"

I nod and lick my lips. "I need to see him." And I realize I've never spoken truer words. In this moment I realize I am not so different than the man I love.

22

Ace

I pause outside the garage door and stare for a few moments, feeling somewhat anxious that Melissa wants to see this fucker.

She's *heard* the damage I do, has heard the breaking of bones and the screams of my victim, but her *seeing* the damage is something else entirely.

We're just now beginning to feel like a real couple. Her walls are no longer up when she's with me and the thought that once she sees with her own two eyes the damage I've done to this prick, that she might pull back from *us,* has me feeling on edge.

"I'm ready, Ace." She gives my hand a slight squeeze as if

to reassure me that she's ready to witness this mangled prick.

Ever since I mentioned to her what this fucker did, that he almost killed me, I can tell that she's been wanting to see the person who was almost responsible for taking me away from her.

There's anger in her eyes and in her voice every time I mention that I'm going out to the garage, but I've made it a point to keep her away from him.

"Once you see what I've done, you can't *unsee* that shit, Melissa." I turn and grab her chin, pulling it up so our gazes meet. "I need to know for sure that you're ready for that. I can't fucking lose you now that you're mine. I won't."

She keeps her gaze locked on mine, a softness in them as if wanting to show me that she's not going anywhere. "You'll never lose me, Ace. Nothing you can do can scare me away now that I know the *real* you." Her hands move up to grip my shirt as she stands on the tips of her toes and brushes her lips against mine. "I'm not going anywhere. Now show me."

I swallow nervously before grabbing the back of her head and kissing her. She kisses me back with a roughness that has me growling against her lips with need.

"Fuck, Angel," I whisper as we break the kiss. "I'm getting really fucking close to taking you upstairs and claiming you instead."

Her gaze lowers to my dick as I reach down to adjust my

erection. A twisted smile crosses her face as she steps in close and runs her hand down my body. "You can claim me after. Like I said… I'm not going anywhere."

Before I can lose all self-control and throw her over my shoulder, carry her upstairs and fuck her like the twisted fucker that I am, I release my grip on her head and make my way over to the garage door to open it.

I step inside first, Melissa following right behind me, so close that I can feel the warmth from her body against my backside.

Troy is still hanging there all bloodied, cut up and bruised just as I've left him every night since he showed up on our property.

He's lucky I've been *kind* enough to provide him with water and food to keep his ass alive. Honestly, I could care less if he starves to death out here, but not getting the chance to hurt him and make him suffer for what he *almost* did is what I can and do care about.

He begins thrashing around at the sight of me, and although there's no way in hell he can get to Melissa to hurt her, I find myself pushing her behind me and growling out in anger.

"Keep fucking moving and I'll have to break all the fingers on your other hand too." The tilt of my head as I stare across the garage at him has him obeying me. He's learned enough over the time since he's been my prisoner what that look means.

I feel Melissa move around me, finally stepping out from behind me to get a look at Troy.

She stands frozen for a few moments, staring up at him as if to take all the damage in.

All I can do is watch her as she watches him, wanting to see every single one of her facial expressions.

At first she looks a little shocked by all the cuts and broken bones, but then her expression changes into anger and determination as if she wants to make him suffer at her hands too.

"He almost killed you," she whispers. "He almost took you from me and possibly even Kadence if he had the chance."

I nod as she turns her attention to me. "Yes."

I watch closely as she walks over to stand in front of me, before kneeling down to reach into my boot for the knife she knows I keep hidden there. The one she's used on more than one occasion to let out some frustration.

She stands and grips the knife, her head tilting to the side as she looks down at it. In this moment, she reminds me a lot of myself. I can almost *feel* her need to hurt him, to cause damage because of the damage he could've and would've caused had he had the chance.

"He hasn't suffered enough yet," she says softly, looking up at me. "I want him to know that if he *ever* hurts anyone that I love that I will hurt him far worse. He needs to know never to come back here again."

I steel my jaw and watch as she turns around and throws the knife at Troy, the blade sticking right into his thigh.

She's breathing heavily, standing still as she watches him.

I feel joy as he screams out in pain and begins thrashing around again. But joy isn't the only thing I feel at the fact that my girl is the one hurting this piece of shit. I feel relief and peacefulness, knowing that Melissa isn't going anywhere.

This moment right here is the confirmation I needed to know Melissa is truly mine for good.

She's not going anywhere.

I don't only want her in this moment, but I *need* her.

It looks like she's about to walk over to grab the knife out of Troy, possibly to hurt him again, but I grab her by the hips and flip her around so that she's facing me.

We're both breathing heavily as I look down at her. My need to have her, to claim her in this very moment, has me gripping onto her body so hard that my fingers hurt. I've never needed to take Melissa as rough and wild as I do right this fucking second.

She doesn't need *gentle.*

She doesn't *want* gentle.

She fucking needs *me.*

With a growl, I pick her up and carry her outside and to the side of the garage where I know no one will bother looking for us. Shit, even if they did, I'm not sure I'd give a fuck at the moment.

The craving to be inside my woman is too strong.

I can see the need in her eyes too... can feel her desire from the rapid beating of her chest against mine as she looks up at me. It has me feeling like a fucking animal ready to strike. With a groan, I set her down just long enough to rip her jeans and panties down her legs and free my cock from my pants. Then I pick her back up, align my erection with her pussy and slam into her so hard that she screams out and digs into my skin, drawing blood.

With each hard thrust of my hips, I push her body up the side of the garage, causing her to scream louder and tear at my flesh as if she's feeling just as wild and animalistic as I am.

"God... Ace..." she pants against my lips, her nails digging in further. The feel of her leaving marks has me going even harder. "Keep going... keep going..."

I thrust into her again and stop, leaning my head back as she pulls on my hair.

"Fuck..." I growl into the night sky, loving the way she's being rough with me. Her roughness is fueling me to fuck her harder... and harder... taking her with every bit of strength that I have without breaking her in two.

I can barely fucking breathe. Both of our bodies are dripping with sweat, but I keep going, giving us both what we want.

Wild, untamed sex.

With the way she's handling me, I'll be covered with bruises and scratches by the time I come inside of her, and of course that shit only turns me on more. I want my woman to hurt me. I want her to do with me as she fucking pleases, because it shows me that she's claiming me as I've claimed her.

My beautiful, twisted angel.

We were meant for each other, in every fucking way.

Being inside of her has me so fucking heated that I end up biting into her lip and drawing blood. When she moans out in pleasure from it, I feel a tug at my balls, fucking ready to bust inside her. "Come for me, Angel," I growl against her mouth. "Right. Now."

Within seconds, her pussy squeezes my dick, drawing the cum straight from my cock. I push in as far as I can and fill her with my seed again, loving that Melissa is the first one to have *all* of me.

Every twisted part of me belongs to her.

I love her, and I'd kill and die for her without a second thought.

This woman, right here in my arms, is mine and I'll do everything in my power to keep it that way.

She sags against me and for long seconds we stand here, panting, breathing each other's air, being in the same headset as the other. I knew the moment I'd seen her that she was mine, that I'd do whatever in my power I could to ensure that. It took a long time, too damn long for Melissa to be claimed by me, but I have her now. That's all that matters. They'll have to cut out my beating heart for me to let her go.

They can try, but they won't succeed. Because when you've got something so good nothing else matters, you'll lay bodies at your feet to ensure you never let it go.

That's what I have with Melissa.

The ground I walk on will be littered with the fallen who try to take her from me.

EPILOGUE

Melissa

Six months later

I stare at the boxes that litter my living room. Anything that means something to me is packed away, ready to be housed in a new location, a new home. Hell, *I'm* about to go to a new place without Kadence.

I'm about to *live* with Ace.

I can't say that I'm not scared, that the anxiety of something new doesn't terrify me. But I'm going to be with Ace, and that's all that matters. I decided that it's the right time to move in together, and although he asked me a month ago, and at first I said I didn't know, it hasn't taken me long to realize this is exactly what I want.

He's exactly what I want in my life.

Forever.

The thought of not being with him... of not touching, kissing or holding him *kills* me. My feelings for him have only grown stronger with each day.

Ace, Sterling, and Aston all come in through the front door to grab some more boxes. They brought their vehicles, packing them full of my stuff. This has been my home for over a year now, one I shared with Kadence. But she and Aston are going to live together now, Wynter is with Sterling, and I'm finally with the man that I love.

I look over at him and can't help the way my heart starts beating faster. It's an instant reaction when I'm near him.

Sterling and Aston grab a few more boxes and head out just as Kadence and Wynter walk in. The whole family has been helping, and I can't help but feel like that's truly what they are ... my family.

Ace pulls me in for an embrace before I even know he's right in front of me. I rest my head on his chest, inhaling deeply, taking in the woodsy, purely masculine scent of him.

"You sure about this?" he asks in his gruff voice.

"More than I've ever been about anything else." I pull back and look at him, smiling as I stare into his face. This is exactly what I'm supposed to do, where I'm supposed to be. After all the shit I've been through with Ace, all the things I've seen, participated in, I know that I was always meant to be with him.

The rumors, the fear I felt when I heard about the Locke Brothers, before I even knew Ace, knew any of them, are distant memories now. These men protect what they hold dear, and to Ace I am his world.

He cups my cheek and leans down to kiss me soundly on the lips. "I love you, baby. So fucking much."

Hearing Ace say those words, knowing that for as hard-core and rough he is, that to him I am everything, takes the breath straight from my lungs. "I love you, too."

He grins and kisses me again. "You ready to live with the most twisted Locke of all? I'll promise no more prisoners in the garage... for a while at least."

"I can work with that." I grin against his mouth when he growls, most likely wanting an answer from me. "And yes. I've been ready for a while now. It just took some time to realize that. There's nowhere else I'd rather be, Ace."

There's no other man or person for that matter that could ever make me feel the way that Ace does.

The excitement.

The feeling of being alive... living on the edge.

The overwhelming feeling of need whenever he's present.

And most of all... the safety and security I feel whenever I'm wrapped up in his strong arms, feeling his heartbeat, is perfection.

Ace is it for me.

He's the one and there's nothing in this world that could ever make me give him up.

I am his world and he is *mine.*

Ace

THE FACT that my brothers and I moved Melissa's things into the Locke house has me feeling like the happiest man on earth.

It took a month for me to convince her to say yes, but I knew she'd eventually want the same as me. That she'd want to fall asleep next to me and wake up beside me every day of the fucking week.

That's what I want.

It's not as if she hasn't been doing that, but it wasn't her waking up in *our* bed or in *our* house and the idea of that has been eating at me deep.

Ever since Melissa and I made things official, Aston and Kadence have been spending most of their time at Kadence's, so it just made sense that Aston and Kadence would live there, and Melissa would move into the Locke house with me.

We're all close and able to have each other's backs and that's what's most important.

All except for Uncle Killian.

Last I heard, he was in a different town busting faces and being the most brutal Locke of us all.

He'll be back eventually. He always is.

He never was one to stay in this town for too long.

I look over and smile at the sight of Melissa pulling the blanket from the back of the couch and wrapping it around her, getting comfortable.

She's been living here for less than twenty minutes and she's already treating my home as hers.

Our home.

Good. That fucking makes me happy.

"Come here, baby." I pull her into my lap and wrap us both up with the blanket. She smiles against my lips, showing me she's just as happy about living here as I am that she is.

"I can't believe that I'm living in the Locke house." She grabs my hand and moves it over her belly. "That this will be *our* home."

My eyes widen as I look down at her stomach. "Fuck, baby. Please tell me that–"

"I'm pregnant," she says, cutting me off with excitement. "We're having a baby."

Hearing her say that she's carrying my child has my heart filling with a happiness I've never felt before. Hell, I never thought this would happen to me, that I'd even find a woman to have by my side, let alone be a father. But if I'm going to do it I sure as hell want to do it with Melissa.

Yes, Melissa makes me happy. She makes me more than happy, but this feels *different*.

She's having *my* baby.

"Hell yeah!" I roar out with excitement before I set her on her feet and drop down to my knees in front of her. My entire body is shaking as I grab her hips and move in to kiss her belly. "I fucking love you and I promise you with everything I am that I will love our baby and protect it always."

She grabs my face and pulls it up until I'm looking at her as she looks down at me. "I believe it with my whole heart. No one loves or protects fiercer than you do."

I grin up at her. She's my world, and the child she carries brings this whole situation full circle. I may be one twisted as fuck Locke, but hell, when it comes to Melissa, to our baby, I'm not very tough at all.

There's nothing better than knowing you've got it good, even if maybe you don't deserve it.

"What's all the fucking excitement in here?" Sterling sticks his head through the doorway and checks me out on my knees, while holding a burger in his hand. "Why are you on... oh fuck."

I nod and stand to my feet before grabbing Melissa's face and kissing her hard. I want to show my brother just how happy I am. "Oh fuck is right. I'm going to be a dad and I'm happy as shit about it. Call the others in here. Now."

Sterling's face turns up into a proud smile. "Shit... I'm going to be an uncle." Ignoring my orders, he comes at

Melissa and kisses her hard on the top of the head. "That's going to be one lucky kid. Us Lockes always look out for each other. *You're* a Locke now too, sister."

I smile at the happiness filling Melissa's eyes. "Thank you, Sterling. Now go get the others."

"Yes, ma'am. You, I'll take orders from." Sterling flips me the middle finger and takes off.

That dick. He's lucky he listens to my woman at least.

I can barely keep my hands off Melissa's stomach while waiting for everyone else to join us in the living room.

I feel as if I'm about to fucking burst with happiness and pride.

Kadence is the first to join us, followed by Wynter and then Aston, who crosses his arms and leans against the wall.

"This better be good. Kadence and I were *busy*." He spins his lock around his finger, while looking over at me.

"Shut up, asshole. I don't want you ruining our moment."

"I'm just going to say it," Melissa says with excitement. "Ace and I are having a baby. You're all going to be aunts and uncles."

Kadence is the first to react. She runs at Melissa and throws her arms around her. "I'm so happy for you guys. I knew it. I *knew* you and Ace would end up together. You have no idea how happy I am for you."

I look over to see Aston finally push away from the wall. His lips curve up into a smile as he tosses his lock aside and walks over to pick Melissa up and kiss her on the lips.

"Hey, asshole. Don't make me cut those bitches off."

Before I can get too upset with Aston for kissing my woman, Kadence laughs and punches him on the arm while we watch Wynter attack Melissa with a hug.

Everyone is surrounding us now, everyone happier than I've ever seen them, and I know without a doubt that our baby will be happy and loved.

We're a family.

We're the Lockes.

We play hard, destroy even harder, but most of all… we love with everything in us…

The End

ACKNOWLEDGMENTS

VICTORIA ASHLEY

First and foremost, I'd like to say a HUGE thank you to Jenika Snow for taking a chance and writing this amazing series with me.

I'd also like to thank the beta readers that took the time to read Pay for Play: Lindsey and Amy. We appreciate you ladies so much!

Lea Schafer for doing a wonderful job at editing and Dana Leah for her amazing design work on our cover.

And I want to say a big thank you to all of my loyal readers that have given me support over the last couple of years and have encouraged me to continue with my writing. Your words have all inspired me to do what I enjoy and love.

Each and every one of you mean a lot to me and I wouldn't be where I am if it weren't for your support and kind words.

Last but not least, I'd like to thank all of the wonderful book bloggers that have taken the time to support our book and help spread the word. You all do so much for us authors and it is greatly appreciated. I have met so many friends on the way and you guys are never forgotten. You guys rock. Thank you!

JENIKA SNOW

A big thank you to Victoria for going on this adventure with me and creating dark and twisted characters that we love to hate! This story wouldn't be possible without the help from so many people: Dana, our cover designer, Lindsey, who took the time to go over the story and give us her opinion, Lea Ann, who is an incredible editor, Ardent Prose for their help in promoting, and of course all the readers and bloggers who support our crazy endeavors.

WHERE TO FIND VICTORIA ASHLEY

VICTORIA ASHLEY grew up in Rockford, IL and has had a passion for reading for as long as she can remember. After finding a reading app where it allowed readers to upload their own stories, she gave it a shot and writing became her passion. She lives for a good romance book with tattooed bad boys that are just highly misunderstood and is not afraid to be caught crying during a good read. When she's not reading or writing about bad boys, you can find her watching her favorite shows such as Supernatural, Sons Of Anarchy and The Walking Dead.

Contact her at: Website: www.victoriaashleyauthor.com

WHERE TO FIND JENIKA SNOW

Find Jenika at:

Newsletter: http://bit.ly/2dkihXD

Goodreads: http://bit.ly/2FfW7A1

Amazon: http://amzn.to/2E9g3VV

Bookbub: http://bit.ly/2rAfVMm

www.JenikaSnow.com

Jenika_Snow@yahoo.com

Printed in the USA
CPSIA information can be obtained
at www.ICGtesting.com
LVHW012300150524
780439LV00033B/1116

9 781723 249242